Always remember to do you!

Brittani Avery

BRITTANI S. AVERY

BLACK
MEREDITH
PRESS

Omaha, Nebraska

ELEMENT UNKNOWN

Black Meredith Press books may be ordered
from your favorite bookseller.

www.BrittaniSAvery.com

Black Meredith Press
4822 South 133rd Street
Omaha, NE 68137

ISBN: 978-0-9971336-1-5 (Ppk)
ISBN: 978-0-9971336-2-2 (Mobi)
ISBN: 978-0-9971336-3-9 (EPUB)

Library of Congress Cataloging Number: 2017950537

Library of Congress Cataloging-in-Publication
data on file with the publisher.

PRODUCTION, DISTRIBUTION AND MARKETING:
Concierge Marketing Inc. www.ConciergeMarketing.com

Printed in the USA

10 9 8 7 6 5 4 3 2 1

CHAPTER
1

THE AUCTION BLOCK, AN UNIMPOSING slab of wood, was equally the most feared and most praised object in all of Maventa. On average, its height only reached a man's chest and its width was only two arm lengths. The platform normally wobbled and creaked with each step, and it looked as if it would collapse beneath the slightest pressure.

Various stains covered the sides. Tops were haphazardly polished, producing an inconsistency of shininess. Yet the appearance of the block, no matter its size or condition, was not what caused fear in hearts or raised sounds of jubilation. It was the symbolism of it: slavery.

While slavery and its moral validity were hot topics among all classes and statuses in Maventa, they were of little interest to fifteen-year-old Rex Marshall, a tall and darkly handsome bad boy of the country's highest social class. Seeing that his father was an abolitionist, Rex realized that he should care more about the welfare of others and join his father in the fight for freedom. But he was just glad it was Saturday and he did not have tutoring lessons or church, the two most boring events in his life. Saturday was his only free day, and all he wanted to do was enjoy the market.

It was the dead time of the market, when the early risers had already finished their morning rounds, and the late bloomers were just now getting up. This was his favorite time to explore. There were fewer people, and therefore fewer disturbances to the sights and sounds.

He admired the giant, brightly colored tents that littered both sides of the street. Vendors of all sorts competed for his attention, calling out their prices and waving their merchandise for sale. With a nod of thanks, he shoved his hands into his pockets and continued through the market. During his wandering, he stopped at random stalls and pretended to be interested in this or that but never bought anything.

Soon enough, he moved on, coming closer to the market's end. The items got bigger and bigger until an elephant, led by an intoxicated man, almost squashed him. After properly swearing at the fool, as any Maventi would do, Rex sighed and walked a little more, finding himself at the shipping docks, which collided with the end of the market.

The wooden ships towered over him, and he looked up, mesmerized at their size and grandeur. His father had strictly forbade him from venturing to the docks, but yet another emergency Maventi Council meeting kept his father occupied.

Rex's curiosity overrode his father's warning. He began to explore the docks, his dark brown eyes taking in the new scene. Eventually, he found himself in a crowd of people standing near a ship's entrance. All kinds of people were there: big and tall, short and small, male, female, elf, fairy, dwarf, human, and… something else entirely.

There was this girl, a very strange-looking girl. Firstly, she was blue—blue as the ocean on a cloudy day. Her hair was an extremely light color, nearly white from a distance. She was also tall and thin, appearing too regal for the skimpy outfit she wore. Rex found her pretty in her strange way and decided that a pretty girl should not be denied the opportunity of conversing with him.

He approached her and the closer he got to her, the more beautiful she became. She was taller than he expected, nearly the same height as him. Her skin, despite the strange color, was flawless. Her hair was not solely white but held purple highlights. Her ears were pointed, splitting into three points at the top. She was indeed something else entirely.

"Excuse me, miss, I've done lost my heart. Did you happen to steal it?" he said, putting on the charm.

The girl turned around to face him, and he saw for the first time a person with two different colored eyes. One of her eyes—the right one—was a lovely dark green, while the other was a deep red. She blinked her two-toned eyes, and Rex could see from the movement that neither was glass. These were her natural eyes.

"You got the most beautiful eyes…" he thought out loud and, upon realizing he had actually spoken, grinned wide in a vain attempt to hide his blunder. She gave him no reaction. He considered the possibility of her being deaf or even mute. He pointed to himself and signed the letters of his name: R, E, and X. With a smile, he waited for some sort of response, and still nothing came. The girl stared blankly at him.

"Deaf?" he asked, pointing to his ear.

She shook her head no and whispered, "Unauthorized to speak."

He stared at her in amazement.

"What are you talking about? You're in Maventa, one of the most liberal places ever! We aren't the Saldur Empire or Churchland."

"I shall be punished if I continue to speak. Please, I do not wish to resort to rudeness. I beg of you to go in peace."

Damn, she's proper, he thought and said, "Oh, come on! A pretty little thang like you gotta have a name to match."

"If I reveal my name, will you go?"

"Tough crowd. Yeah, I'll go. What's your name? I'm Rex."

"I know. I can sign as well. My name is Meenal." She signed the letters as she spoke.

"*Mee-Nuh?* With a silent *L*? What kinda name's that?"

"You said that you would leave. Please, I wish not to be punished."

"Why you keep saying you gonna be punished? Who gonna do that? Your dad? Ah hell, is he one of them overly protective dudes that think girls get pregnant just by talking to a dude?"

"N-No?" Meenal paused, looking panicked. "Sir, please, you must leave me."

With that, she turned her back to him, and he heard a rattling. He looked down and noticed chains on her bare feet and wrists, squeezing against her joints. His eyes quickly flashed from dark brown to red. She was a slave, and the thought infuriated him. He could not understand how someone like her could become a slave. She looked to have more class and proper training than some of the duchesses and princesses he had met. But here she was, chained like an animal and unauthorized to speak.

He narrowed his eyes and spun her around. Her head instantly dropped, and the sight of her bowed head only increased his anger.

He barked, "Lift your head!"

She obeyed and said, "I apologize."

"You're a slave, not spineless! Hold your head up."

Meenal stared at the strange boy, fighting the urge to drop her head again. She had been taught all her life never to look at anyone of authority in the eyes, and this boy was telling her the complete opposite. She began to examine him in detail now.

He had brown skin with a red undertone and wide dark-brown eyes, which now held a slight reddish tint to them. His hair was dark brown and messy though clean. He smelled of lavender and fresh cotton, signaling that he was of the upper class. However, his clothes lacked the style and grace of such status.

Overall, his appearance confused her, but she did not voice her confusion for the threat of discovery still loomed. She needed to remove him from this place at once before the driver returned.

"Does this satisfy my master?" she asked, holding her head as high as she could manage.

Rex rolled his eyes, saying, "Don't call me that. I'm not your master. Did I buy you?"

"Right, of course. My apologies, sir."

"Sir? Nah, none of that either. We're pretty much the same age! How many years you got, anyways?"

"I am uncertain."

"What? Really, you seriously don't know?"

"That is correct, sir. I do not."

She heard movement from the front of the pack of slaves. Her eyes widened. She needed to act quickly.

"What's wrong?" Rex asked again.

"Please, you must go. I shall be punished."

She stepped further away from him, but it was too late. She felt a rough hand on her forearm yanking her away from the boy. She suppressed her cries— screaming would only worsen the punishment—and she was already too tired from the long journey at sea.

The slave driver spoke harshly to her in his native tongue of Jaak. She replied, telling him that the boy had spoken to her first. Not believing her, the driver smacked her and busted her lip open. He then proceeded to scream at her, gesturing wildly in Rex's direction. Meenal said nothing as the man berated and shook her. The panic in her eyes faded, and a lifeless expression filled its place.

Rex stared at the scene playing out before him and a boiling hatred rose within him. He launched himself at the slave driver and landed on top of him, throwing blow after blow. Blood spattered up and covered both men. The driver begged Rex to stop, but his words fell on deaf ears.

Commotion approached as a man rushed over to aid the slave driver, his muscular legs flexing with each step. His large hands grabbed Rex by the collar and pulled him off, holding him back securely. Another man approached slowly. His giant stomach and fat chin made walking—or rather waddling—labor intensive. He was breathing heavily once he finally reached the place of action. Shaking his head, he glanced down at the man lying on the ground.

"Stupid Jaak," he gasped, trying to catch his breath.

The Jaak coughed, spitting out blood and a couple of teeth, and then slowly got up to his feet. His left eye was bruised, swollen shut. Black and purple blotches covered his face.

"Stupid boy messin' wit' slave," the man said in his thick Jaak accent, pointing at Rex. With a menacing, doglike growl, Rex fought violently against his hulky captor's hold.

"He hit her, Titus!" Rex growled, his eyes a chilling red color.

"Rex? Whachya doin' here? Your father be havin' ya head if he caught ya down here. You shouldn't be puttin' ya nose in business that don't concern ya," Titus said.

With more ease than before, Titus waddled over to Meenal and roughly grabbed hold of her chin, twisting it around to examine the damage. He pressed his thin lips together in disgust and smacked her shoulder.

"Ack, the boy got a point though… The Jaak done messed up the girl for today's auction. We gotta wait for that lip to heal in order to get top coin."

"We could get a healer and still sell her tonight," the man holding Rex said with a shrug.

"Dru, that cost money and while she'll make a pretty penny, she ain't worth a healer. Go on and let him loose."

Dru, the big man, released Rex, and Rex glared at him, his eyes slowly returning to their original color of dark brown.

"Run along now, Rectavius. Ya daddy's callin'," Titus teased.

"I'm fifteen now, Titus," Rex said. "Don't treat me like a child."

"Hot damn! Fifteen! My apologies then, Sir Rectavius. If ya an adult, then I should call the authorities and have ya arrested for assaultin' my employee."

Rex stood his ground and made an inappropriate gesture to Titus.

"You can arrest me for that too, you jerk," he said.

Titus laughed hard, his fat jiggling in rhythm. He waddled over to Rex and patted him on the shoulder. He then directed Dru to take hold of Meenal's chains while the Jaak followed behind, cradling his broken jaw. Her head lowered as the four of them walked away. But before walking out of sight, she turned around and caught Rex's eyes. She mouthed something to him and right before they turned the corner, he finally got it: *Thank you.*

Δ

"Then he hit her! *Whack!* Right across the face, even busting her lip," Rex exclaimed, his outrage still lingering since his encounter with the strange-looking Meenal. He had tried to get her out of his mind, but she remained, her sad and hopeless eyes staring at him as if asking him to do something. It was driving him insane.

"Yes, I know," Leeni said as she set down the dinner plate. "You have repeated yourself multiple times, and I do believe that you have quite plainly made your point."

"Oh, leave him alone!" Tiffanie said, kissing Rex on the cheek as she picked up his salad plate. "Let him express himself! And 'sides, not everyone can read minds like you."

"I don't read people's minds. I can recall their memories," said Leeni. "There is a difference."

"Goodness, you Earth elementals are so 'Everything must be correct.'"

"And you Air elementals are all about partying and having fun, even when it's illogical."

"Ladies… can we focus more on me?" Rex said, calling the two servants back from their ongoing argument. Tiffanie nodded with a smile while Leeni just turned and faced Rex, crossing her arms.

"Your father is still at the council meeting and will not be joining you for dinner," Leeni said, and Tiffanie glared at her.

"I was supposed to tell him that!" she shouted.

Leeni just blinked at her. "And when did you plan on doing so? He is already eating his main course. He probably already figured it out."

"Still! It was *my assignment*!"

"Ladies, please! On me, I kinda got a dilemma…" Rex said and once again, the two servants turned toward him. Rex gestured toward the chairs, and Tiffanie quickly joined him at the small dining room table. Leeni hesitated slightly, but eventually joined after some friendly coaxing from Tiffanie. Rex sighed and started to speak but stopped himself, putting his hand on his chin. He sighed again and then shook his head.

"There's gotta be something I can do!" he said.

"About what?" Tiffanie asked, her big blue eyes watching him intently.

"About who, not what. I feel like I *have* to help her—the blue girl."

"Meenal, you mean?" Leeni said.

Rex glared at her. "Quit that! It's intrusive."

"That is like telling me not to breathe. If you wish my death, then say so."

"Okay, Leeni, happy thoughts!" Tiffanie said with a big smile. Leeni rolled her eyes.

"I was being humorous… or at least attempting to be so." Tiffanie gave a forced laugh, and Leeni sighed, "Never mind. As for the slave situation, there isn't much you can do for her. She'll be auctioned off soon, going either to a collector or a brothel, based on her appearance."

"A collector?" Rex asked.

"Ew! One of those creepy slave owners who think people are like coins or stamps or dolls or something," Tiffanie sneered.

"A collector is a slave owner who attempts to own slaves who are of a unique species or who possess particular powers. So yes, to them, slaves are collectible stamps. If Titus is smart, he'll wait until next Saturday to auction her off. There is going to be a collector's convention. He'll make the most money then."

Rex shot up from his seat.

"Where are you going?!" Tiffanie shouted after him, but he ignored her and hurried to his father's bedroom.

He changed into one of his father's suits, scooped a couple of moneybags into his pockets, and popped on a large top hat and a scarf. Looking at himself in the mirror, he noticed that he needed something else to give him more of an adult look. He spotted his father's old reading glasses and tried those. *That'll do*, he thought with a last look in the mirror.

Stepping out in the warm summer night, Rex set his haphazard plan into action. His mind jumped around, trying to come up with a more reliable plan, but the only thought that kept resurfacing was of Meenal and the hopeless look in her eyes. He walked briskly, keeping his face covered and his head down. He sprinted toward the city's center, the lanterns decreasing and the shady characters appearing.

He spoke with a couple of gentlemen, and they pointed him in the direction of an event hall, which looked more like an abandoned shed. Stepping inside, he tried to find Titus, but the fat man was nowhere to be found.

The next best person to find was Antigua, his right-hand woman, keeper of the books, and wife. He found her at a corner desk and walked over to her, making sure the hat and scarf covered most of his face. He wished not to be recognized; he needed to be treated as a respectable adult, not the teenage son of a councilman.

"Evenin', sir," she said.

"Evening, madam. Can you tell me which slaves are going to be auctioned off in the next couple of nights?" he said, deepening his voice. Antigua looked through the various papers and started listing off descriptions. None matched Meenal's. He waited until she had finished before asking, "I had heard about a different sort of slave—a girl. She has unique coloring, particularly in the eyes, one being green and the other red."

"Oh, that slave," Antigua said, grinning. "You gonna have to wait 'til next Saturday. She's gonna be in the collectors' auction."

"I see. Tell me then, is there a price that will change your mind?" He pulled out the moneybags, dropping them obnoxiously onto the desk. A couple heads turned toward the ruckus and Antigua's eyes widened, shifting back and forth.

She pressed her thin lips together and with a sad shake of her head, she said, "There's no price that's gonna change my mind. I know what she's worth and I doubt you got it."

"You doubt my interest? I have two hundred silver coins to prove it."

Antigua stared silently.

"Three hundred?" Rex asked, but again, the woman kept her silence. Rex continued to increase his price incrementally, all the way up to five hundred silver coins. Each new offer was greeted with silence. Eventually, he took the money and bid Antigua farewell.

Δ

The next week dragged on. His efforts to discover Meenal's location for a rescue attempt proved futile.

Tiffanie and Leeni attempted to cheer him up without success. His tutoring sessions suffered as his mind drifted off to his encounter with the unique slave girl. There was something about her that marked her as different than any other person he had ever met. Tiffanie called it love at first sight, Leeni called it déjà vu, and Rex believed neither of them. Yet, whatever it was, he was determined to find out.

Saturday had once again arrived, and he was readying himself to go to the auction. He had no idea what he was going to do there, but he knew that Meenal would be walking out with him. He heard a knock on the door and after giving permission to enter, he saw Leeni appear and bow. Rex was slicking his hair back and stopped, returning her bow.

"I am the servant, therefore it's unnecessary to bow to me," she told him.

He shrugged. "What you need, Leeni? I gotta go soon."

"I can come with you and help you bid. I was part of a collection once before, so I know how their minds work. Meenal will most likely be the last to be auctioned off; therefore, it would be wise to wait until much later in the evening to depart."

"Why are you helping me?"

"As I said, I was part of a collection."

Much unlike Meenal, Leeni was very plain in her appearance. She had slanted green eyes, light brown skin, and light brown hair. Very little was physically interesting about her. Rex raised an eyebrow. With a roll of her eyes, Leeni pointed to her head, and he instantly got it. Her collector was more into powers than appearances.

"There is a very slim chance she will go to a brothel. The collectors will fight over her," Leeni said. "Do you want my help or not?"

"You apparently got a better idea than I do. I was just gonna take her."

Leeni sighed and left the room. Rex waited for her to return and when she did, she looked nothing like her plain appearance before. Her eyes were covered with a dark red eye shadow and outlined heavily. A hint of blush was on her cheeks and a lovely burgundy was on her lips. Her hair was pulled back into a tight and stylish ponytail and she wore one of Tiffanie's flashy dresses, white, and tall red heels. Rex tilted his head and stared at her, shocked by the transformation.

"Damn… you're kinda pretty when you actually do something with your hair," he said. She punched him hard in the arm. He laughed, rubbing the spot.

"Do not get used to this. I am only dressing in this fashion for Meenal. You are supposed to be a collector, and collectors love for their pieces to look their best. I would look out of place in my normal style of dress," she said.

"You okay? I know this is close to home."

She shrugged and turned away. "I'm hungry."

Rex allowed the conversation to drop and trudged off behind her. She instructed him in the way most collectors acted, saying that they do not view their pieces as living beings but as objects. They were to be used for whatever skill the collectors wished to exploit. The only skill that Meenal had, in Rex's opinion, was her use of language, for she spoke with no accent—in Jeletho with him and in Jaak with the slave driver. Leeni told him that she most likely would not be used for her language skills.

The hour had come when Leeni deemed it late enough to enter the auction. They made their way past the busy and gaudy side of downtown Chance and entered into one of the rougher patches of the city. After getting directions from various people, they arrived at a warehouse of sorts.

Rex kept his top hat low and scarf up, allowing Leeni to do all the talking. She sounded sweet and soft, coaxing the bouncer to allow them in. It was weird to Rex, and he had to keep himself from laughing. Once inside, she briefly displayed her displeasure with another solid punch in his arm. After that, they both returned to character.

Leeni guided Rex to the main part of the hall, following the sound of shouts and cheers. There was the auction block, in all its infamous glory, and upon it was another unique slave. She had light purple hair, matching eyes, and fluttering wings. Her only clothing accessories were chains bound to her wrists and ankles. Her naked thin frame stood alone on the block as booming voices fought against each other. Suddenly, a loud "Sold!" was heard, and the fairy's eyes went wide with fear as her new owner came to collect his prize.

"Meenal should be next. We'll stay in the shadows," Leeni said, turning to Rex and stopping short, "Rex— are you all right?"

"What?" he said.

"Your eyes—They're… They're glowing red."

He pulled down on his hat, covering his eyes. It was neither the time nor the place for such questions, despite her strong curiosity. Leeni had heard the rumors of his mother's eyes changing in the same fashion during times of distress. Yet, Rex's eyes had always been blackish-brown and nothing more.

Leeni pressed her lips together and led Rex to one of the unoccupied corners. She recalled the memories surrounding her, confirming her assumption. Meenal was next, and the excitement was great. She glanced at Rex again, the haunting red still visible. Shivering, she focused on the block and forced back her own memories.

"If this is too much, I can bid for you and you can wait outside," she said, but she felt a tight grip on her shoulder.

"Meenal's up," he said.

All eyes turned toward the block as big burly Dru entered into the spotlight. He held chains in his hands and, after some loud clanking noise, yanked them and pulled Meenal directly into the spotlight. As with the fairy before, the only thing she wore were the chains on her wrists and ankles.

Her eyes held the same hopeless expression as the fairy while she attempted to cover her exposed body. Her hair was no longer a matted mess but straight and flowing along her back, the purple highlights clearly visible now. Her skin seemed to shimmer in the light, causing "oohs" and "ahs" to sound throughout the crowd.

Rex gripped onto Leeni's shoulder tightly and fought off his rage, disgusted by their gawking and by them describing Meenal as if she were some sort of dog.

"Rex, are you sure you're all right?" Leeni asked again.

Realizing just how tight his hold had gotten, he let Leeni go and said, "Yeah, what's the plan?"

"We should wait until the bids start to die down. Due to her unique appearance, most of the visual collectors will fight over her, driving her cost up. If she is described as having powers, the power collectors could also help drive the price up. Once it appears that the price has outweighed the excitement surrounding her, we'll start bidding, but not a moment before."

She turned to face him and curled her finger. He leaned closer, and she whispered, "Keep silent, and she'll be free. Speak and you'll probably never see her again."

His eye color intensified, becoming more of a fiery red. Leeni stared at him in awe. Yet a loud and familiar voice caught their attention.

"Ladies and gentlemen, your attention please!" Titus said. "This beauty is slave number one six five zero, a visual collector's dream! I don't even need to describe her gorgeous white hair streaked with purple, her red *and* green eyes, her beautifully thin shape, and her sparkling blue-toned skin. Honest, it shimmers!"

He poked her with the butt of a whip, and she moved, twirling in limited circles. The shimmers bounced off the walls and only brightened as the spotlight briefly flickered out.

"She is the species of—*unknown*!" Titus continued. "Alien, creature X, mutant—she's it! That last piece to finalize even the most completed collection. And she's not just a pretty face and sweet body. This young one here's strong, stronger than an ox, indeed! She got skin like one too, able to withstand the harshest of punishments. I mean, really, we've tried to hurt her. There are no marks, I repeat, *no marks*, on any part of her little body! They just disappear, like magic." He gestured an imaginary cloud of smoke.

"*She's* magic, for she cooks, cleans, *and* listens. One more very important thing…" He started to chuckle, his fat jiggling in sync, "According to past owners, she is an interesting little creature in bed. Perfect for those brothel owners out there, she'll definitely fetch ya some nice change. So, folks, we gonna start this bid a little higher due to her *unique* abilities. Opening bid: two hundred silver coins. Who's up first?!"

The flood of bids was not immediate, as Titus and Leeni had both believed it would be. Silence filled the room as a single man in the back shouted, "You lying! Magical? Bah, prove it then!" He incited the crowd into a chant, "Prove it! Prove it!" and soon it grew louder.

The prospective buyers were not going to have a higher starting bid without some concrete evidence that she was as magical as Titus claimed. The chant became an ear-splitting cry. Meenal attempted to cover her ears with her bound hands as a frown settled on Titus's lips. Scanning the crowd, Titus shook his head and then waddled up to the girl, screaming, "Y'all want proof?!"

He turned her back against the crowd and cracked the whip against it. She hollered out and staggered. The sounds of the whippings silenced the chants as Titus threw his strength into the motion. Eventually, his fat body could not keep up with the demands of the crowd as they celebrated her spot-free back, wanting more.

Dru readily took over and started the process again with such vigor that Meenal could barely keep rhythm in her screams. Her cries rang out until she was quiet, slumping against Titus. He forced her to stand as Dru continued with his brutal assault.

Leeni had closed her eyes as soon as the whip appeared. The mere sight of it brought flashback after flashback of her experiences on different blocks. She attempted to mute the sounds, forcing herself to remain strong. But soon, it was too great for her, and she turned toward Rex to ask if she could leave. But he was gone.

"Enough!" Rex's voice rose above the applause as he attempted to snatch the whip away from Dru. The big man, startled by this interruption, yanked the whip away from the well-dressed gentleman, but Rex was quick. He dodged the whip, took hold of it, and swung the whip and Dru off the stage. Piece after piece of the gentleman's ensemble fell away during the scuffle, and the son of the abolitionist councilman was revealed. All cheering had ceased.

With fierce red eyes, Rex said, "I know this man here—Titus; he's the uncle I never had. I thought he was a good family man who treated others kindly. Seeing him *abuse* this girl—who's more than property, more than some ridiculous collection piece—ain't right in the slightest sense. She's a living, breathing creature. She has thoughts and dreams and fears, just like all of us. Somebody's daughter. She shouldn't be treated worse than some of y'all treat stray dogs. She must be respected like the person she is."

His words were met with silence, and Titus coughed awkwardly. Rex's eyes slowly returned to their brown color, and he smirked. "But of course, I'm asking too much for you lechers. Your minds are too one-tracked to broaden your horizons, and you'll be forever stuck between stupid and pitiful."

Angry buzzing started among the audience, and Titus tried to steer Rex off the block, but with one harsh shove, Rex sent him off the stage as well. Silence again.

"Let's up the ante. We gonna start the bidding that you sick lowlifes are asking for, but with a more interesting price. My bet's five hundred gold coins."

Gingerly returning to the block, Titus wrapped an arm around Rex, but quickly took it off once the red color of Rex's eyes returned. He waddled in front of Rex and opened his arms wide, encompassing the scene.

"Well, folks," Titus said, his loud voice almost too loud for the quiet, "we got ourselves a real auction. Current bid is five hundred gold coins. Yes, indeed, I said *gold*. Anyone willing to go five hundred and ten?"

A bidding war commenced, and soon enough it was only Rex and another man going back and forth, until the other man had the higher bid at seven hundred gold coins. Leeni had managed to squeeze her way toward the front, and Rex briefly looked down at her. She raised her eyes up, thinking, and then sharply nodded. Rex bid again and crossed his arms. The man pressed his lips together and dusted off his shoulders, signaling defeat.

"Current bid, seven hundred gold coins and two silvers. Any other bids? Going once?" With a broad grin on his face, Titus said, "Going twice…?"

Silence.

"Sold! To this crazy donkey over here, Rex Marshall!"

Despite the rough start, Rex did manage to get quite the applause for his purchase. He frowned deeply and spat. Dru, having recovered physically (his ego was still quite bruised), shoved Meenal toward Rex, and she landed in his arms. She looked at him with those same sad eyes, and remembering her place, she lowered her head.

Rex narrowed his eyes and wrapped his suit jacket around her. Surprised, she stared at him in amazement. Leeni tapped his leg and then handed him a folded piece of paper. He took it and opened it. He smirked and then showed it to the audience. In bold print, appearing at the top, were the words: "Application for Legalization of Residence."

"I'm not buying her for me, you disgusting pigs!" Rex shouted, pride increasing the volume of his voice. "I'm giving her a chance at a normal life. She's gonna be free!"

Meenal stared at him, her eyes showing the first spark of life he had seen. The audience booed and cursed him, declaring it wasteful to free such a fine specimen. Rex ignored them. He paid Titus his money, received some acceptable clothes for Meenal, and signed the transfer-of-ownership papers. They exited the hall and quickly moved past all the envious eyes of those who clearly disbelieved that Rex was actually going to free her. He silently answered their accusing glances with a smirk of his own, daring them to call his bluff.

CHAPTER 2

MEENAL WALKED BEHIND HER NEWEST master... not master, not owner... the latest man to purchase her—her benefactor, she finally decided. She heard brief snippets of the conversation he held with his faithful companion—another slave, she assumed. She heard the words "father," "freak out," and "slave" exchanged repeatedly, but she tried her best not to interfere. It was not her place to dip into the business of her benefactor.

Eventually, they stood in front of a grand manor. She admired the old architecture and majesty of the place. She recognized the structure as being from around 1700 BGC (before the Great Cataclysm) and she was amazed at the quality with which it had been restored. Slowly she stopped walking. Leeni turned around, nudging Rex. He turned around and watched her.

"Meenal?" he said, and she instantly snapped out of her daydream and bowed lowly.

"I beg for your forgiveness, benefactor. Please punish me as you see fit."

Rex approached, and Leeni tried to stop him, but he waved her away. Carefully, he took hold of Meenal's hands, and she flinched.

"Hey, it's okay; I'm not gonna hurt you. And I'll make sure no one ever will again, okay?" he said.

She raised her head, and his eyes surprised her.

"My benefactor's eyes are like one of mine," she said.

"Call me Rex. No master, no benefactor. Just Rex, aiight?"

She nodded, wondering the meaning of "aiight." He released her hands, and they continued, knocking on the door. The butler, Edmond, opened the door with a solemn expression that quickly turned to shock as he spotted the blue girl. Rex glared at him with red eyes, and Edmond quickly closed his mouth, clearing his throat and opening the door wider.

Leeni stepped in first, and Meenal hesitated, looking toward Rex. He waved her inside and with a deep bow toward Edmond, she entered. Her dazed look appeared once again as she gazed at the grand entryway and the chandelier glittering and mimicking her skin. Edmond blinked and looked over at Rex, giving him a questioning look. Rex mouthed, *Not a word.*

Rex and Leeni led Meenal up a flight of stairs and down a hallway. She glanced at all the different artwork on the walls, admiring the craftsmanship of each piece. Rex looked back and forth between her and the pictures. Meenal caught him one time and stared at him, but he instantly looked away. He opened a door and invited Meenal inside, but Leeni turned on Rex.

"Are you putting her in here? In your mother's old room?" she said, and Meenal widened her eyes at Leeni's grand show of disrespect.

He sighed. "Where the hell else am I supposed to put her?"

"Not here! This is Ms. Bala's painting room! You can't put her here!"

"You got a better idea?! You said my dad would freak. He don't come here."

Leeni narrowed her eyes and then stormed away. Meenal watched her and then turned back to Rex, noticing his eyes becoming red again. She quickly glanced down when he looked at her. For some time, they stood awkwardly in silence.

"Is there something that I may assist you with?" Meenal said, bowing.

"Stop with the damn bowing. You're free now, and we're equals," Rex said. "Hold your head up and do you."

She stared at him blankly. "'Do you?' I am unfamiliar with the expression."

"Dude, where you been? 'Do you' just means be yourself; don't be fake."

Meenal nodded slowly and wondered how in the world she was going to "do you." Usually, she was presented with a list of duties that would please her master. After a very short time, she would learn which words would please him and which would anger him.

From there, she would develop her default mode of behavior. However, Rex was presenting her with the opportunity to be herself, whoever that was.

"But ah, um… you gonna stay here 'til I find a way to talk to my dad about you," he said, scratching his head.

"Will I bring displeasure to your father?"

"Not if I can get your legal papers straightened out first; then we'll be cool."

"Will you be punished for your actions?"

"Yeah, probably, but…"

She dropped to her knees and bowed low.

"Please allow me to be punished on your behalf, for I owe you my life. I am indebted to you."

Rex raised his eyebrows. "Okay… just go on to bed. I'll see you in the morning."

She slowly lifted her head and watched him leave the room, praying that her overzealous attitude had not angered Rex, her strange new master.

Δ

The next morning was quiet. There was no heavy snoring or murmuring against her ear. No smacking against her neck, no nuzzling into her chest. When Meenal's eyes fluttered open, she saw that the first streams of light were brightening up the room.

She slowly sat up and then froze. Nothing ached, neither her head nor her body. Amazed, she moved to the right and then the left, not bumping into another person. She hesitantly kicked her legs, but still there proved to be no one. She let out a giant sigh, the first time in her life waking up alone.

Adhering to her strict orders, Meenal climbed out of the bed and explored her limited surroundings. The room was colored a light gold, and there were lovely, dark wood furnishings including an easel, a desk, and a full-length mirror.

She noticed an unfinished picture upon the easel and saw the same painting style as all the others. *This must be an unfinished work of Rex's mother.* Meenal envisioned her to be a woman of high ranking and grace due to the status of Rex's father, a councilman of Maventa. The craftsmanship of the strokes and attention to detail clearly revealed to Meenal that the woman was talented, possibly taught by one of the finest teachers of art.

Meenal scanned the rest of the room, noticing that it was rather sparse. She frowned, for this would make her discovery of her new landlords much more difficult. She picked up this knickknack and that trinket. She looked at each individual picture and admired each painting.

One framed picture caught her attention. She stopped in her exploration and picked it up. There was a man with light skin and dark hair and eyes, a woman with all dark features, and a young boy with a very similar appearance to the woman. Staring at the boy, Meenal recognized him as a younger version of her benefactor. The man most likely was his father, and the woman his mother. She tilted her head to the side and tried to imagine the atmosphere Rex had experienced in his childhood.

"Whatcha looking at?" She heard a voice and jumped, nearly dropping the photo. She quickly replaced it and turned around to see Rex with a tray of food. She bowed and upon rising, she saw him frown.

"I apologize if I have upset you," she said.

Rex ignored her and set the tray on the desk. He started to walk out of the room, but she stopped him.

"Rex?" she whispered.

"What?" he said, turning around.

"I simply wish to express my gratitude toward you in giving me freedom. I am uncertain as to how to repay you. Is there something in particular that you would like?"

"Wow—so formal. Um… no…?"

She bowed. "If you change your mind—"

"Stop, just stop. I gave you freedom because I wanted to, not because I wanna get anything from you. You got nothing I want anyways."

Shocked, Meenal said nothing and bowed. Once again, Rex frowned. A knock on the door drew his attention, and Tiffanie and Leeni popped their heads into the room.

"Your father just woke up. You should get ready for church," Tiffanie said, eyeing Meenal curiously. Meenal, glancing over at Rex for a sign and then half bowed and half nodded in Tiffanie's direction. Tiffanie narrowed her eyes at Meenal and whipped her head out of the doorway, her long brown hair following behind. Leeni rolled her eyes and shrugged, retreating from the room. Rex pressed his lips together and followed them out.

The next few days continued in the same manner, with Rex sneaking away and giving Meenal her meals. He repeatedly apologized for the lack of comfortable amenities and told her that the process of approving her alien residence was harder than he had originally thought.

During their brief moments together, Meenal tried to follow his speech. Yet, there were plenty of times when she was lost in translation. His use of slang was frequent, and his overall manner of speaking was much different from the majority of her previous owners, who had been high officials or even royalty. She thought he would be more refined, being the son of one of the country's leaders.

She also tried to get to know Rex on a more personal level. These attempts were even more of a failure than her translations. He was locked up tight, especially whenever she brought up the paintings and the artist who created them. He only confirmed that his mother had done all of them.

Δ

Some days later, Rex was out, wrestling with the legal system in the hopes of getting Meenal legalized.

Meenal, as always, waited alone in her chambers, admiring the outdoors and looking toward the sea.

When she was not trapped inside a boat in a cramped holding cell with hundreds of other slaves, she found the ocean to be beautiful and calming. She wondered if she would ever be able to enjoy it as her masters and their families did.

The door opened, calling her attention away, and she stood in the center of the room, waiting to greet her benefactor. But it was not Rex. It was his father. He stood tall with his head coming close to the top of the door. He had a thin frame and pale skin, but his dark eyes held a look that easily intimidated Meenal. She quickly bowed, remaining in her bowed position until he spoke.

"What are you doing here?" he asked, his voice revealing his irritation.

"Awaiting your son's return, sir," she said, bowing again.

"Your speech and respect for authority is greater than the others. What is your name?"

"Meenal, sir. What others? If it would please you, perhaps I could spend my time with them."

"What are you talking about? Are you not Rectavius's latest female companion?"

Meenal blinked at the use of Rex's proper name, as well as the mention of her true purpose. She cursed herself for believing that his words were truth.

She bowed. "You possess more knowledge than I will ever, sir. I was unaware of his true intentions in regards to my purchase."

The councilman's eyes narrowed and he stepped closer to her. She lowered her head and knew that she had misspoken, forgetting that Rex's father would be angry with him in regards to her. She cupped her hands together and waited for the punishment to come.

"Purchase?" the councilman said through gritted teeth.

"Yes sir. I was purchased by your son and he—"

"Get out."

"Sir?"

"I said get out!"

The councilman swung the door wider and pointed to it. She bowed again and made her way out. Once she was out, he slammed the door behind them and then screamed for the butler. Edmond appeared with his same solemn expression, as the lord of the house instructed him to usher out this slave, a disgrace to his family's name. Edmond nodded, and the councilman trudged off, calling his son every curse word in the book.

As Edmond and Meenal walked in silence to the door, she replayed the conversation in her head, wondering what she had said to warrant being thrown out onto the streets. She had assumed that she would be beaten for her lord's mistake and things would continue as if nothing had occurred. When they approached the door, she pleaded with the butler to allow her to stay, at least until Rex's return.

He, however, stayed true to his master's words and slammed the door in her face.

She stood there, hands clasped and face worried, hoping for someone else to take pity on her and allow her back inside. As time passed and the sun sunk lower, she knew that no such pity would be taken. It was a long walk toward the city, and she was completely unfamiliar with the land.

Going off alone could easily lead her to worse trouble than being a personal slave. She could find herself in one of those awful brothel houses. She shuddered and decided to wait for a little while longer, at least until sunset.

The sun continued its descent and soon enough, it was barely visible above the horizon. Her hope decreased, and she started to stand, preparing herself for the night. As she walked away from the manor, she noticed someone approaching—Rex. She immediately bowed. He cursed and grabbed ahold of her hand, yanking her back toward the door. He pounded his fist against it and barked, "Open the bloody door!"

Slowly, the door creaked open, and Rex impatiently shoved it fully open, dragging Meenal along with him. Leeni backed out of the way as Rex fumed, swearing loudly. She tried to calm him, but he would not stand for it and demanded to know where his father was. Leeni shook her head, and Rex grabbed her arm.

"Tell me where he is," he said, his eyes turning the haunting red color again.

"I told you not to leave her in that room. Your father is out. He will speak with you tomorrow at breakfast before your lessons," she said and shook herself out of his grasp.

"You didn't say anything! I've never seen him in there!"

"He goes in every once in a while; it's not consistent. I thought you knew and assumed that her holding there would be temporary."

He huffed and trudged away. Leeni looked at him and sighed, turning to Meenal. It, of course, would be her duty to deal with the confused slave.

"Follow me, and I will show you to your new quarters," Leeni said and began to walk.

Meenal quickly followed the small girl into a darkened hallway. Leeni took a lantern from the wall to light the way. There were no beautiful paintings on these walls, and there was no warmth at all. She suppressed the memories of the cold and damp holding cells, knowing that it was not going to last forever. She took a deep breath, and Leeni stopped, holding the light to her face.

"There is no need to worry, Meenal. This will not be like those other times," she said. Meenal tilted her head in shock.

"Are you a prophet?" she asked.

"No, I am simply an Earth elemental with the ability to recall memories, especially when those memories are brought to the fore by another. I can promise you. This will be different."

Meenal nodded slowly, still unsure of what the prophet-like girl spoke of. She had never heard of an Earth elemental. But she put the strange term away and focused on what was in front of her: a large and menacing door.

Leeni, with the slightest touch, opened the door and revealed a quaint and cozy bedroom. Meenal slowly walked inside and smiled at the sight of the bed and fireplace. She turned back toward Leeni, but she was already gone, leaving just as silently as they had come.

Alone, Meenal curled up onto the bed and prepared herself for the do-or-die moment of breakfast.

CHAPTER 3

KADMUS XAVIER MARSHALL WAITED AT the head of the table inside the secondary dining hall. He was not in the best of moods. The anniversary of his wedding to the love of his life was approaching, and she remained missing, having not been found alive or dead. The agony of having no closure ate away at him every year as their supposed celebration came and went.

Now, it seemed that his son, Rectavius, would add to his troubles, having purchased a slave. Rex well knew of his father's opposition to slavery. The council had passed countless motions on the abolishment of it, and Kadmus fought with all his power to make them law. However, he was in the minority, for every other council member enjoyed the use of slaves and they proclaimed that Maventa would fall to its knees without free labor. The council would surely humiliate him for his son's latest adventure.

Holding his head in his hands, he sighed as he heard the sound of footsteps coming into the dining hall. Looking up, he saw Tiffanie and her right-hand companion, Leeni. Leeni gave an awkward bow while

Tiffanie curtsied prettily. Completely different in their personalities and tastes, it was a miracle that they were friends at all. But as Tiffanie gave the menu for the breakfast in her loud and confident voice, Leeni quietly corrected her many mistakes. They were an interesting, though balanced pair.

Just as Tiffanie finished, Kadmus placed his order, and she gave a sharp nod and walked off, but Leeni remained for a brief moment. Kadmus looked at her expectantly, irritated that she remained. He wished to be left alone in order to prepare himself for the meeting with his son. He did not want to deal with whatever issue Tiffanie was causing. He had much bigger problems at hand.

"What is it?" He sighed. Leeni stared at him long and hard before speaking. Despite his speech about freedom for all, respect and order were highly ranked in his set of values. He would not stand to be given such impertinence.

"Do not be trifling with me, Leeni. I am not in a pleasant mood," he said. She kept her silence, staring him down. He returned the stare, narrowing his eyes in annoyance and waiting for her to fall through the ice.

"Councilman Marshall," she said, bowing, "I know that you are of good heart and sound mind and therefore it is unnecessary of me to remind you of your son's good intentions in regards to the slave. But nevertheless, please, my lord, be kind to him."

She bowed again and took her leave. Kadmus softened his eyes and sighed once again, wondering what that powerful girl had seen in his memories: His outburst at the poor slave, who had been thrown into the situation against her will? The names he called his son? Whatever it was, it was enough for her to speak in favor of Rex, specifically mentioning his good intentions. Yet, good intentions were useless without a well-thought-out plan.

More footsteps came, and Kadmus turned his attention to Edmond, who had appeared, announcing Rex and Meenal. They stepped out of the shadows, Rex looking ready for war and Meenal looking ready to run. Her entire body was stiff and on edge, and her eyes darted everywhere to avoid eye contact with Kadmus. Kadmus berated himself for his previous behavior in regards to her, for she obviously was not the one who had placed herself in his wife's painting room. It was misdirected rage, and now, he had a chance to settle the wrong.

He stood and approached the slave, ignoring his son promptly, and bowed. Meenal still avoided any eye contact. Deciding that it would probably be better not to mention it, Kadmus said, "I wish to apologize for my behavior the previous day. While this is no excuse for such a poor disposition, I was caught off guard by your presence in my wife's painting room. Please, accept my apology."

Meenal stared at him, shocked. But she played her part exactly, accepting the apology and joining

Kadmus and Rex at the table. Tiffanie and Leeni returned to collect Meenal and Rex's orders, hurrying away to leave the three of them alone. Once they left, Kadmus faced Meenal and said, "I am curious, Miss Meenal, about your place of origin, your people, and your culture. What place do you call home?"

"I am uncertain of my origin or heritage. To be quite honest, my good gentleman, I have never had a home, for with a new master came a new place. I have never stayed with one particular man long enough to consider his land my land or his people my people," she said with exquisite professionalism and no accent in her speech.

"How—I don't understand. You cannot be much older than Rectavius."

"I have been the slave of twelve different men. I have been the concubine of a crowed prince, a part of the winnings of a poker game, and the caretaker of a village doctor's children. My previous master, a chieftain of one of the most powerful tribes in Navistan, was killed during a revolt, and the rebels deemed me too strange in appearance to be of any use to them besides profit."

"What of your parents and siblings?"

"I have neither."

Kadmus shook his head and sighed deeply. Her life story made him admire his son for his courage in freeing this pitiful creature. Yet, the issue of buying a slave at all remained.

"Did you enjoy your time at the slave auction?" he asked, taking a sip of his tea.

Rex glared at his father and said nothing. Meenal looked from Kadmus to Rex and back again, waiting for either of them to speak.

"Rectavius, I asked you a question and I wish for you to answer it. Did you enjoy yourself at the auction, seeing all the lovely women flashing in front of your eyes? Then you saw her…"

Kadmus turned his dark eyes toward Meenal, and she looked away, picking at her fruit salad.

"When you saw her, you had to have her for yourself, didn't you?"

"I bought her freedom," Rex muttered.

"Oh, yes, you did buy her—bought her for your pleasure, and had her locked up in your mother's painting room to have your way with her."

"I bought her freedom," Rex said, his voice growing louder.

"Did you even consider my reputation as an abolitionist or my position on slavery before purchasing this girl? What will the other council members think of your most recent acquisition?"

"I did," Rex growled, his eyes fading to red briefly.

"In what way? You are the son of a prominent abolitionist, the heir of a leader in the fight against slavery. You purchased a slave, brought her into my home, hid her away in my wife's personal room, and colluded in a conspiracy with my own employees! Strangers knew more of what was occurring in my own house! So please, tell me how you considered my reputation. Educate me."

Rex remained silent with his eyes shifting between brown and red as his father waited for an answer. After some time, Kadmus continued with a renewed sense of disappointment.

"If you wish to join me in my fight, you are going about it in the most ineffective way. People are not going to associate your stand with the abolishment movement. They will believe that you purchased her for her uniqueness. Still others will believe that you made a pact with Titus to raise the bid to ensure that only you purchased her. Most will only remember your outburst and how you handled that poor man Dru, an honest man simply completing his work. Thankfully, you did not kill him or leave him with any life-changing injuries. But is physical assault the way of a peaceful movement?"

Rex stood and an inhuman sound emitted from his mouth, a mixture between a snarl and a roar. His eyes had become fully red. Kadmus had never seen such a transformation in his son before. He stared in frightful awe as heat radiated from Rex. Meenal watched as Rex inched forward, the humanity slowly disappearing from his eyes.

"Master," she called out and drew his attention away from the councilman. He cocked his head and like lightning, he was on her, his hand covering her mouth and nose. Her eyes widened as she tugged at his hand, but he ignored her struggles and narrowed his eyes in displeasure.

"I'm not your master," he said, his voice distorted and raw. "I bought your freedom, not you. You're nothing to me."

"Rex, let her go," Kadmus shouted. "Will you kill her before she can even experience freedom?!"

"Kill her? I freed her! Those *honest* men, they would've killed her! I'm not like that!"

Meenal clawed at his hand and beat on his arm, but he would not budge. Rex stared down at his father as though threatening him not to come near.

"Let her go! She cannot breathe!" Kadmus tried again, and finally Rex felt her death-grip on his arm and turned to see Meenal with wide eyes. He jerked away from her, and she dropped to the floor, gasping for air. He glanced down at his hand and turned toward his father, his familiar brown eyes pleading for understanding.

Kadmus shook his head and backed away. Rex looked down again at Meenal and staggered back, racing out of the dining hall.

After receiving medical attention at the insistence of Kadmus and comforting the poor councilman on his son's burst of rage, Meenal decided to search out her benefactor. While it seemed illogical, being that he had nearly suffocated her to death, part of her knew that it had been an accident. An emotion had overtaken him, and he lost himself. She had dealt with much more violent masters who never showed remorse for their actions. Rectavius Marshall, while strange, was nothing like those so-called honest men Kadmus spoke of.

She traveled through the hallways, seeing dark wood dominate the furnishings and the floor. She ran her fingers across the walls, distinguishing them from the doors. She heard bustling and talking in the shadows, but she did not bother to follow the sounds. She continued her exploration when she noticed some light at the end of her current hallway. It was bright like sunrays from a window.

Meenal moved closer and in doing so, she heard soft piano music. It was beautiful. Keeping her steps quiet, she tiptoed and then peeked around the corner. She could see nothing of the pianist, the piano hiding him. Suddenly, the music flared to a dramatic conclusion, and the pianist slammed down on the keys. The sound reverberated off the walls and made Meenal's ears ring. She rubbed her ears and slowly approached, but the pianist stood up.

"Stay away," Rex ordered, taking giant steps back and holding his hands out.

Meenal tilted her head in confusion but nodded and said, "Please pardon my interruption. I did not wish to—"

"Shut up with all the damn apologizing. It's annoying, and besides, I should be apologizing to you. I almost killed you! How are you gonna act like nothing happened?"

"If I may speak frankly, your father was being melodramatic. I have been in much more serious pain. I doubt your ability to kill me easily."

He slammed his fists against the keys. "Cat vomit! Don't belittle what I just did to you! I attacked you for no reason."

"I caused you to become upset, therefore it is my fault. Punish me, if anyone should be punished."

Meenal fell prostrate before him. She waited for some time before looking up to see him staring at her in bewilderment.

"Mas—?" she called but his stare only hardened. She tried again, "Rex…?"

"Get up. You look like an idiot on the ground," he said, and immediately, she stood, apologizing. He rolled his eyes and returned to the piano, starting again. Meenal remained silent and listened respectfully as he perfectly played a piece from the famous composer Ulrich M. Penna, the dwarf who challenged the stereotype that his kind was not creative. She watched Rex's hands move all across the piano, and she envied his talent. She had no musical ability in her bones.

Rex stopped again and stared at her. She bashfully looked down at her feet until she heard him bark, "Look up!"

She did and with a frown on his face, he stood up from the piano bench and patted it.

"Pop a squat," he said, and she gave him a look of confusion. He chuckled and translated, "Have a seat."

She sat down and waited for further instruction. He told her to place her thumbs on the middle key and lay the rest of her fingers down accordingly.

With extreme caution, she did so. When he directed her to play, he repeatedly prodded her to hit the key with any force. Eventually, she played this note and that note, creating a familiar tune. Once he finished instructing her, he said, "Congratulations, you just played 'Fairy Fields.'"

"I did not realize that a child's song would be so complicated," she said.

"Nah, you're just a crappy piano player. Too stiff in the fingers—well, too stiff everywhere. You gotta loosen up and quit being such a stick in the mud."

She tilted her head at him, equally intrigued and frustrated with his use of idioms and sayings. Standing up from the piano, she asked, "How do you wish for me to be? I do not understand what it is that you want. I am stiff because I have not been instructed on the proper behavior for my position."

"What?"

Meenal glanced down and remembered the words of Kadmus, telling her that she was yet another special lady friend of his son. She folded her hands and said, "To me, you are my benefactor, since you insist on not being my master. However, I have no idea what I am to you."

"Um..." Rex said, scratching his head, "does it matter? Ah, I guess you're right. No, I'm not your master; nobody is. And 'benefactor' makes me sound old and creepy, like I expect to be repaid or something."

"You do not wish to receive payment for purchasing my freedom?"

"No... I just wanted to do something nice. Can't a guy do something nice for a girl without wanting anything in return?!" Meenal stared blankly at him, and he sighed. "Forget it. But you aren't anything to me. You can be whatever you want. I mean, we can try to be friends."

"Friends?"

"Yeah, friends. You wanna be friends?"

"Yes, though I am unsure of what a friend is supposed to do. You shall be my first."

"That's kinda sad, Meenal. But a friend is someone who's always there for you, through thick and thin. Someone who tells you when you're being a butt-face, and they'll bail you outta jail... or be in jail with you, depending on the circumstances."

"I believe that sounds... interesting. I shall try my best to be your friend."

She bowed, and he rolled his eyes, standing up and walking away. She hurried after him as he gave her the lowdown on being his friend.

"Rule Number One: You are only allowed to be Miss Prissy Proper around other proper folks. Otherwise, cut with the bowing and apologizing crap. It's annoying."

CHAPTER 4

REX STOOD TALL, HIS HAIR SLICKED BACK. He wore a pale blue button-up shirt and a light gray wool jacket and matching slacks. His shoes were black and clunky, but he ignored that unstylish part of his attire. He was looking his best, and it was certainly a night for celebration.

It was Meenal's one-month-of-freedom anniversary, and according to the majority of onlookers, it had been quite the successful month. After Rex calmed himself and Kadmus assuaged his fears, they discussed Meenal's outcome.

Kadmus pushed for her to go to a convent or some other sort of women's shelter, where they would properly care for her needs and teach her basic life skills. Rex pushed for her to remain with them at Marshall Manor, since women were usually taken advantage of inside those so-called safe havens.

Of course, with the threat of another outburst and a rational argument on his side, Rex won, and Meenal was permitted to reside with the Marshalls as a long-term guest. However, she had to obtain legal alien residency, a respectable occupation, and a modest wardrobe; otherwise, the agreement would be null and void.

The first two requirements were easy to accomplish once the councilman became involved. Using his influence, Meenal earned legal-alien residency (despite never having been a legal citizen of any country) and a governmental job as a translator. She had never realized how valuable her knowledge of language was, and her broad and formal vocabulary only sweetened the deal for both the council and Meenal.

The final requirement of a modest wardrobe was difficult to acquire at first, since she had never been allowed to choose what she wore. Yet, with the help of Leeni as well as Tiffanie, who quickly befriended Meenal once she realized Rex was not romantically interested in the former slave, Meenal's attire was stylish and modest. Since she was doing so well and never had experienced an official night out on the town, Rex thought it best to show her how the Maventi threw down and partied.

He continued to admire himself for a few minutes more, making kissing faces in the mirror before he was interrupted with a cough at the door. He turned and spotted Tiffanie and Leeni. Tiffanie, looking sharp as well, wore a form-fitting red dress and dazzling silver sandals.

Leeni, on the other hand, looked washed out in her beige shirt, light-brown pants, and clunky shoes similar to Rex's own pair. Her hair seemed to be struggling against the braid that Tiffanie had obviously constructed. Tiffanie sashayed toward Rex and stood on her tippy-toes to give him a kiss on the cheek. He accepted the kiss with exaggerated appreciation while Leeni just rolled her eyes.

"What's the matter, grumpy-pants?" Tiffanie said.

"If you two would stop flirting, we could make our reservation," Leeni said, crossing her arms.

"Ugh! You're such an Earth!"

"And you are such an Air. Now both of you, let's go. We still have to find Meenal."

Rex laughed and gave Tiffanie a sloppy kiss on the cheek, causing her to squeal, much to the displeasure of Leeni, who turned out of the room and started toward Meenal's bedchamber. Tiffanie giggled, gave Rex a hug, and then pranced out of the room, following Leeni. Rex did a double-take in the mirror before joining the ladies in Meenal's room.

He heard whistles and shouts upon entering. He looked at Tiffanie and correctly assumed that the screaming had come from her. What caught him by surprise was Leeni. She was whistling, showing an emotion other than pissed-off. He finally looked at whatever had their attention, and it was Meenal. She was... absolutely beautiful.

She was sitting on the stool in front of her vanity, adjusting her pinned-up hair. She had a hint of color on her lips, a pretty purple. She wore a dress nearly the same shade as the purple on her lips, with a single white line running from under her bust to the bottom of the dress.

She looked up, and Rex noticed a gemmed eye patch covering her left eye, her red eye. He wondered why she would cover up one of her most distinct features. Her eyes made her stunning. He felt the sudden urge to rip the patch from her face, but he contented himself to frown, displaying his disapproval from that angle instead.

She smiled at them in the mirror and slowly stood, turning around and giving them a bow. Tiffanie skipped over to Meenal and kissed her on the cheek. Leeni's enthusiasm left just as soon as she heard the clock tower belling out eight o'clock. Tiffanie hung her arms around Meenal's shoulders, causing Meenal to hunch over in an uncomfortable position. Yet, Meenal's small smile only grew. Tiffanie, seeing the grumpy expressions on Rex and Leeni's faces, sighed and released Meenal.

"You look nice. You'd look better without the damn eye patch," Rex said, and Leeni hit him hard in the side. Tiffanie stuck her tongue out at Rex and hugged Meenal tightly.

"Shut it, Rex! Did you consider that she prefers the eye patch? Gives her a sense of comfort? Maybe she doesn't want to stand out for once?" Tiffanie countered. Rex rolled his eyes and shrugged.

"If it would please my friend, then I shall remove it," Meenal said quietly.

"Do what you want, Meenal. I've told you that already."

She nodded, removed the eye patch, and placed it on her dresser. She stood and slipped on her flats for the evening. Finally all put together, Rex and the ladies walked outside and got into their carriage to take them to one of the fanciest places in all of Maventa's capital, Chance: the Melody Pearl Bar.

Upon arriving at the Pearl Bar, they all had forgotten about the awkward conversation regarding Meenal and her different-colored eyes. They were laughing, joking, and enjoying each other's company. Rex particularly loved his time with Meenal, since he deemed it his goal to make her blush.

Meenal was still stiff, only giving a well-practiced smile that had probably made all her old owners happy. But Rex was searching for her genuine feelings, wanting to know the real Meenal, not the fake slave version of her.

The carriage stopped in front of the restaurant, where dozens of people stood in a long line that wrapped around the building. The diversity that this type of restaurant pulled was evident. It was loud, with shouting and squealing and chattering circling all around them.

Meenal stayed close to Rex, her eyes wide and one hand covering the ear facing the crowds. He looked over at her and wondered if it was the right thing to do to bring her to the busiest bar on her first night out. She smiled softly to the ones who greeted her and she seemed to be fine. But still, she was a master of hiding her emotions, so just to make sure, Rex leaned over into her ear, but she jerked back.

"Sorry! I was just gonna whisper in your ear," he said, somewhat offended that she had reacted so violently.

She smiled regretfully, swallowing her apology, and nodded for him to continue. She still flinched as he whispered, "We can leave whenever you want. It's your party."

She smiled again and nodded, returning her eyes back to the entrance. As they neared it, the noise grew louder as the line waiters noticed who was entering the restaurant. The reporters threw questions at Rex, wondering who his mystery guest was. Admirers wished to learn the name of the beauty who was on his arm.

Tiffanie and Leeni pushed Meenal through as Rex shoved a clear path. Meenal looked at her friends and frowned, unsure of what to think of them distracting her from answering the reporters' questions.

They stopped at the entrance of the restaurant, and after Rex stated his full name, the guards eagerly ushered him and his party inside. The heavy doors shut behind them, and the loud shouting of questions disappeared. Soft, upbeat music played in the background. Hushed conversations overpowered the instruments.

Waiters and waitresses served hors d'oeuvres and champagne to the guests seated at tables covered with golden cloths. A waiter came over and gracefully directed them to a table in the middle of the room.

The band grew slightly louder, and Tiffanie was already dancing, wagging her bum in the waiter's face as he pulled out her chair for her. Meenal gave her a strange look but returned her attention to the band. Her eyes followed the movements of their hands and mouths. The tempo sped up and slowed down, the loud drums pounding in her chest. She tapped her foot and hummed softly as she bobbed her head from side to side.

Her body froze as she suddenly felt a touch on her shoulder and a memory jumped to the forefront of her mind. She could feel an imaginary breath against her neck and invisible hands exploring her body further.

She closed her eyes and wished the memory away, trying to convince herself that she was not trapped in that dreadful room with her sadistic master. Yet, the memory replayed in her mind each second the hand remained on her shoulder.

Meenal opened her eyes and saw Leeni looking directly at her with an understanding expression. Taken aback, she looked away and stood abruptly, nearly bumping into someone. Finally noticing the newcomers, she bowed, saying, "Please pardon my fidgetiness, for this is my first official outing to enjoy Chance's nightlife. I am inexperienced and certainly on edge from all the exciting new things. Oh, but where are my manners? Allow me to introduce myself. I am Meenal Libéré."

She bowed again and fixed her face into a look of calm, hiding the fear from the previous minute. It did not fool Leeni at all as she watched Meenal with concern. Meenal ignored her and looked at the person who had touched her, a young man with features too small for his broad frame. In a high-end black suit with lavender accents, he stood eye-to-eye with her, his light brown eyes widening upon meeting hers. He raised his chin slightly before giving her a deep bow. With an awkward smile, he quickly readjusted his floppy brown hair and smoothed out his suit. His pale hands were cold as he took hers and gently placed a kiss on them.

"Charmed. I am Septimus Maxence, the seventh son of Lord Seneca Maxence of the Emerald Region. I have wanted to make your acquaintance ever since I heard the rumor of Rectavius Marshall, son of the abolitionist councilman, buying a *slave*," he said with a slimy voice and a smile broadening from awkward to sly.

"Sorry to disappoint, Sept, but I didn't buy a slave. I bought her freedom. Big difference, cuz," Rex said, rising and standing in between Septimus and Meenal. He glared down at his cousin, silently daring him to say something else stupid. Septimus blinked and looked behind Rex to meet Meenal's eyes.

"But you did beat out the other participants in the *slave* auction, did you not? And you were handed her *slave* papers, right? Rectavius my cousin, you indeed bought yourself a slave. How have you been enjoying her? She is quite the fine specimen, and I love her two-toned eyes."

He reached out to touch Meenal, but Rex slapped his hand away, glaring at him. Septimus smiled that sly grin again and continued to stare at Meenal. He held out a sweaty palm.

"Would the lovely slave like to dance?" he asked, his eyes roaming up and down her body. "With such a lovely form, you must be a graceful dancer. Come on, show us you're worth the seven hundred gold he paid."

Meenal lowered her head and slowly took his hand. His grin widened, and he walked her over to the dance floor. Despite the upbeat tune playing in the background, Septimus pulled Meenal in close and draped her arms around his shoulders. He settled his hands on her lower back, and throughout the dance, they lowered ever so slightly.

Rex watched the two of them together at the edge of self-control. Tiffanie and Leeni said nothing, as Septimus's and Rex's shared companions, Thaddaeus, Jackson, and Jacqueline, joined them at their table. The twins, Jackson and Jacqueline, talked softly among themselves while Thaddaeus tried to remind Rex of a story from their childhood that included Septimus. Rex turned his attention to Thaddaeus and demanded, "Why you hang with this guy? He's such a prick!"

Thaddaeus frowned. "'Ey, what you blamin' me for? I'm doin' what I gotta do. His father owns some of the biggest theaters in Maventa. I gotta get my big break somewhere and he's my best bet."

"Oh, my bad. Never mind we've been friends for ten years. Being bros must not mean much anymore."

Rex rolled his eyes, and Tiffanie patted his arm, hoping to soothe him, but he turned away from her. She sighed and stood, stretching. She turned to Jackson and demanded that they dance together. Jackson agreed and led her to the dance floor. Jacqueline soon followed suit with Thaddaeus, who received more angry glares from Rex. Only Leeni and Rex remained at the table as Septimus and Meenal returned. Rex could not read Meenal's expression. As usual, it was completely obscure. His eyes faded red as he turned his glare toward Septimus.

"Thank you for the lovely dance," he said, kissing Meenal's hand. "I would love to see what else you can do. Perhaps your owner can loan you to me sometime."

Meenal glanced down and stared at her hands. In a flash of movement, Rex grabbed Septimus's shirt collar and lifted him off the ground. Yet, despite the fury that was in his eyes, he kept his voice down and muttered into Septimus's ear, "I don't care if we're related or not. I'll kill you if you insult Meenal again. Now leave and don't bother her anymore."

Septimus turned stark white and once Rex released him, he quickly dismissed himself. Leeni sighed and nudged Rex on the shoulder.

"I'm happy you took care of him before I did," she said.

Rex said nothing. He just sat with his arms crossed.

"Rex…" Meenal whispered, and he shot her a glare. She glanced away from him and dismissed herself, heading toward the restroom. Leeni smacked Rex on the back of the head and called him stupid. He hissed at Leeni, and she rolled her eyes, crossing her own arms in disappointment. Minutes passed, and the couples returned. No one asked where Septimus had gone, but Tiffanie instantly smacked Rex on the back of the head with her purse.

"Where's Meenal?" she said. When he didn't answer fast enough, she whacked him again. He cursed at her but stood and said that he was going to go look for Meenal. When Tiffanie started to follow him, he ordered her to stay behind.

She stutter-stepped and pouted. "I should go too, so you're not alone. You're the one who chased her away in the first place."

"And that's the whole reason why I should go *alone*," he said.

Tiffanie started to protest, but Rex silenced her with a hard glare. He turned away and started toward the restrooms. As he left, he heard her yelling at the waiter for a drink, a Golden Rod with a triple shot.

Meenal sat on a stone bench at the fountain just outside the restaurant. She stared at her reflection in the water, wondering why so many people deemed her beautiful. She was nothing of the sort. White hair, blue skin, and a bizarre red eye made her nothing close to human, which had become the default standard of beauty. She frowned and turned away from her reflection. She stared up at the moon and closed her eyes, taking in the silence of the night, the slightest smile creeping onto her face.

Hearing someone approach, she opened her eyes and waited. The footsteps were heavy and fast, though they did not sound angry. She relaxed when she saw it was Rex appearing from the shadows. He gave a short, awkward wave and took a seat diagonally from her on another bench.

They sat and said nothing to each other for some time. Her curiosity compelled her to meet his gaze, which never seemed to leave her. Her previous slave training, however, forced her to look away and stare at her hands, seeing the little sparkles that appeared on her skin during the night. They were like stars, shimmering as she breathed and shifted.

"Please excuse my ignorance, but I do not understand your reasoning for anger," Meenal said.

"Really? You don't get it?" he said, his voice giving away that he was still upset.

"Yes, I do not understand. Sir Maxence was only stating the facts of my previous state as a slave."

Rex cursed, and Meenal dropped to her knees, begging Rex for forgiveness. He stared at her.

"Get the hell up! That's just it, you're not a slave! Not anymore. He was mocking us. You didn't have to dance with him or anyone else. You got the right to choose what you want. You're not my slave! You're just you!"

She lifted her head. This was not good. She had displeased her benefactor, her friend. He wanted more from her. He wanted her to be herself, but she had never had such an opportunity before and she was floundering under the weight of it. A month had already passed since Rex had purchased her independence, and she believed that she had made strides of progress. Yet, it was not enough to satisfy Rex.

She stood and stared at him. "I am me? I apologize, my friend. I still do not understand what it is you want from me."

He frowned, crossed his arms, and said, "You want to know what I want from you? Fine. Kiss me."

"What?"

"You heard me. I wanna kiss."

"I do not under—"

"Enough of that!"

Meenal glanced down and bit her lower lip. He made no sense. First, he claimed that she held nothing he wanted and that his sole wish was for her to be herself, an independent person with her own opinions and thoughts. Now he demanded a kiss. She raised her head to face him and saw a deep frown on his lips, which was off-putting. Nevertheless, she continued in order to please her complicated friend. Before she actually did kiss him, though, Rex put his hand over her face and pushed her back. She stumbled and then stared at him in disbelief.

"No," he said.

"No?" she said, ever more confused.

"Yes. No."

"Rex, please be plain with me, for I am lost in your way of speaking."

He sighed. "You got the right to tell me and anyone else no. Some are pricks and won't listen to you, but I'll make damn sure that those around me will."

He demanded again, "Kiss me."

"I apologize, but I must refuse."

"Eh, close enough. Congratulations, you've graduated from obedient slave to opinionated resident."

Meenal smiled softly and nodded, thanking Rex for his guidance in the land of freedom. He gave her a shrug and led her back to the party, where the rest of their crew was waiting for them.

After Tiffanie hounded Meenal for details about her alone time with Rex (for which he received plenty of whacks on the head from her and Leeni), they pulled her to the dance floor and joined the pulsing crowd of partiers. She was quite uncomfortable at first, staring at the others for instruction on their sort of wild dancing. Yet, soon enough, she joined in with graceful moves and flawless rhythm.

Meenal, in time, found herself dancing in between Jackson and Jacqueline, the redheaded brother and sister duo she had met that night. Jacqueline moved with just as much grace as Meenal did, while Jackson was offbeat and awkward. She smiled and forced her movements to mimic his unusual dance style.

Jackson saw that she was dancing with him and beamed a bright grin. He grew bolder and took her in his arms, twirling her in a circle before just as quickly releasing her. She laughed loudly above the music. While the laugh was loud, it flowed with the sounds, and the crowd cheered, believing the band had done it. Jackson widened his eyes at Meenal, and she slowed her movements, embarrassed. But he beamed that bright grin again and her concerns quickly vanished.

The music continued, and Meenal felt her worries slipping from her fingers. Her body took on a life of its own, binding with the music. Jackson and his awkward dance steps floated away, as well as the other hundreds of bodies crowded around her. It was only her and the band as she spun and swung her hips. Carefree bliss engulfed her for the first time in her life. She heard no voices. Only the music sung to her.

The restaurant was closing down as the town clock struck three in the morning. Rex and Thaddaeus slurred their feelings for each other, reestablishing their close friendship with a manly embrace and handshake.

Meenal, Tiffanie, Leeni, Jackson, and Jacqueline, all sat in a booth, sleepiness and/or drunkenness glazing over their eyes. As Rex and Thaddaeus joined them, Tiffanie moved to sit on Rex's lap while Leeni leaned against Jacqueline with her head on her shoulder. Jackson and Thaddaeus were using each other to prop themselves up, their heads bobbing up and down to the rhythm of oncoming sleep. Meenal, unlike all of them, sat properly and straight. Yet, despite her rigid back, she felt herself easily dozing off.

A loud clap jarred all of them awake, and Jacqueline even materialized a fireball in her hands, ready to incinerate the noisemaker. The bouncer held up his hands and softly asked if they could leave the restaurant. It was closing for the night. One by one, they all moved from the booth and headed out the door.

Rex then found his place beside Tiffanie and nuzzled his face into her neck. Thaddaeus took Jacqeline's hand and laced their fingers together. Leeni listened silently as Jackson stammered and stuttered through a story about his latest adventure in the arenas.

Meenal looked on at everyone and smiled. It was strange not being paired up with anyone, yet she enjoyed the solitude. It was calming, and watching the others interact was interesting. And none of them seemed to notice her absence, which was the complete opposite of her previous life.

The fact that she could disappear overwhelmed her with possibilities, and she stopped in her tracks. Never before had that option been available and yet now, here it was, working itself out. With a new sense of excitement and a desire for discovery, she quickened her pace to rejoin the others.

The group reached a crossing, and the party split. Thaddaeus, Jackson, and Jacqueline went to the right, while Tiffanie, Leeni, Rex, and Meenal went to the left. They waved and disappeared into the night. Tiffanie and Leeni huddled against each other in the brisk early-morning breeze. They walked quickly, leaving behind Rex and Meenal. He slowed down to match her pace, and she smiled at him softly before returning to her stoic expression.

"Had fun?" he asked.

"Oh yes. I do believe I know why these restaurants and… clubs are so addicting to the people of this land," she said.

"Yeah… we party."

He held out his hand and nodded to it. Meenal politely shook her head and said, "Thank you for the lovely gesture, Rex, but I must decline. I enjoy walking on my own."

He blinked and frowned. She then started to place her hand in his, but he snatched it away, scowling at her.

"Nah, stick to your first answer. Don't change just because someone gives you a pouty face or some sad story. Only change if it'll benefit you or save you from harm. Got it?"

She nodded, and he tried it again; she refused. He gave the pouty face, and she still refused. He dropped to his knees and pleaded with her to hold his hand. She stepped back, attempting to cover up her giggles. She shook her head, and he grinned. Jumping up onto his feet, they walked together back to the Marshall Manor—back home.

CHAPTER 5

EENAL AWOKE AT DAWN WITH THE sun barely visible above the horizon. She felt it was going to be a busy day. She moved straight from the bed to her desk. She lit a candle and continued her work from the previous night. She was currently translating a government announcement, seeking the registration of all residents within Maventa, wanting name, occupation, head-of-household status, and legalization.

The council had promised that those residing within the country illegally would not be deported but given a certain amount of time and substantial assistance in earning legal residency or even citizenship. However, if the resident did not register with the council within the allotted time frame, he and all his dependents (or other family members in his care) would be banished from Maventa and either deported to their original country or to Aharra, the prison territory.

Meenal was unclear of the reasoning behind registering each person inside the country's boundaries, and she brought her query to Councilman Marshall.

With the initial shock of her history gone, and the proof of her ability to be a hard worker made known by the past year and a half, Meenal found herself in Kadmus's good favor. He even deemed her his favorite of Rex's entourage. Due to her status, she had asked Kadmus for the reasoning behind the new law.

"The registration has two goals: one, to gain an accurate status of the current population of Maventa in order to gauge who would be available for a military draft, and two, to capture all the drug lords and their subordinates. It's assumed that they will not register with the council in time and therefore will be banished. All those who register with the council will be given a small invisible tattoo stating their status as a legal resident of Maventa. The tattoo will be placed on the inside of the resident's wrist and will only been seen by a special elemental frequency, which certain Fire elementals emit. The process of registration is not difficult and doesn't even cost the people money, making it as painless as possible."

He assured Meenal that it was in the country's best interest. She accepted his explanation, knowing that he understood the Maventi way of life. In all honesty, she still found the people and culture strange at times.

The sun slowly rose and eventually made the candle useless. Meenal blew it out and continued translating, moving from the third language to the fourth. She sighed as she heard a knock on the door and quietly allowed entrance.

Leeni entered and announced that breakfast was served. Meenal thanked Leeni, but said that she would eat later in the morning. Leeni frowned and bowed, quietly shutting the door.

Meenal continued, and the morning passed, her delicate handwriting scratching against the rough paper. She thought about the various expressions and words that would best suit the strong and authoritative tone that the council wanted. She finished a sentence and set down her pen as she heard another knock on the door. She glanced at the window and saw that it was no longer morning at all.

Tiffanie did not wait for an answer from Meenal and barged into the room. She walked over to her and squeezed her shoulders. She looked at the document that sat on the desk and scratched her head.

"What are those?" she asked.

"It is an announcement from the council regarding the registration of all Maventa residents, both legal and illegal," Meenal said, stacking the announcements into a neat pile. "Is there something I may help you with, Tiffanie?"

"Nothing much. We're just going to the beach and we want you to come with us."

"To the beach?"

"Yes, the beach. Don't tell me you don't know what a beach is. A place with sand... right next to the ocean, yes?"

"Oh yes, I know of a beach. However, I have plenty of work to do, and this announcement is very important according to Councilman Marshall."

"Councilman Marshall says everything is very important. Come on; it can wait. Don't you want to go swimming?"

"Swimming? In the ocean?"

Tiffanie laughed. "Of course, where else?"

"I am saddened to say that I have never been swimming before and I am very fearful of drowning."

Tiffanie grabbed Meenal's arm and dragged her up from the chair. Meenal tripped over one of the dictionaries on the floor and stumbled into Tiffanie's arms. Tiffanie squealed and shouted for Leeni. They collapsed onto the floor on top of each other with Meenal's face inside the crook of Tiffanie's neck.

Leeni charged into the room with a look to kill and a martial art fighting stance. She glanced down at her two friends on the floor and raised an eyebrow. Tiffanie cut Leeni a look and shoved Meenal off. Meenal was dazed and slowly got up into a sitting position.

"Never swim!" Tiffanie shouted.

"What do you mean?" Leeni asked, helping Tiffanie up.

Pointing at Meenal, still sitting on the floor, Tiffanie shouted, "This girl has never been swimming!"

"Never? Do you actually know how to swim?"

"Uh—no... I..." Meenal stammered.

"That is it! You are going! No buts, no nothing. Work'll wait!" Tiffanie said as she grabbed Meenal's hand and yanked her up from the ground. She half-trudged, half-dragged Meenal out of the room with Leeni following close behind.

Meenal attempted to protest, using work, her lack of swimming attire, and her nervousness as excuses. Tiffanie and Leeni would not listen, and they began to prepare Meenal for a day at the beach. They talked with Councilman Marshall, who allowed Meenal to have the day off work, especially after hearing of her dedication to her work and inability to swim.

They went shopping and picked up a modest swimsuit: a light pink tank top and skirt combination. Next, they changed and contacted the others, explaining to all of them that Meenal needed to be introduced to the ocean.

All, minus Meenal, were excited as they walked to the beach that sat behind the Marshall Manor. Tiffanie and Meenal walked hand in hand, Tiffanie swinging their hands like children. Meenal walked cautiously, avoiding the small rocks inside the sand.

Rex was behind them both, watching with flirtatious eyes. Leeni caught up next to him and whacked him on the back of the head. He glared at her but then laughed and rubbed his knuckles in her wild hair. Thaddaeus walked hand in hand with Jacqueline. Jackson was the last in line, talking with another man that Meenal had not yet met.

"Tiffanie, do you know the young man speaking with Jackson? I have never seen him at the Manor before," Meenal asked.

With a big grin on her lips, Tiffanie said, "His name's Alcon. He works in the stables, so that's probably why you haven't seen him before. He tends to like horses more than people."

"Oh, he works with the horses then?"

"Yeah, he's actually the *head* stable boy. Councilman Marshall saw him handling the horses of his cart when he called for a carriage to an important meeting. After the meeting, he offered Alcon a proper job and of course, Alcon accepted. I met him on his first day at the Manor, as I do with all new employees. We became fast friends and now, he's my boyfriend, for about a year."

Tiffanie's eyes sparkled as she leaned in closer to Meenal and whispered, "I love Alcon with all my heart and soul."

Meenal tilted her head in confusion. "Rex and you have quite the flirtatious relationship. How can one love a man while expressing affection toward another?"

Tiffanie ignored the question and sprinted off. Meenal stopped and looked at Tiffanie racing into the water, the droplets splashing all around her. It looked safe enough, but for someone who had never been in any large body of water, it was absolutely terrifying.

Rex stood next to her and nudged her shoulder. She stared at him, giving a nervous smile. He frowned and asked, "You okay?"

"Yes, I am fine," she said and brightened her smile, accidentally showing off her pointed teeth. Rex raised an eyebrow, fighting back a laugh at her vain attempt at seeming calm.

"You're not fooling me, Sharky. What's the matter? You nervous?"

"Sharky? I do not understand."

"You got sharp teeth and you're blue, so you're like a blue shark. But anyways, don't be nervous. The water's not gonna hurt you."

She narrowed her eyes in disbelief. "I have seen water kill. Water is nothing harmless. It only appears to be."

He rolled his eyes and shook his head. The others eventually walked past them both, heading toward the water. Their friends began swimming and splashing around. They heard laughter and giggling, and Rex tapped his foot as he stared at Meenal.

Her eyes looked off into the water with intense caution as she nervously twiddled with her fingers. He sighed and nudged her shoulder again. She turned to him and gave another tiny smile, the nerves hidden beneath the surface of her expressionless eyes.

"I can introduce you to the water," he said and she glanced back to where Tiffanie was getting dunked by Alcon.

"That would be wonderful. Mind you, I am still fearful of water. I witnessed a drowning and I do not wish that destiny for myself."

Rex nodded and trudged off. Meenal followed him closely, moving to the left each time he did and to the right as he did. She would not leave him with the dangerous water only a short distance away. But that distance grew as they climbed up a small cliff. Her eyes darted back and forth as she realized that they were getting further and further away from the water. She had assumed that an introduction to the water should be made closer than on a cliff.

When they reached the top, she felt the wind against her skin and shivered. Taking a step away from the edge, she bumped into Rex, her hand smacking against his bare chest. Her eyes widened and she immediately jumped forward, nearing falling off. Rex reached for her arm just in time and heaved them both back onto the grass. She tripped over a rock and he tripped over her, causing both of them to roll nearly halfway down the hill.

"What the hell?! You trying to get us killed!" Rex hollered, dusting off the sand and dirt from his arms.

"I apologize, but I touched you without permission. And say nothing about freedom, for that is rude regardless," she said, her voice possessing a little bit of a chill.

"Now, you wanna show some goddamn backbone. You don't need to freak all out and nearly kill yourself, though! Dammit Meenal."

"Again, I apologize sincerely."

He cursed again and stood, muttering insults and trudging back up the hill. Meenal slowly stood and called after him, "Rex, I am confused. Should I be introduced to the water by actually being near it?"

He shouted a curse, which more or less told her to follow him, and so she did. They reached the top of the cliff again and she stood her ground carefully, making sure to avoid all contact with her benefactor.

As she glanced over at him, she noticed the tension leaving his shoulders, and the frustration in his brows softened. He faced her and, for the first time since their meeting, extended his hand without any hint of play or test. She stared at his hand and then his eyes, seeing the anticipation growing in them.

"Take my hand. We're jumping together." His voice was soft, an odd sound coming from someone who was usually either swearing or shouting boisterously.

"I am too fearful to jump. Is there not a more gentle way to be introduced?" she pleaded. He grinned. "Nope!"

With that, she took his hand, placed a death-grip on it, and closed her eyes. Rex laughed and slowly brought her closer to the edge. Her grip grew tighter with each step. He cursed at her to ease up and she did—barely.

"You really should open your eyes. You're missing a wonderful view," he said matter-of-factly.

"I am about to plummet to my death, and you wish for me to enjoy the view? I do not understand your logic," she said.

"You're not about to die. Geez, drama queen much? Just hold your breath and jump when I get to three. One… two… two and a half… two and three-fourths…"

"Rex…"

He laughed. "Fine—three!"

They jumped with Rex whooping and hollering as they went down. Pencil straight, Meenal kept a tight hold onto Rex's hand, but on impact, she lost contact with him and began to panic. Rex opened his eyes to see Meenal searching for him and he hurried over to her. As he took her hand, she instantly calmed down, and with a nudge from Rex, she began to kick and move her arms to stay above water. He smiled wide and swam with her. She started to panic whenever Rex let her hand go, but she picked up on the movements of swimming much quicker than he had initially expected. She grew bolder and confident in the water and eventually wanted to dive deeper than Rex's body could handle. So, he resurfaced and was welcomed by a wonk on the head.

"What the hell, Rex? Are you crazy?! She's never been swimming before!" Tiffanie shouted. She dove down, searching for the lost blue girl. Rex rolled his eyes and noticed the looks on the others' faces.

"Oh, come on! Y'all can't possibly think I'm *that* stupid! I know how to rescue and do mouth-to-mouth and stuff. She's fine!" he said, but still the crowd was not amused.

Tiffanie popped back up, her pale skin flushed from exhaustion.

"I can't find her," she said.

"What you mean you can't find her?" Rex said with a growl in the back of his throat.

"I can't… find her!" Tiffanie hollered and dove again. Rex and the others followed suit, searching for their lost friend. Alcon, Jacqueline, and Rex were the last to come up to find their friends dejected. Rex splashed the water in rage and started to head further out.

Tiffanie called after him and began to chase him, but Alcon held her arm and forced her to stay with him. Jacqueline cursed and followed him, telling the rest of them to go ashore just in case Meenal was already there. When she had barely caught up to Rex, she splashed him and yelled, "Where are you going?"

"I'm gonna find her!" he growled, continuing on. She huffed and swam quickly in front of him, blocking his way.

"This is not the fastest way to find her. You'll tire out before you do... Rex... Rex!"

He ignored her, swimming further out. He shouted Meenal's name and received no answer. He tried again and again. Suddenly, someone was shouting his name, and in the distance, he saw a hand. He shouted Meenal's name, and the person shouted back with an enthusiastic wave.

"How in the world did she get way over there?" Jacqueline asked. Rex shrugged, too happy for words. Meenal swam toward them and upon reaching them, Rex greeted her with curses and damnations as Jacqueline threatened her with death if she ever scared them like that again.

Meenal did not understand their concern, for she was obviously a natural swimmer, yet she allowed them their feelings, and the three of them returned to the beach where cheers welcomed their arrival.

Tiffanie raced into the water and hugged and kissed Rex on the cheek, then hugged Jacqueline, and finally—and very briefly—hugged Meenal. She deemed that a celebration should take place for their safe return and she did not take no for an answer. She sent Jackson back to the manor for some food and entertainment and improvised while they waited, dancing around with everyone and asking Jacqueline to start a fire. Jackson returned with food and musicians, and the real party commenced.

The afternoon disappeared into evening and evening into night, and the young people were quietly sitting around the fire, which Jacqueline rekindled every so often with a shot of fire from her hand. She was sitting in Thaddaeus's lap as he played with her long red hair. Jackson sat next to them with Leeni beside him, softly conversing among themselves, along with the servants and musicians who had stayed behind.

On the other side of the fire, Tiffanie sat in between Alcon and Rex, while Meenal was on Rex's other side, staring off into the water. Rex was halfway listening to Tiffanie talk about some topic that only held his interest for a second.

His mind drifted to Meenal, wondering what she was looking at. She had not spoken a single word since her time lost at sea and she continued to stare into the ocean as if engaged in conversation with it. Yet each time he was about to ask her what she was thinking, Tiffanie distracted him and forced him to pay attention to her. When she finally finished her twenty-odd tales, Rex started to speak, but Alcon said something first, calling the entire group's attention.

"Tiffanie..." he said.

"What you want?" she said, her wide blue eyes blinking anxiously.

He opened his mouth then closed it. He swallowed hard and stood, sinking to one knee. Tiffanie covered her mouth in disbelief.

"Alcon..." she whispered as he pulled out a modest black box. He opened it and revealed a diamond ring.

"Ever since we met years ago, I knew that you were something special. You care about everyone and do your utmost for them. You have a heart of gold, and with it you captured mine. Tiffanie Poirier, I want you to be my wife and show the world that our hearts tightly hold each other. Will you marry me?"

All were silent with their eyes glued to Tiffanie as she sat motionless. Her eyes darted back and forth from Alcon to Leeni to Rex and back again. Slowly, she nodded and held out her hand. Alcon slipped the ring onto her left ring finger.

Applause erupted among the group as Tiffanie and Alcon kissed. Jacqueline and the female servants immediately went over to her to get a better view of the ring, but Tiffanie ignored all of them and rushed over to Leeni, who dismissively glanced at the ring while Tiffanie waved it back and forth, watching it shine in the moonlight.

"You're making me look bad in front of Jacqueline," Thaddaeus teased Alcon.

Meenal, unfamiliar with the after-proposal celebration, remained in her spot and watched the others interact. Tiffanie was happy, so Meenal was glad as well. She turned to Rex to express her joy and saw his eyes glowing bright red. He was upset, nearing the edge of livid.

"You disgust me," he said, standing up and looking over at Tiffanie. Meenal watched him, standing slowly with him. She could not understand why he was so upset, for this appeared to be a joyous occasion. Alcon narrowed his eyes and stood, staring Rex down. Rex ignored him and directed all his attention to Tiffanie.

"What?" Tiffanie said.

"So quick to change your mind when something better comes along, you attention whore!"

Alcon rushed Rex and shoved him. "Don't talk to my fiancée like that!"

Rex pushed him back. "You sure you wanna marry *that*? She'll probably replace you too when a richer guy comes along."

Alcon struck Rex square across the jaw, and Rex launched himself at Alcon, holding him down on the sand and punching his face repeatedly. Alcon tried to block the blows, but they kept coming. Jackson rushed over and tried to pull Rex off. Tiffanie screamed for him to stop and she tried to shove him off, but he slapped her across the face.

Alcon's anger blazed and he managed to overpower Rex, throwing him onto the sand and clocking him good in the head. The male servants split into two groups and managed to pull Alcon off Rex and separated them enough to prevent any further hits. Rex snarled and growled, his eyes the same fierce red.

Alcon easily composed himself while Rex nearly broke the hold that the servants had on him. Leeni suggested that they take him away from the rest of group and allow him to calm down. She then went over to Tiffanie and attempted to comfort her as she cried.

Once again, Meenal was confused and decided to speak with Rex, unable to provide comfort to Tiffanie and unable to feel comfortable enough to speak with Alcon. So, she silently slipped away and followed the men and Rex.

The glow of the fire became less bright the further she followed the voices of the men. She heard various accents and words of comfort, none of which aided in calming Rex down. He continued to snarl and growl more like a caged animal than a human male.

They stopped at the beginning of the cliff she recognized from earlier, and Rex ordered them to leave. One refused and said that he would stay to provide company, but Rex threatened him with a pay cut if he stayed. Eventually, the servant was convinced to leave, and Rex was alone.

He walked back and forth, muttering and hissing curses to himself and calling Tiffanie every name in the book. While he did not look like Kadmus, he definitely was his son and swore just like him. His vocabulary was very colorful, and Meenal found some of his swears humorous and giggled softly.

Rex looked up and growled, "Tiffanie!"

Meenal quickly stepped out of her hiding place and lowered her head. He narrowed his eyes at her and said, "What you doing here? Shouldn't you be comforting your friend?"

"Tiffanie has plenty of comforters while you are alone. You are my friend, my very first friend, therefore I am here," she said softly, staring down at her hands.

Rex's eyes instantly returned to their normal brown color, and he sighed, running his hand through his hair. He pressed his lips together. Meenal watched him and tilted her head as he paced back and forth. He suddenly stopped and sighed deeply.

"Thanks, Meenal. You're a good friend," he said.

Meenal smiled softly and nodded, finally looking at him. He was the Rex that she recognized with warm, brown eyes and a smirking smile. She was unsure of the raging red-eyed monster he became whenever his emotions got the better of him. She started to turn back when she heard someone approaching. She stepped out of the way and Tiffanie trudged into the clearing.

"How dare you embarrass me!" she hollered and shoved Rex hard in the back. He barely stumbled but all the calm that had come during Meenal's arrival vanished, and the red-eyed beast returned.

"Embarrass you?! How do you think I felt when you said yes?!" he screamed.

"Why should you care?"

"Because *I love you*, you stupid wench! I even told you before y'all started dating! But you freaking blew me off!"

She narrowed her eyes. "Why didn't you tell me?! I blew you off, so what. That hasn't stopped you from getting what you wanted before."

"Oh, I forgot how limited your memory is. Let's see if this rings a bell. 'I love you, Tiffanie, and I wanna marry you.' 'Oh… yeah, I like you too, Rex.' You did that five different times, each time I said the *exact same words*! So, why him? Why him over me? Is it because he's fully human? Because he's *normal*?"

"Rex, that has *nothing*—"

"Liar! That has everything to do with it! Ever since my eyes turned, you've reeked of fear whenever you're near me."

"That's not true! I love you—"

"Shut up!"

Rex raised his hand to smack Tiffanie, but Meenal came out of the shadows and took hold of his arm. He glared at her, his red eyes fierce and threatening. Yet, she kept her blank expression and shook her head.

Slowly, she lowered his arm and pushed him against a rock. His eyes flickered in color as Meenal held his face in her hands. She closed her eyes and breathed deeply. Rex fought the calm and fidgeted in her grasp. She remained still, unnerved by his movements.

Tiffanie watched in amazement at the effect Meenal had on him. No one had been able to calm him down as quickly and as effectively as she had. She had done this all without a single word.

"Calm yourself. Tiffanie is not worth you losing control and giving in to the rage. It is obvious that she does not love you in the manner that you wish. Leave her to her own conscience." Meenal's monotone voice hummed softly against his ears as she leaned into him, holding him down.

The fidgeting slowed and eventually stopped all together. His eyes never left Tiffanie, following her as she backed away. Meenal narrowed her eyes and turned his head to face her.

"Pay her no attention. Allow her to return to her fiancé," she commanded. Rex finally looked away from her. Tiffanie looked at the two of them with distrustful eyes before she rushed back toward the light of the fire. Meenal listened carefully as Tiffanie's footfalls faded into the night. Once satisfied that the foolish girl was far enough away, Meenal stepped back and removed her hands from Rex.

"I apologize for my rudeness by intruding into your personal space. I simply did not wish for any harm to come to Tiffanie for her actions," she said, staring at her hands. Rex said nothing but stepped closer to her and lifted her head with his pointer finger. She blinked, surprised he had touched her so boldly.

"Rex… are you all right? Do you wish to be left alone?"

He dropped his finger from her chin and took hold of her hand, lacing their fingers together. She tilted her head at him curiously, wondering what he could be doing. While he was indeed calm, his eyes remained red, and this only added to her confusion. He smirked and then took his other hand and brushed a bit of hair out of her face.

As they stood, she noticed a major difference between the feelings she had for him and for her previous masters. In their arms, she had felt frightened, bored, or abused; in his arms, she felt safe and comforted. She suddenly realized that she never wanted this to end.

Rex moved his hand to cup her face and rubbed his thumb against her cheek. She widened her eyes, the comforting warmth spreading throughout her body. He leaned in closer, and her grip tightened on his hand.

He stopped just short of kissing her and looked into her eyes. She silently pleaded with him to continue. Her lips parted just slightly as she inched closer to him, and he closed the distance completely. And when he did, something happened.

A fiery blaze flowed through Meenal's blood as Rex felt a powerful lust. The two stood passionately kissing, their hands exploring the other. Minutes passed and suddenly someone was standing over Rex and Meenal, who were lying tangled in each other's arms in the sand.

Leeni's eyes widened as her mouth dropped. The color drained from Meenal's face, and she quickly removed herself from Rex's embrace. She could not meet either of their eyes as she walked briskly back toward the others. Rex watched her go, a hunger for her still beating in his chest. He licked his lips and then just as quickly shook his head to clear his thoughts.

He turned toward Leeni, who was already walking back. He ran up to her, and she turned toward him and stared. She pressed her lips together in disgust and trudged off, disappointed in her friend. Rex had sunken to a new low.

CHAPTER 6

THE EXCITEMENT OF AN UPCOMING wedding changed the atmosphere of the Marshall Manor, and the only detail of the trip to the beach mentioned was Alcon's proposal to Tiffanie. People soon forgot about Meenal's time lost at sea, Rex's outburst at the proposal, and the altercation between Alcon and Rex.

Tiffanie romanticized the proposal, adding extra fanfare with each telling. Indiscreetly, she revealed to all Rex's true feelings for her and how she absolutely had to reject him to marry the love of her life, Alcon. Others mentioned how she had previously talked about becoming Rex's wife, often calling herself the latest Mrs. Marshall. She denied the claims and dismissed her former nickname as wishful thinking on Rex's part and a childish crush on her own.

The gossipers moved on to more relevant topics, like choosing the theme of the wedding, determining the colors of the bridesmaids' dresses, and finding the type of flowers they should use. The most important aspect of the wedding still hung in the air: what would Tiffanie wear?

The options were endless and Tiffanie, having turned into a monster bridezilla overnight, would not rest until she had the perfect dress. Months passed after the proposal, and the perfect dress was still at large.

Tiffanie hunted throughout the city, going from the humble dressmakers to the chic boutiques of the rich in order to find the dress, *her* dress. But nothing was up to her standards. Leeni attempted to convince Tiffanie to be more reasonable, but Tiffanie refused to listen, screaming that her dress was out there somewhere.

During this time, Meenal distanced herself from Tiffanie and the others due to Tiffanie's recently discovered dark side, as well as her guilt about the close encounter with Rex. She remained engulfed in her work, cranking out translation after translation.

Councilman Marshall commended her impressive efforts, but when he asked if she wished for another day off, she pleasantly but firmly refused. When work did not come fast enough from the councilman, she sought out additional work from other government officials. She began to develop a reputation for quick turnarounds and exquisite craftsmanship.

Meenal tried her hardest to use her talents for good in order to combat her feelings of shame, but her efforts were in vain. The glaring disappointment from Leeni always made an appearance in her mind after each completed translation, zapping any joy she would have experienced from her success. Her stomach churned each time she saw Rex, and she dashed in the opposite direction.

Her mind berated her for destroying her group of friends. She longed for the quiet days of months past, when she felt nothing but confusion when dealing with cultural differences. Now, she only suffered discontent and remorse for her unspeakable actions.

Meenal was carrying her most recent translation to the councilman. She could feel the guilt creeping back into her mind. Leeni's look of shocking disappointment flashed in and out of her sight. She clutched the papers tighter and slowed her walk.

The strange, passionate desire she felt for Rex reappeared and fought against her shame, begging her to seek him out and press her lips against his. She craved the fiery sensation she had felt as his hands explored her shoulders, back, and hips. She shuddered and shook her head, removing the lustful thoughts.

She stopped walking and took a deep breath. *I cannot remain preoccupied with the past,* Meenal told herself. She had to focus on the words of business and government. The new Resident Registration Act was gaining ground, and its enforcement was beginning to take effect. This was not a time for what-ifs.

She regained her focus and resumed her journey down the hallway. Yet, her emotions continued in flux between lustful rage and shameful grief. Her walking pace increased; her heart raced. Sweat on her hands smeared the ink from the papers as they slowly fell away onto the floor. She closed her eyes, shaking her head to banish both sets of thoughts. Constantly they fought and continued to crush her fragile spirit.

She collided with the heavy doors to the councilman's office. A loud thud echoed in the empty hallway as she looked up at the ceiling, seeing the last bit of her latest work fluttering down toward her face. One piece of paper rested briefly before it was lifted up, and there appeared the man of her obsession.

She stared at his smooth brown skin, full lips, and dark eyes. He held the same look of great intensity as he had that night. She glanced away. Nothing was said for several seconds. Soon enough, however, the silence outstayed its welcome.

"What happened?" Rex asked, the concern evident in his voice. Meenal's eyes danced wildly and simply refused to focus on anything. He bent down closer to her on the floor, but she jumped up and started to run away, stomping all over her translated pages as she went.

Rex dashed after her. He tried to get ahold of her arm, but she dodged him by turning a corner. She sprinted but was suddenly stopped by a jerk on her arm. She felt a deep growl against her neck.

It had been three months since his last meeting with Meenal, since that eventful night on the beach. With all the commotion regarding Alcon and Tiffanie's wedding, Rex had only seen Meenal in passing, always facing the opposite direction.

He had attempted to find her in order to speak to her about the strangeness of their first kiss, but she was a master at disappearing. Whenever he went to her room, she would be gone to the capitol building. Whenever he searched the capitol building, she would be gone running errands. Even late in the night, after all the businesses had closed and the council members returned home, she would still be up, preparing yet another translation and not wishing to be disturbed.

After the sixth week of this act, Rex understood that she was avoiding him, purposely keeping herself inhumanly occupied. He brought up his concerns with his father, and Councilman Marshall agreed with his son's findings, decreasing Meenal's workload; he even offered her another holiday. However, to Rex's disappointment, she refused the holiday and sought more work from other officials. Despite that, he never let go of his determination to find Meenal and speak with her face to face.

Now, it appeared that he would finally have his chance. She stood with her back to him and her wrist in his grasp. He wanted to lessen his hold, but he feared that she would dart off again, commencing the chase once more. He narrowed his eyes and growled softly.

"Why are you avoiding me?" he asked, his voice no longer concerned. Irritation was the only emotion he felt for her now. Her behavior reminded him of the childish antics he had used during his youth to dodge

Professor Ostby when it came time for his tutoring lessons. This was nothing like the mature Meenal to whom he had become accustomed.

She said nothing to his question and so, in anger, he forced her to face him. She would not look up, so he grabbed her chin and stared at her with red eyes. He examined her face and noticed a bruise developing on the side of her forehead. Her eyes were still unable to clearly focus, and she was biting down on her lips. She had never acted like this before. It was strange; it frightened him.

"Meenal?" Her eyes finally stopped jittering around and landed on him.

"My apologies. I have a very important translation to deliver to your father," she said with a smile so fake that it made Rex cringe.

"You're trying too hard. What's the matter?"

Meenal did not answer him and began to walk back to where she dropped the translation. Rex followed her. As they walked, she shook her head and mumbled to herself in some foreign language. Rex rolled his eyes and watched her movements, looking for signs of possible head injury.

They spotted the mess of papers on the floor and picked them up, each avoiding physical contact with the other. Soon enough, all the papers of the translation rested in Meenal's hands, and she started to leave, but Rex blocked her way. He was determined to get some sort of answer from her.

"Meenal, I haven't seen you in three months," he said, and she blushed, hiding herself behind the papers.

"You have noticed..." she whispered and tried to escape again.

Rex stepped in front of her. "Hell yeah! I haven't got you out of my mind since that day on the beach."

"I-I really don't... I must be..."

She tried to push pass him, but he thrust her against a wall and leaned in close. She squirmed and stammered some gibberish, but as soon as he rested a hand on her cheek, she stopped moving, nearly stopped breathing. Their breaths synced together as the minutes passed, and Rex's eyes remained hauntingly red, despite his calm demeanor.

The translation dropped to the floor as Meenal wrapped her arms around his neck. The coolness of her hands caused a chill to rush down his spine, and he smiled at the sensation. She blinked and started to ask a question, but he shushed her with a single brush of his thumb against her cheek.

He leaned in closer and said, "Do you want this?"

She looked at him with her two-toned eyes. He could see the gears working in her head as she developed an answer. He was unsure of which answer he wanted. That kiss on the beach had been the focal point of every dream he had had in the past three months.

Each time he watched her dash away, that moment replayed in his mind and his body jolted with yearning for her. Yet, whenever he did not see her, his mind wandered and was engulfed in all the other female specimens of the city. The strong yearning he felt for Meenal was never present for any of these other women, even when he managed to land one in his bed. He would satisfy her and himself, but soon his body began to crave Meenal again.

His desire was bizarre, for she was beautiful but odd, intelligent but naïve, kind but unconfident. She was nothing like the women he usually preferred. Still for some unknown reason, he wanted her.

"Tell me..." he whispered, running his fingers through her hair. She closed her eyes, shuttering out a sigh.

"I-I... ye—n..." she said and then violently pushed him away.

"Meenal, what—"

"I cannot. I do not know what these feelings are. I am confused, and this is nothing like I have ever experienced before. I-I must go. I am sorry, Rectavius; I must go."

With that, she turned and sprinted away, leaving her translation on the floor. Rex did not follow her. He had received his answer.

Δ

The national holiday for the independence of Maventa from the Saldur Empire had arrived, and while it was not widely celebrated during the day, all government buildings, as well as many businesses, were closed.

Meenal looked through her window and noticed the empty square, saddened that she would not be receiving any work. She needed something to distract herself from the thoughts flying in and out of her head. She decided to leave the manor for the time being, perhaps visiting some of the landmarks within the city.

As soon as Meenal stepped out of her door, Tiffanie glared up at her with disgust. Meenal blinked, frightened by the bridezilla, and quickly glanced down at her hands. Tiffanie tapped her foot and hollered at the pack of groupies following her, Leeni at the head.

"Where have you been?" she demanded, her foot-tapping speeding up.

"I have been occupied with translation work for the government in accordance with the new Resident Registration Act," Meenal said.

"You know you could have just said you've been busy at work, right?" Leeni said, smirking.

Tiffanie's look of disgust transformed into one of hatred and irritation. "Screw work, you're coming dress shopping with me."

There was little Meenal could say to stifle Tiffanie's aggressiveness, and therefore, she found herself dress shopping. She walked at the back of the groupies, looking at the unfamiliar neighborhood of Mystic Quartz, the richest part in all of Chance.

The shops displayed dresses that probably cost slightly less than what Rex had paid for her freedom. She could not understand how someone could purchase a piece of clothing that expensive.

When she brought this point up with a groupie, the groupie rolled her eyes and shook her head, calling Meenal a stupid fashion noob. She did not know the meaning of the word "noob," but she interpreted it as an insult and refrained from speaking with any of the other groupies from then on.

Disinterested in the rows upon rows of shops with irrationally priced clothing, Meenal thought about leaving the group to explore. Yet, as soon as the thought entered her mind, a loud squeal pierced her ears.

Tiffanie was standing directly in front of a shop with her wide blue eyes zoomed in on the window. She blinked in excitement, and lots of pointing and shouting commenced, causing quite the scene in the upscale neighborhood. The dress that caught her attention was a long white gown with dark blue and turquoise gems.

"Ahh! Loook!" Tiffanie screamed, and the others girls crowded around the window. They began all talking at once, and Meenal quickly developed a headache from all the chatter and started to walk away from the noise. Tiffanie, a bloodhound for anyone not paying attention to her, noticed and pounced on Meenal, blocking her way. The groupies saw that their leader had found a new target and began encircling Meenal.

"Yes, Tiffanie?" Meenal asked.

Tiffanie pointed an unsteady finger at the gem dress in the window.

"This. *Is*. The dress," she whispered with a bright smile on her lips.

Leeni had remained staring at the dress. With a shake of her head, she pushed her way through the hoard of groupies and shouted, "This?! Tiffanie, have you lost your mind?! This dress is—at least—twenty-six years' worth of wages!"

"I don't care! I must have this dress. I'll just get Rex to buy it for me. He gives me everything I want anyway and besides, he says he loves me. He should show his love by actions not words only, right?"

"You selfish little—ugh!" Leeni trudged off, leaving Meenal and the rest to deal with the bridezilla.

Tiffanie whirled on Meenal and said, "You probably think this isn't such a good idea either, huh? Well, screw you, lil miss not-so-perfect! Don't think I don't know what you tried to do. Just remember, Rex is all mine, and this marriage to Alcon will *never* change that."

The groupies readily agreed with Tiffanie, while Meenal stared at her in disbelief. Questions flooded her mind: Had Leeni told Tiffanie what had occurred between Meenal and Rex? Had someone seen them in the hallway and assumed the worst? Did others know and look upon her in shame? She lowered her head and allowed the others to continue into the store, Tiffanie now leading the group and marching with unbeatable determination.

CHAPTER 7

TREES WHIPPED BY AS REX PUSHED HIS black stallion further, hoping to fight off the troublesome thoughts in his mind, which concerned the two most important women in his life.

The first woman, Tiffanie, was the hottest gossip within the manor. The upcoming wedding had overshadowed his outburst over her acceptance of Alcon's proposal.

However, a few knew of the intensity of his feelings for her and how much his heart ached by her deliberate refusal. Rex felt betrayed and abandoned. As soon as he started changing, she dropped her old thoughts of becoming the next Mrs. Marshall and concentrated on snatching up a full-blooded human.

The second woman, Meenal, had not contacted him personally since their brief though intense meeting in the hallway. She avoided all the places he frequented, and if they did find themselves in the same room, she would acknowledge his presence and even give him a friendly greeting. But her words were void of all feeling.

Playing his part, he kept the exchanges pleasant, brief, and formal. But each time he saw her, a feeling of lustful need beat in his chest as if it were a caged animal desperate to be freed. His eyes would change to a dark red, and he knew that his body wanted her. His mind, though, was caught between the old love that rejected him and the new one that confused him.

With these conflicting thoughts, he tried to put on a brave face. He had purchased that extremely expensive dress Tiffanie had wanted. He had given Meenal space and avoided her completely. But the wedding was less than two weeks away. No one was available for him to talk about his plight. His brave face was disappearing.

All that he saw in front of him were greens and browns, merging together into a blurred mash of colors as his horse, Thunder, galloped through the forest. He heard nothing and attempted to think of nothing. But the thought of rejection and betrayal always reappeared.

"Rex!" a voice called to him. He ignored it at first. But as the voice persisted, he gradually slowed Thunder down to a trot and allowed the person to catch up. Thunder neighed upon seeing the other horse, a beautiful white mare and his mate, Lightning. She hated to be ridden, and only one person was brave enough to ride her. Alcon rode up next to Rex, starring at him with worried eyes. "You all right? People are looking for you."

"Do folks think I might wanna be by myself?" he muttered under his breath and rolled his eyes. "What you want?"

"I just wanted to thank you for purchasing Tiffanie's wedding dress. She would not go through with the wedding unless she knew that she had that dress."

Rex shrugged. "No worries."

He quickened Thunder's pace and started to leave Alcon behind. Alcon immediately matched his speed. Rex glared at him, but Alcon said nothing. They rode in silence for some time as each collected his thoughts.

"I also want to apologize for the both of us. I should have controlled my temper, and Tiffanie should have told you much earlier that we were serious. I told her to tell you since I knew that you had been together at one time and were still very close," Alcon finally said.

Rex pulled Thunder to a halt and moved him to face Alcon.

"We gonna set some things straight," he said. "Tiffanie and I, we were never together. Fooled around when we got drunk once, and then some more for like three months after that. When she got with you, I kept my hands off, even though she begged me not to. Second—"

"Hold it. You had relations with her?"

"Yeah, and damn near all the guards did too. She gets around, but I'm her favorite," Rex laughed. "It's kinda funny. I'm not human enough to be her husband, but I'm more than enough to be in her bed."

"You're lying. She told me that she hasn't had relations with anyone since being employed by your father."

"Oh yeah, I'm totally lying. You got me. I'm lying. *Please*… Why would I lie? I got nothing to gain and nothing to lose. I don't want a lying tramp as my wife anyways. She's a whore and always will be."

"Really? So what of your precious Meenal? Lest the rumors are true and you had her too."

Rex drew out his sword with decisive skill and held the point only inches away from Alcon's neck, his red eyes glaring.

"Disrespect Meenal again, and I'll cut you up into little pieces and feed you to the horses."

Alcon swallowed hard and nodded, but Rex held the sword in its place.

"Second," he continued, "don't believe everything you hear in the rumor mill. I haven't touched Meenal."

Rex lowered his sword and returned it to its sheath. His eyes faded from red to brown as he turned and led Thunder deeper into the forest, saying, "Ask Leeni if you don't believe me. She'll tell you the truth."

He did not wish to concern himself anymore with weddings and old loves. While his heart still flipped back and forth between loving and hating Tiffanie, he had spoken the truth about not wanting an untrustworthy woman.

He was an heir to one of the richest fortunes in all of Maventa. His father was a powerful government official who held the unpopular belief of freedom for all. It would not be in his best interest to marry Tiffanie, especially since no one in his snobbish family liked her very much. She was loud, uneducated, and flirtatious. She would not blend in well with his upscale family.

He silently wished luck to Alcon in his search for truth. Marriage was final. It would be difficult for Alcon to be chained to a lying whore until death did them part.

Night had fallen by the time Rex and Thunder returned to the manor. His body ached, and his horse was exhausted. As he returned Thunder to the stables, he expected to see Alcon there, seeing that he was the head stable boy, but he was nowhere to be found. He asked a young stable boy where Alcon was, but the lad had not seen him since that morning.

Rex handed Thunder to the lad, figuring that Alcon and Tiffanie were spending time together, planning this and deciding that. He gagged and firmly decided that he would never have a wedding, even if his father arranged his marriage. He and his fiancée would elope.

During his journey back to the main part of the manor, he heard an ear-splitting scream. It sounded like Tiffanie. He rushed toward the sound as the wailing echoed throughout the entire servant wing. His body protested, but the screams grew more distressful the closer he came. When he and ten others came to the source, they discovered it was indeed Tiffanie, holding a note and screaming, "He left me!"

The comforters came immediately to her side as Tiffanie wailed about her lost love. They assured her that Alcon would return and gave her numerous reasons for his disappearance. Yet, nothing could be said to control her sobs.

For days, Tiffanie continued like this. She remained locked in her room, soaking her pillow and blankets with tears and slobber. During the night, all in the manor heard her cries for Alcon and they pitied her. But after a week, everyone returned to their normal schedules, finding the riots against the Registration Act more interesting. Only Meenal and Leeni seemed to care about the abandoned bride.

It had been ten days since Alcon left Tiffanie and his employment at the manor. Earlier in the day, Tiffanie spoke with Councilman Marshall to discover the reason for Alcon's resignation. She remembered him speaking so fondly of all of the horses in his care. She did not understand why he would leave a job he that loved so much and that paid so well.

Respecting the man's privacy, the councilman only revealed it would have been too difficult for Alcon to remain an employee at the manor. He gave no other reason, which did nothing to ease Tiffanie's confusion. Sitting on her bed, she fiddled with the note from Alcon, an abstract message that did not make any sense to her. She reread it again for the hundredth time. Nothing came to her.

At the beginning of the end of her wedding, she was determined to uncover the hidden message herself. Alcon had left it for her and her alone. She did not want to share this with anyone else. Yet, as she continued to read the note, her confusion grew into frustration at her incapability to crack the code.

A soft knock sounded on the door and Tiffanie muttered, "Come in."

Meenal slowly peeked her head around the corner and said, "I wish to provide you company."

Tiffanie signaled Meenal inside and continued to concentrate on the note. She did not notice Meenal at all, but her friend stood silently, apparently waiting for instruction. Eventually, she heard a sigh, a quiet but obviously bored sigh. Irritated, Tiffanie cursed and thrust the note in Meenal's face.

"Yes?" Meenal asked.

Tiffanie narrowed her eyes and pushed the paper closer in Meenal's face.

"Read it," she spat. "Alcon left it for me, and I don't get what he's saying."

Meenal sighed softly and took the note in her hands. Tiffanie narrowed her eyes and made a hurry-up gesture with her hands. Meenal then read the note aloud:

> *Tiffanie,*
>
> *I am sorry, but I can no longer marry you.*
> *"It is hard to find the perfect wife. Her value is far more than that of emeralds. Her husband trusts her deeply, and he wants for nothing in the world."*
>
> *—Axioms 29:11,12*
> *Alcon*

"I do not understand what you are misinterpreting," Meenal said and held out the note to Tiffanie. Tiffanie smacked the note out of Meenal's hands, cursing. She quickly stood and rebuked Meenal, who attempted to interject with an explanation, but Tiffanie cut her off.

"What could Alcon be referring to? Has there been a case where you betrayed his trust?" Meenal managed to ask.

"No! I was *good* to that foot-licker! I gave him everything he wanted!" Tiffanie yelled.

"He did not believe so, and quite frankly, I agree. You did not give him loyalty and you behaved like a woman of your former occupation."

I am the victim in this twisted situa—

Tiffanie stopped mid-thought as Meenal spoke. Her wide blue eyes narrowed into slits as she walked up to Meenal. She puffed out her chest and glared at her. Her face reddened and she balled up her fists.

"Just what are you saying, Meenal?" Tiffanie asked.

"You still do not understand? You behaved like a wanton woman, the prostitute you were formerly, and proceeded to lie about it."

A hard slap came across Meenal's face as Tiffanie spat, "Don't you dare call me that! I am not a whore—not anymore. I was always completely faithful when me and Alcon were together. I never cheated on him!"

"Perhaps that is true," Meenal continued, "but you did lie to him. I heard it. You said that you did not have relations with anyone after receiving employment from the councilman, but I know that you and Rex were sexually involved at one time."

Tiffanie stared at Meenal and shook her head. "You're wrong! Alcon loved me! He would have never left me for the past, especially not because of some good-for-nothing spoiled brat! Rex isn't even human anyways; I wouldn't marry *that*! You stupid or something? I would never curse my children with whatever *disease* he's infected with, to become some raging lunatic!"

Outraged, Tiffanie continued in her rant against Meenal.

"I am the one who has been left at the altar. I am the one who has been betrayed. I was faithful to Alcon. Rex violated *me*. I told him no, but he was drunk and forced himself on me. Then he told everyone that we were together as a couple so that no one else could have me. He manipulated me and made me think he loved me. It was selfish lust! I am the victim in all of this." This was what she was determined to make Meenal believe.

Tiffanie's rage increased against Meenal and her disbelief. She soon felt a chill in the room and began seeing her breath in the air. Looking at Meenal, Tiffanie noticed her narrowed eyes and the dark expression on her face. Meenal had never looked so menacing. She stepped forward and stared down at Tiffanie, unmoved despite the cold.

"What are you doing?" Tiffanie shook, her breath growing more pronounced.

Silence answered her as Meenal simply stared, saying nothing. Quietly, whispers circled around Tiffanie and she kept looking toward Meenal, who stayed silent. The whispers grew into screams and Tiffanie twirled around, attempting to find their source. Black chains rose from the ground and strapped around her ankles and wrists, dragging her down to the ground.

"Meenal... what's going on?" she asked, but Meenal had disappeared, and in her place stood Ares, her first consistent client. Her eyes widened as she jerked the chains. He grinned that same sickening smirk, and her stomach dropped.

"Wh-What are you doing here?"

"Giving you what you want. You wanna be convincing, don't you? So, you gotta know how it works," he said, his grin broadening.

"I don't work for Keyx anymore!"

"Keyx? He's not important in this matter. I'm doing this for your benefit and my enjoyment. You were supposedly raped, right? Call me your genie."

He came closer to her. She tried to yank at the chains clenched around her hands and feet, but they grew tighter with each struggle. Before she knew it, he was right next to her, his breath holding the same stench of weed and alcohol. He touched her waist, and she screamed. He stopped in his attack and closed his eyes, his hands covering his ears. As long as she raised her voice, he stayed away. But, eventually, her voice and her strength gave out.

A hand grabbed her wrist, jarring Tiffanie awake, screaming, fighting, and biting her way to freedom. More hands came and tried to force her down. Tears fell as she begged for him not to take her. As if on fire, the hands flew off her body and she opened her eyes.

Ares was gone, and so were the chains. Instead of screams, there was a soothing melody. She saw her friends all around her: Leeni, Rex, and a few fellow servant girls. Alcon was not there, of course, for she remembered he had left her only two weeks before their wedding. Yet, she noticed another was missing.

"Where's Meenal?" she asked. Rex's eyes faded to red and back again.

"She's lying down," Leeni said. "We found the both of you on the floor of your bedchamber. You collapsed."

She blinked and did not remember falling. The last thing she remembered was Ares. She shuddered, which Leeni mistook for a chill, placing another blanket on top of Tiffanie. She did not protest; she was freezing after all.

Suddenly, Rex stood and seemed to be leaving. Tiffanie reached up and took one of his hands. He was warm, and she smiled, missing the heat he provided. He looked down at her with hard eyes and said nothing.

She called his name, but he only glared at her and removed his hand from her grasp. Her mouth opened at the rejection, and she glanced away. First Alcon had left her an unwedded bride and now her stronghold, the man who was always in her corner, was leaving her.

"Where are you going?" she asked before he left, but still he did not answer her.

"He's going to see Meenal," Leeni said softly. "She has not yet recovered."

Tiffanie's eyes narrowed and in a huff, she buried her head underneath the covers. She was no longer the apple of Rex's eye.

Fear and death had permeated Tiffanie's bedroom when Rex found Tiffanie and Meenal on the floor. A frost similar to one on the tops of mountains lingered in the air. Eerily still, the women were collapsed on the ground, and when he had checked their pulses, the fear spread into his heart.

Tiffanie's pulse beat at a rate faster than he had ever felt before. With Meenal, he felt none. As he approached Meenal's room now, Rex fought off the fear of her death. Despite their strange relationship, Rex blamed himself. He had bought her freedom and placed her in such a hostile environment.

The guard stationed at her door saluted Rex sharply and opened the door for him, after giving him a warning about the temperature. Rex nodded but still cursed as soon as the cold burst hit him. He rubbed his hands and arms to build up some warmth, but it was useless. He walked over to the healer at Meenal's bedside, and she smiled upon seeing him.

"How she doing?" he asked, noticing the condensation of his breath.

"She's still alive at least. I have no idea if and when she'll wake up. Can you watch her as I warm up a bit?" the healer said.

Giving him her coat, she left. Rex stared down at Meenal and sighed. He took hold of her hand and felt the block of ice it had become. He almost let go, but she suddenly tightened her grip. Her lips started to quiver, and she kept whispering something.

He leaned in close but could not make out the language she was using. He nudged her shoulder and whispered her name, but she remained unconscious. Soon, her quivering intensified, and her entire body began to shake uncontrollably. His eyes widened, and he tried to break free from her grasp to alert the healer, but she refused to release him.

He yelled for the healer and tried to restrain her. She continued to convulse. He yelled again for the healer, who rushed inside and immediately raised her hands over Meenal's body. But as soon as her hands began to glow, the healer jerked back and collapsed onto the floor, crying hysterically. The guard rushed over to Meenal, but Rex stopped him, barking, "Don't touch her!"

Suddenly, Meenal's eyes snapped open, and the chill within the room vanished. She released Rex's hand and sprung out of the bed, falling onto the floor. She dragged herself toward the healer and held her face in her hands. Slowly, her crying stopped and the healer was asleep.

"What the hell?" Rex said as the guard checked for a pulse. With a strong nod, the guard picked up the healer and carried her out of the room. Meenal watched them go, dragging herself into a sitting position. She then tried to stand, but her legs collapsed beneath her. Hearing the thud, Rex shook himself out of his shock and lifted Meenal up onto the bed.

"What the hell did you just do?" he asked. "First, you and Tiffanie freaking knocked out on the floor. Now she screaming about some Ares dude, and then the room gets all cold and crap, and then you made the healer... What the hell?"

Meenal stared at him blankly for a moment and then looked down at her hands. He sat down on the edge of the bed and placed his hands on her shoulders. She stiffened, but he ignored it. She had endangered his friends, including herself, and he wanted to know what had happened.

He looked into her eyes. "Tell me what happened."

"No," she muttered, still staring at her hands.

"What... happened?!"

The sharpness in his voice caused Meenal to jump, but her eyes remained on her hands. Rex rolled his eyes and demanded again, threatening to banish her from the manor. Her eyes went wide and finally, she softly nodded and began to speak.

"Tiffanie asked me to interpret the note Alcon had left her. She did not understand its meaning, and therefore I explained that Alcon was referring to her lie about her past relationships, including the one she had with you. I called her a wanton woman, declaring that she was acting like a worker of her former occupation. However, I only spoke truth, but I did not know that she would take such offense. She began to curse you, deeming you less than human. She even stated that she would have never married you and that you had violated her. At the destruction of your reputation, I grew upset with her."

Rex frowned and dropped his hands from her shoulders. To envision Meenal upset nearly made Rex laugh. She was the peaceful one who calmed him down when he was irrationally angry. He turned his laugh into a cough, and Meenal looked at him with concern. He cracked a tiny smile and took one of her hands, noticing the warmth returning to it.

"Tiffanie's a lying slut. She deserves whatever she got," he said.

She shook her head. "No, Rectavius. She may be promiscuous, untruthful, and disloyal. However, she does not deserve what I did to her."

"What's that?"

"That is the part I fear most. I do not know. I remember nothing in my anger and something occurred to make us both collapse. Now you say that she is paranoid about the presence of some man? She does not deserve any of that. I should have controlled my rage. I am at fault. I should be punished."

"Meenal… don't talk like that…"

She slid her hand from his and lay with her back to him. He sighed and reassured her that expressing herself was not the issue. "You need to express yourself more. You're too controlled." But he could tell that his words meant nothing to her.

She kept her silence, never agreeing with him once. Eventually, he left her, feeling as if his time had been wasted. Shoving his hands in his pockets, he returned to his own room, questioning whether he should have brought her to the Manor at all.

CHAPTER 8

WEEKS PASSED, AND TIFFANIE REGAINED her health, becoming her old flirtatious self, having learned nothing from her lack of a wedding. She started dating one of the guards—incidentally, the same man who was stationed outside her door during her recovery. She apparently had not chased him off with her temporary insanity, and they were now a couple.

Leeni and Tiffanie were also back on good terms, as inseparable as ever. The talk of what had occurred faded from the main news within the manor, and soon enough it was no longer brought up in conversation. New news had replaced it. All was forgotten.

However, Meenal had not forgotten. Her conscience tormented her, and she worried about the damage she had caused her friends. She sought out Leeni and Tiffanie to apologize, but only Leeni listened and accepted her apology. Tiffanie ignored Meenal, declaring, "I smell the stench of fake friend and hear an irritating buzzing sound in my ears."

Nothing anyone said convinced Tiffanie to listen to Meenal. Eventually, at the advice of Leeni,

Meenal stopped trying. Rex and Meenal still approached each other only in the most formal settings. Otherwise, he kept his distance, and despite her puzzling desire to be near him, to feel his hand wrapped around hers, and to hear her name whispered from his lips, she avoided him as well. In one way or another, she had lost each of her friends and was now alone in the strange world of freedom.

Meenal did not recognize the person she had become, having changed from a cool, calm slave into a ball of desultory emotions. Due to her instability and broken friendships, nightmares stole her sleep, leaving her with less than three hours of rest each night.

She used the time she was awake to work on translations by candlelight. Her superiors praised her even more than before, and she felt some relief. Each night, though, the guilt and confusion returned and sleep became unbearable. She requested a heavier workload from Councilman Marshall. But as soon as the word left her mouth, he shook his head and denied her the work.

"With all due respect, councilman, I am growing disinterested in the amount of assignments I am receiving from you. I wish to receive more in order to make better use of my time," she said.

Kadmus sighed and stood up from his desk, walking to the front and leaning against it. He gave her a hard once-over, and she wondered if he saw the traces of sleeplessness in her eyes. Her feet kept shuffling, and she fiddled with her fingers.

"Meenal, how many hours of sleep have you had?" he asked.

She lowered her head. "Very few, sir."

"Why are you working yourself into an early grave? From the looks of you, you are around the same age as Rectavius, and therefore, you have your entire life ahead of you to work. Right now, you should live your life and stop being such a workaholic. Yes, you are talented. Yes, you are intelligent. But you are *young*. You are *inexperienced*. You have to find yourself."

"Is this similar to the expression of 'Do you'?"

Kadmus laughed. "Not quite. To find yourself is a precursor to 'Do you.' You must know who you are first. What makes you tick? What are you made of? Where do you come from?"

"Councilman, there are no records of my birth, and I do not understand how I can tick."

Kadmus sighed, rubbing his eyes. He pushed himself off the desk and stood in front of her. She looked up at him and blinked expectantly.

"What's your favorite color?" he asked.

She widened her eyes. "Pardon?"

"What's your favorite color? Favorite animal? Favorite season, though there aren't too many choices here, just dry and rainy. But the principle remains the same. Can you name these things that are unique to yourself and not those of your previous masters?"

Meenal thought about this for a moment. She had never considered her own preferences for colors, seasons, and animals. All colors were beautiful in their own ways, and all animals had practical purposes, as did the seasons. She stared at the councilman and gave an awkward shrug.

"Exactly," he said with a nod.

"Sir?"

"The Marshall family is having our biennial Winter Ball within three weeks, and during those three weeks, you will be on holiday from work. You will not be able to translate, touch, or even think about anything involving the government."

"But sir!"

"Uh-uh, no buts whatsoever. This is final. If you go against my word and attempt to seek governmental work from another official, I will fire you."

"Sir!"

"This. Is. Final!"

Meenal bowed her head. Her shoulders slouched forward. Dread swallowed her up. Nothing would prevent the sleepless nights. Her insanity was imminent. This could not be allowed to proceed. She lifted her head and narrowed her eyes at him. She realized that she was acting more out of character, giving in to the strange rise and fall of emotions, but she did not care. She was determined to be heard.

"Meenal?" he asked.

"If I am now forbidden from my employment, then what else shall I do with my time? I had originally come here to obtain more work. However, I have less than I did at the beginning. Please tell me, Councilman, what am I to do to fulfill the empty spaces within my day? Find myself? As I stated, there are no records of my birth. Where do I begin in this search for something that is of no importance to the grand scheme of life? Please—enlighten me."

Kadmus stared at Meenal in silence, and as the seconds ticked by, worry replaced the brief confidence she had mustered up. She started to take back everything, stumbling over her words. Kadmus raised his hand, and she was quiet, utterly embarrassed.

"Do not retract what you said, for you speak the truth. You asked for more, and I gave you less. I have done you an injustice and I apologize wholeheartedly for that. Also, you should speak up more. It suits you."

"Sir?"

"You should attend Rectavius's schooling lessons with him. Those usually last all day with plenty of opportunities for further research to use up much of the evening. I also know Darius would love to have a willing student for a change. Besides, he would be a much better person to help you in your self-discovery and its significance. Sometimes, I'm still figuring out who I am."

Perhaps the councilman was right; she had misjudged the importance of discovering herself. The great man before her was still in the process of finding himself, despite the amount of years and influence he had in comparison with her. He never trifled with useless adventures. Therefore, if he spent his valuable and limited time in the goal of self-discovery, why should she not as well? She was delighted to learn more about her preferences and her heritage. An opportunity she had never before been offered was finally available, understanding the complex web of her emotions and self.

Yet, her heart pounded at the anticipation of seeing Rex. According to the reports from Leeni, his top-three priorities were to explore Chance's nightlife and women, to investigate the conflict between citizens and government in regards to the Registration Act, and to study. He asked nothing of Meenal. Leeni always assured Meenal that her friends cared for her and that this strange time between them would pass.

However, Meenal was unconvinced. Rex barely spoke to her and firmly respected her wish for distance. She thought she would be more at ease without him paying attention to her; she would concentrate on her own feelings in this complex world. Instead, she felt more restless than before and part of her was even saddened by his apparent rejection of her, which she would not admit to anyone. Her request for distance had backfired.

"Meenal? Do you wish to join Rectavius in his studies—at least for the time being? We can reevaluate your status after the ball," Kadmus said.

Despite that tiny sorrow in her heart, Meenal knew she needed to simplify the input of her life, and Rex's question of a romantic relationship was not simple.

Therefore, it was necessary to shove her complicated feelings for Rex down into herself. It was best for everyone. With a nod, she said, "Yes, an excellent idea. Thank you, sir."

Kadmus then dismissed her, returning to sit at his desk. Yet she stood there, waiting. He raised his eyebrows and asked, "Is there something else, Meenal?"

She bowed. "Please pardon my ignorance, but I am unsure as to where Rex holds his lessons with Professor Ostby."

"Follow me."

Meenal could hear two distinct voices converse as she walked through the halls with Kadmus. One droned monotonously while the other interjected often in an attempt to liven up the boring one. Soon enough, the lecturer grew tired of the interruptions and there was a loud whack. Meenal glanced up at Kadmus, and he just shook his head with a sigh. Upon entering the room, Meenal saw Rex glaring at an older gentleman with shoulder-length white hair and beige skin.

Rex mumbled something under his breath, and the professor whacked him on the head with a rolled-up paper. Kadmus cleared his throat, and the two men looked up. The older gentleman greeted them both with a warm smile, age lines curling around his lips.

He was losing the battle against time: wrinkled skin, hunched back, slight quiver in his voice. However, his purple eyes were bright, full of life and wisdom. Rex spotted his father and smiled widely, but his smile twitched as he noticed Meenal. His eyes narrowed, and he glanced away, wondering why she had interrupted his lessons.

She had wanted space, and he had given her space, excluding the strange occurrence between Tiffanie and her. Now, she was invading his private lessons, his personal time with his best friend of sorts, Professor Ostby. He crossed his arms and stared out the window.

"I thought you'd be working. Gotta save Maventa one translation at a time," Rex mocked, refusing to look at the newcomers.

"Councilman Marshall has so graciously given me the next three weeks reprieve from my duties," Meenal said, and despite himself, Rex smirked. He knew that Meenal had a backbone somewhere. It looked as if it was beginning to show.

"I'm doing this for your own good, young lady," Kadmus barked.

"No matter the occasion," said the professor, "we are delighted for this unexpected visit. Kadmus, my friend, it has been far too long since the last time you sat in on one of your son's study sessions." The professor smiled wide and gestured for the two of them to take a seat. Both Kadmus and Meenal seemed to hesitate, but after much encouragement from the professor, they eventually sat down.

"I won't be staying long. I just came here in order to show Miss Meenal where she will be spending the majority of her time for the next three weeks," Kadmus said.

"Excellent! Though, I do believe that a formal introduction is in order. You two have been keeping Miss Meenal from me," the professor said, standing up and towering over Rex, despite the hunched back. He bowed low and continued, "My name is Darius Ostby, professor of the geography of lands, the cultures of peoples, and the languages of foreigners. I am quite pleased to finally make your acquaintance, miss."

Finally taking his eyes off the window, Rex watched the flamboyant greeting from the professor: bowing low, sweeping his hand across the floor. Meenal blinked with astonishment and confusion evident in her face. Rex smiled at her discomfort, enjoying the scene playing out before him.

Despite his lack of correct speech and gracious behavior, Rex knew how to turn on the professional charm when necessary. However, Meenal appeared lost. He realized that it had turned out for the best, her rejecting him. She would never be able to stand by his side and mingle with the rich snobs of his society.

Meenal stood and bowed even lower than the professor and said, "It is my pleasure to meet someone of such a high educational background. Thank you for your introduction, and I look forward to learning a great deal from you, professor."

Rex rolled his eyes. She had handled the situation better than he would have. He glanced out the window again, embarrassment coloring his cheeks.

"Enough with the stupid pleasantries," he shouted. The others glanced at Rex, and he could feel their eyes on him, but he kept his focus on the window. He would not give them the satisfaction of seeing him ashamed by his own assumption.

Professor Ostby changed the subject. "Rex and I were just discussing the political flare of the land, in particular the reactions of the Registration Act. Most are unconcerned since it is free and relatively painless. Yet, some are attempting to escape the registration due to their lack of an actual residence or employment."

"Better to get the leeches out of the rich soil of Maventa." Kadmus said.

"Oh, I disagree," Professor Ostby said. "Maventa is a rich but tough mistress. Hard times have fallen on plenty of people."

Kadmus would not see the other side of the coin, and before their discussion could grow into a heated debate, he took his leave, wishing Meenal and Rex a fine study.

As his friend left, the professor sighed and shook his head, mumbling something under his breath. Rex knew it was a one of the many foreign languages he knew. Meenal immediately answered back in the strange language, and both Rex and the professor stared at her wide-eyed.

"You know that language? It is believed to be dead," Professor Ostby said.

"The village of one of my first owners spoke that language. I have traveled throughout many different lands during my servitude; I simply believed that I had traveled out of the language's geographical area."

"Incredible…"

Rex looked back and forth between the two nerds and rolled his eyes, grumbling under his breath. "Great, now I'm surrounded by language lovers."

These were supposed to be his private lessons, instructing him in the ways of educated men in order to handle his inheritance of the Marshall fortune and family reputation. He was being one-upped by a slave who did not understand the simple and common expression of "Do you." Still, part of him was proud of her and proud of his decision to free her. If anyone could survive the transition from enslavement to freedom, it had to be Meenal.

"Meenal, do you have any recollection of your earliest memory?" Professor Ostby asked. Meenal tilted her head, pressing her lips together in thought. After some moments, she lowered her eyes in shame and shook her head.

"Please, I wish not to reveal it," she whispered.

"My apologies, miss, I meant no offense. Your delightful and upbeat personality has allowed me to forget your past," the professor said with his hand on his heart.

Rex narrowed his reddening eyes. He cursed himself silently, ashamed of his childish thoughts. He had also forgotten her harsh background. He realized that she had been a slave, most likely even a sex slave. He could only attempt to imagine the duties she performed.

Yet, he was ashamed of being one-upped by her. *Perhaps my father was right by saying I am unprepared for the title of heir,* Rex thought. *I am self-centered, disrespectful, and irresponsible.* He was now determined to fix things between Meenal and himself and prove his father wrong.

"What's your happiest memory from your past?" Rex asked.

Meenal looked up and smiled. He shrugged, and slowly, his eyes returned to their normal brown.

"I was young, perhaps the human year of seven judging by size and speech patterns. I was with my mistress and her two children, both younger than me. She was attending to business elsewhere, and I held control of the children. Each one held a hand of mine… and we were watching a parade of sorts with dancers dressed in the colors of the woods. They twirled leaves and dirt around as they danced. One single dancer solely wore white. She moved so gracefully, and after convincing the girls, Lesedi and Osumare, we joined the woman in white in her dance. It was wonderful. The girls talked about it for weeks after."

Professor Ostby's mouth dropped. His purple eyes widened, and he eventually recovered and closed his mouth. Rex looked at him, demanding an explanation. The professor cleared his throat and shook his head again.

"It was the festival of the moon goddess, correct?" he asked and Meenal nodded. "This is incredible! Outsiders are not allowed to see that festival, for it is sacred, and the Chitachi people believe that outsiders will scare away the moon goddess from taking hold of the woman in white, which I have called the sacrifice. I have been trying to get access to that festival to include in my book on the Chitachi people since I was a lad, wet behind the ears as a researcher. And you… You actually participated. You must tell me all that you know!"

The professor grew louder with excitement, and even Rex was much more interested. Meenal looked down and fought off a smile. Ostby took out a clean sheet of paper and quickly jotted down all the important details she gave, including the fact that the woman in white was not a sacrifice but a privileged one, considered beautiful and graceful like the moon.

They discussed the other traditions of the Chitachi people, such as marriages and funerals. He shook his head and began to mutter to himself in yet another strange language. Rex turned to Meenal and asked for an interpretation, but she simply shrugged. The professor looked up and blushed. Coughing lightly, he neatly stacked his notes in a pile, sitting them aside.

"I apologize to the both of you. I have not had new information like this in some time," he said, a happy smile on his lips.

"No sweat, prof. But you killed all our time for today." Rex smirked and stood up. The professor sighed and laughed, beaming and glancing constantly at his new notes. Meenal frowned and folded her hands against her lap. Rex noticed and nudged her. She looked up, and he saw anxious concern in her eyes.

This only fueled his determination to remove the strangeness between them and return to the way they used to be. He would not allow his bruised ego to destroy their relationship completely. She was his friend after all; she belonged to him.

"You aiight, Sharky?" he asked.

"I…" she hesitated and then turned to the professor, who held a strange expression on his face. She sighed and smiled, showing her pointed teeth. His eyes widened in surprise and he blinked a few times.

"Wow, that's incredible, my dear—simply incredible! You are certainly a uniquely made individual! Do you know what you are?" the professor asked.

"No, I do not and, until recently, I never considered my genetic makeup. Normally, it had little effect on my duties. There are no records of my birth, and my unique appearance was more than enough to satisfy my masters, who were visual collectors. It was unnecessary to consider my origins. However, Councilman Marshall suggested that I should discover my heritage, my preferences—myself. I do not understand the purpose of such discovery, though I am interested in learning more about myself now that I have the opportunity. Yet, from where does one begin to find oneself?"

"That Kadmus is a wise one indeed. A little stubborn, but we all have our bad tendencies."

"Yeah. Yours is talking too much," Rex said. The professor shot him an unamused glare.

"And yours is being a rude and rebellious nuisance. As for your questions, Meenal, self-discovery is part of the maturing process. One cannot be a useful member of society if he or she does not fully understand what and how to contribute to bettering society. Full potential simply cannot be reached. So, do you wish to make the best use of your liberation from slavery?"

"Yes," Meenal said eagerly.

"Then you must understand who you are. Yet, that is more than your genetic makeup or even your heritage. It is about your strengths, your weaknesses, your skills, and your preferences. From there, you can determine the best way to aid society. An appropriate start to self-discovery is finding one's element. It can lead to finding out about one's heritage, personality traits, and occupation choices. It's a fine start to learning about yourself. But, on an unrelated note, if you wish to continue your studies with Rex and me, you will most certainly have to excuse us. We have a tendency to argue amongst ourselves."

Rex stuck out his tongue but then nodded with a shrug. "So, you gonna study with us, or what?"

"Yes, I would like that very much. However, I do not wish to impose myself on your private lessons, Rex. This was just a suggestion—"

"Shut up with that," Rex cut Meenal off.

"Rectavius!" Professor Ostby shouted.

"She's used to it. Oh, well… not like that. I mean, we got an understanding. It's fine."

"Yes, professor. It is quite fine." Meenal chuckled softly. "Are there to be assignments or additional research for the evenings?"

With a shake of his head, Professor Ostby sighed. "Yes, of course. Your first assignment, Meenal, is to find your element and, using the common strengths and talents associated with it, determine how you may aid society. Finally, if you wish, you can make speculations on your heritage. Rex, you are to help her and also find out any new information regarding your element."

Rex frowned and crossed his arms. "You know I don't believe none of that. It's like that astrology crap."

"Actually, Rex, it is not. Leeni is an extraordinary young woman with the ability to pull memories from deep within a person and bring them to the forefront. She is an Earth elemental, and plenty of other Earth elementals have been documented with the same ability. While we are unique, we can be collectively grouped into specific elements, usually by personality types and/or species types. It is not astrology, for I agree with you that that is a pseudoscience. However, this—elementology—this is *real* science."

Rex rolled his eyes and mumbled, "Fine."

Meenal stood and bowed, thanking them both for the interesting time together. However, the professor wished to present a gift for the new student. Rex watched as Professor Ostby moved to one of his bookshelves. His thin and elegant fingers moved across the spines, and they stopped on a dark-blue book. With a smile, he pulled out the book and handed it to Meenal, who stared at it as if it were some foreign object. Rex walked over and looked at the book. In dimmed gold letters, it was titled *Discoveries*.

"What's this?" Rex asked.

The professor opened it and skipped pages with scrabbles of notes. Once he arrived at a blank page, he pointed to the subject and date lines.

"This is an old journal of mine. It is lightly used, unfortunately. Nevertheless, I wish to give this to you in order for you to document your future discoveries, Miss Meenal," the professor said.

A bright, sharp-toothed smile shined on Meenal's face. The professor nodded and dismissed them both saying, "I want reports of your findings from you both in a week."

CHAPTER 9

MEENAL, EVEN THOUGH SHE WAS slightly frustrated at being denied her translation work, poured her heart into the research of elementology. After taking her leave from the professor, she immediately went to find out as much as she could on the strange subject.

Elementology, the study of the classic elements, and their effects on sentient beings, is a relatively new science. The classic elements of Fire, Water, Earth, and Air were considered the buildings blocks of the world until the discovery of chemical elements. Yet, despite being discredited as critical for life's existence, these four classic elements have played vital roles in entertainment, literature, and pop culture for centuries. It appeared as if that pattern would continue for as long as sentient beings remained on this planet. But the Great Cataclysm, the event during which myth became reality and fantasy creatures became our everyday neighbors, changed that for all.

—The New Science of Elementology: The Discovery, the Research, and the Predictions

Meenal hesitated to ask Rex for help, but Rex did not allow her to vacillate. He dragged her to the library and showed her the elementology section.

Yet, that was the extent of his aid. He was more of a distraction, asking her all sorts of questions about her past and teasing her about whatever topic he fancied at the moment. The awkwardness between them had decreased. They were slowly returning to the way their relationship had been before the kiss.

Soon, though, the more Meenal discovered about elementology, the more she wished to be alone in her work. Once she made her request known, Rex almost happily moved away from her and allowed her to concentrate. When she did look for him again, he was already flirting with one of the younger librarians.

She read the brief descriptions of each element and immediately matched the types of elementals with her friends.

For instance, Rex was definitely a Fire: loud, quick tempered, passionate/flirty (depending on one's definition), impulsive, and from time to time, violent.

Tiffanie was definitely an Air: outgoing, bubbly, vain, flighty, and judgmental.

Leeni was the opposite, which explained their constant bickering. She was an Earth: responsible, honest, rational, quiet, and socially awkward.

While she recognized her friends' elements with ease, she had trouble knowing which she represented. She knew that she was not a Fire like Rex, since he was often too boisterous and impulsive for her liking.

She knew that she was not an Air, for Tiffanie's behavior irritated her greatly—or "rubbed her in the wrong way," to use one of Rex's many idioms.

She thought she could be an Earth, for that was the opposite of Tiffanie, and she did not view herself as an opposite of Rex because they shared similar viewpoints, despite their different ways of expressing them. So, after much consideration, Meenal decided to start her in-depth research with the element of Earth.

Earth elementals were declared to be the most rational of all the elementals, proving to be some of the greatest scientists. One of the scientists who developed the theory and the eventual science of elementology was an Earth herself.

They were honest and impartial, making them work well as doctors and other types of righteous business professionals. They made some of the best friends since they always told the truth, even if that truth was difficult to bear.

It had been noted in research that Earths usually had strong family bonds, also common among dwarves and elves. However, this was due to their sense of responsibility and view of taking care of their own.

They were hard workers who thrived with duties or assignments. Their hard work and sense of responsibility, however, did not translate well into leadership roles. Earths were naturally shy and socially awkward, frequently missing social and cultural cues.

They often had trouble making decisions, and change was an Earth's worst enemy. Earth's opposite was Air, and while relationships with the opposite element were possible, those in such a relationship would deal with many arguments.

Meenal sighed as she looked up from the reading and considered the possibility of her being an Earth elemental and having a dwarf parent. She was abnormally tall for a female, so she decided against that.

Her build was similar to that of an elf. She envisioned a tall, majestic woman with honey-colored skin and mud-brown hair. Her eyes were the same green as Meenal's right eye, and she smiled down at the little-girl version of herself.

She frowned and shook away the fantasy. She was the color of the water, after all. There was the possibility that Water was her element. Yet, according to her brief research, the Water element was common only among humans and sea creatures. Sea creatures did not have the capability to breed with land creatures.

Therefore, by process of elimination, she determined herself to be human. She looked down at her skin and sighed. But she made the decision to further research Water, deciding that there was nothing to lose.

Water elementals were the peacekeepers, and while Earth elementals were advocates for peace as well, they only pursued peace because of logical reasoning—life was simpler without the threat of war looming.

Water elementals, on the other hand, kept peace because they were actually concerned with the welfare of others, particularly their mental and emotional health. Waters were outgoing like Airs but never selfish, always looking for ways to help others.

They were also affable and patient. Yet due to their overzealous desire to help others, they usually lacked self-confidence and looked to others for approval.

Water's opposite was Fire. While the Water was maintaining peace, the Fire was often attempting to destroy it. Relationships between these two elementals were difficult to keep and often dissolved before they truly started.

Therefore, from all her research and comparisons, Meenal determined that she aligned closest with Water. Still, questions of her heritage remained. So, she continued to search through Water's description until she came upon the topic of common creatures and races for Water elementals.

Again, she saw human, but she could not believe herself to be human at all; she looked too strange. Moving down the list, she noticed other races such as mermaids, sirens, cilophytes, and other sea creatures.

One creature that she did not recognize was a water nymph. She knew that nymphs were the embodiment of the element itself and were forever bound to that element, never being able to explore the world around them. Yet, she had heard the legend.

BRITTANI S. AVERY | 133

It was said that a nymph could transform her elemental body at will into a fleshly version of herself, and if she could capture a man's heart and bear his child, she would be free from the forest, volcano, or water source to which she was chained.

Perhaps her mother was a water nymph, which, according to the pictures of the greenish- and bluish-hued women, would definitely explain her skin tone. The streaks of purple in her hair and her single red eye were another story, but at least now she had a possible idea about her heritage.

She finished the day studying some of the powers associated with Water and Fire types and then returned to the manor, hurrying to her room. She dumped the books onto her desk and crashed onto her bed.

The next three weeks flew by, and Meenal became increasingly engrossed in the subject of elementology. She became so educated on the subject that she could identify someone's element with limited interaction.

She recognized that Kadmus was an Earth-Water elemental, having Earth as his primary element and Water as his secondary. Tiffanie was an Air-Fire, and Leeni was strictly an Earth. Alcon, Tiffanie's ex-fiancé, was an Earth-Fire—logical but with a temper. Meenal became known as an element guru, and many went to her with their relationship troubles.

She embraced her title as guru and her element as Water. Yet, with her newfound freedom, she was starting to believe that she was more than a Water elemental. She had to have a secondary element, but what was it? She also thought Rex had to have a secondary element.

Back and forth, she racked her mind around the possibilities, and after returning some of the books to the library, she searched for other books that would unlock the key to understanding secondary elements.

She scrolled her finger across the spines of the books in the section on elementology and shook her head. There was nothing, and her frustration grew. She needed to determine hers and Rex's secondary elements if their relationship was to continue.

She bumped her hand against another's and looked up to see the man of her mind's constant attention. She tilted her head and then quickly bowed.

"What I say?" he smirked.

"I apologize. You caught me off guard; I did not expect to see you here. Last time we spoke, you were not of the researching type," she said and returned to browsing the books.

Rex chuckled and turned his attention to the books that she was browsing. His eyes followed her hands with a hunter's precision. She felt his body heat radiating off of him, and his lavender and fresh cotton scent tingled her nose.

Clearing her throat, she tried to ignore him, but he further invaded her space. The same feeling of need consumed her, but she fought the feelings down. She did not wish to entertain any thoughts of them romantically being together. He—or more correctly, his father—probably had another woman in mind to be Rex's wife. She was not wife material; this much she knew of herself.

Her hand jerked as she felt his breath upon her, and she grabbed the first book her hand came in contact with. Her eyes widened as they landed on the title: *The Facts and Myths of Secondary and Special Elements*. In all her research, she had not heard of special elements.

She started to open the book, but Rex snatched it away. This was no time to play games, especially when she was on the brink of discovering the key to maintaining their delicate relationship. She glared at him, and he only smirked.

"Get it from me," he said, his smirk broadening.

"No, a gentleman would return it to me. A true gentleman would not have taken the book to begin with," she said.

He twirled the book on one finger and danced it in front of her face. She crossed her arms and did not move, watching the book. In a sudden dash, she snatched the book from his hands and trudged off toward a table. With a laugh that granted him a stern shush from the nearest librarian, Rex joined her at the table, plopping down with a wide smile. No sarcasm was present in it, so she allowed herself to smile back.

"What you looking for?" he asked.

"I am searching for the process of determining secondary elements accurately."

"But you already know Father's and Tiffanie's. Whose secondary are you trying to find?"

"Ours."

"Why?"

"You are very inquisitive today."

She glanced up from the book and stared at him, mimicking his playful smirk from earlier. He just shrugged and repeated his question, "Why are trying to find out my secondary?"

She sighed. "I am concerned. We are opposite elements. I believe that we will be spending more time together since I shall be remaining in your household for the extended future—"

"Can't get enough of me, huh?" Rex wiggled his eyebrows, and Meenal gave him a small smile.

"I will admit to enjoying our time together. Yet, I have noticed that you are becoming more easily agitated, and I believe that our opposing elements are the cause. I question if there is a connection between our secondary elements that will ease the conflict between our primary elements."

She returned to staring at the book, but Rex closed it and shoved it away. Meenal glared at him again, but he met her gaze and after two long seconds, she dropped hers. He narrowed his eyes and took hold of her chin, making her look at him again.

She blinked in embarrassment. Neither said anything for some time, their breaths syncing in timing once again. She wished to look away, but each time she tried to do so, his grip on her chin tightened.

She whispered his name, a near whimper of desire. *I just wish he would take me in his arms*, Meenal thought as Rex released her chin and sat back in his chair. She looked away from him and hugged herself.

The game of yes-but-no had caught her again, and she criticized herself for falling for it. He was not interested, according to Leeni, and Meenal had to convince herself that he never would be. Besides, due to the damage her previous life as a slave had done to her mental health, she did not know if she could ever love him, and as a Fire, he needed love more than anything else. Without it, he could never feel whole.

"Sorry… and it's not you. I bother you because I need an escape from crazies at the house," he said. "I act like this every time. I hate them."

"Who do you hate? And what is the source of the intensity of this hatred?" she asked.

"The Marshalls."

Meenal blinked. "I do not understand. How can you hate those that share your blood? A common saying is that blood is thicker than water."

"Yeah, in other families. To them, I'm not Kadmus's son. I'm too dark. I don't look like them, so Ma must've cheated."

"They believe that your mother was unfaithful?" Meenal was shocked that his own family would suggest something so distasteful to his face. She shook her head in rage and disbelief.

Rex shrugged. "Calm the hell down! It's good. I'm used to it. So, don't you be going all crazy, looking for stuff that don't matter. I haven't known what my secondary is for the past few years, and I'm doing all right. It don't matter."

His eyes were the beautiful brown she remembered from when they had first met. Yet, the power and strength behind them were gone. He stood and held out his hand, a silent plea to abandon her studies and come with him.

Meenal stared up at him and blinked, wondering where this gesture would lead them. The hopeful part of her wished for something slightly more romantic, while the rational side of her fought off those desires, stabbing them to death.

Their relationship had to stay platonic, for she had never loved anyone before and she doubted she had the capability. Still, her friend seemed to need her, and she would sacrifice herself for him. He was her benefactor and very first friend. She took his hand and squeezed it. The book would be there for another time.

CHAPTER 10

"**W**ELCOME TO THE ELEVENTH BIENNIAL Marshall Winter Ball!"

Cheers roared throughout the crowd as Titus, the flashy showboat himself, introduced the end-of-the-year tradition within Chance, which eventually expanded to the boundaries of all Maventa, Jaace, and Navistan.

It was not a celebration of the New Year like the ancient ones held before the Great Cataclysm. This celebration had no religious connections, did not celebrate some random baby's birthday, and dealt nothing with the God of the Sun.

Kadmus and Bala, before her disappearance, simply wanted to have a party with their closest friends to enjoy each other's company, and Bala's business dramatically slowed down during the winter. For them, it made sense to have the party at that time. And slowly, the news of the party spread to include most of Chance's upper class. Eventually, it became the way to celebrate the end of the year.

Since Bala's disappearance, the party for Kadmus was just a celebration of the life of his wife and all that she stood for: living adventurously and giving generously. Ever since her disappearance, he started each celebration with a little speech about her.

In the beginning, he pleaded for any news or hints as to her whereabouts, but as the time passed, he turned it into a memorial service, attempting to convince himself that she was indeed dead. He would not accept any other answer.

He glanced at himself in the mirror, his dark eyes boring into him. He stood straight and held his chin up, knowing that it was what Bala would want. She hated his slouching and she always berated him for it, saying, "An important councilman, who one day will change the world, cannot slouch. It's unbecoming and allows others to intimidate you." She would then straighten his collar and jab his side with her elbow. He would look at her, and she would wink, sashaying out of the room.

He sighed. He could not do this, not another year. All he wanted to do was crawl into his bed and be left alone until the party was over. Bala, the firecracker that she was, loved these parties. All her friends would be there, and their family members—the ones who liked Bala, anyways—would come from near and far to join them.

She loved being around them, and they felt the same. She always brought the best out of everyone, especially Kadmus. Now she was gone, and the world just seemed less bright without her. Kadmus stared at his reflection again and saw the shell of the man she had fallen in love with. She would be so ashamed of him now.

The door opened, and he turned to see Darius, the man who had been his own teacher in years past. Despite being a father and a councilman of Maventa, it was still strange to call him Darius, and from time to time, the title of professor still slipped out.

"Professor, it's good to see a friendly face," Kadmus said, turning away from the mirror.

"Indeed it is. Indeed it is. And we shall see plenty more tonight!" The old man smiled and reached up and patted Kadmus on the shoulder. Kadmus sighed and moved away from Darius.

"I don't know if I can do this for another year. It's been twelve years since Bala disappeared. Why have we not found her? Or at the very least a body? I need some answers, professor. I cannot take not knowing for much longer. Where is my wife?"

Kadmus slowly sunk to the floor, tears falling on his cheeks. Darius frowned and creakily followed him, cursing his old bones, and then pulled his friend into a hug. Kadmus was utterly embarrassed to be comforted for the billionth time in regards to Bala. He had to receive comfort from his professor, from a servant, and even his son.

It was illogical to shed tears over someone who was no longer with them, for she could not know that he was still mourning for her. Yet, he continued to cry, call for his love, and grip tightly onto Darius. Time passed. Slowly, Darius shook the still-sobbing Kadmus and eased him up onto his feet.

"Titus is eventually going to be unable to stall," Darius said, fighting back tears himself.

"What? You're joking right? That man could talk in circles about nothing for hours," Kadmus said and cracked a small smile.

"That's the man I know. Let us go and address the crowd."

They walked out onto the balcony above the main entrance of the manor, and hundreds of creatures of all races were there, including those from the foreign countries nearby. *This will be good for building Maventa's allies*, Kadmus continued to tell himself.

He turned to his right and noticed his son and his constant companion, Meenal. He turned to his left and spotted Titus, still jabbering away about nothing. He rolled his eyes and then cleared his throat. Titus turned around, and his eyes widened with delight. He introduced Kadmus, and the crowd exploded into applause.

Kadmus stood tall and pushed Titus out of the way, looking over the crowd with the classic look that all upper-class children learned, which seemed to say: "Hush now, for I have something important to reveal." The crowd obeyed, and he began to speak.

"Brothers, sisters, and honored guests, it is my pleasure to welcome you all to the Eleventh Biennial Marshall Winter Ball!" He paused to allow the crowd to erupt into more applause. He fed off their energy and he felt as if he could do this, at least for one more year.

"I know that you all are waiting to see the inside and dance the night away, so I shall keep this short, sweet, and hopefully to the point," he continued. "You have been with me and my family eleven years, and we appreciate that. Through the best of times and the worst of times, you have been there for us."

He turned toward Rex and held out his hand. This was a first, for Kadmus never invited anyone else to join him in his opening speech for the Ball. Rex looked over at Meenal, and she stared at him expectantly. He narrowed his eyes and faced his father, taking his hand. Kadmus locked Rex into a one-arm hug and shouted, "Thank you! We thank you all for your support throughout these years! May it continue well into the next and ten more after that!"

Kadmus pushed his fist into the air, and the crowd cheered. Rex looked at this strange man who seemed to have replaced his father. This quiet, logical man was thanking random people and moving them to action. Rex smirked and shoved his own fist into the air, and the crowd went wild. Meenal covered her ears and slowly retreated back into the shelter of the manor. Darius noticed and followed her, taking hold of her elbow. She looked up and smiled.

"The noise is unbearably loud. How do you stand it, professor?" she said.

"It's only going to get much louder, my dear." He laughed. "Here take these."

He handed her two small pieces of clay. She took them and stared at them in awe.

"What are these, sir?"

"These little wonders are earplugs for your sensitive ears."

"This sensitivity is not normal then…" she mumbled with a sigh, putting in the plugs.

"Well, not for humans of course, but for elves it is quite normal." Darius grinned, and she widened her eyes.

"For elves? I am Elfin?"

"Well, at least half, Meenal. By your personality and appearance, including your sensitive ears, I would definitely say you are some sort of elf. Starting with the most common species first, of course."

Unable to control herself, she hugged the professor tightly. He laughed and patted her back. She quickly released him and blushed, a darker blue on her cheeks. He happily shooed her away, allowing her to return to Rex's side. Kadmus and Rex were just exiting the balcony, and Meenal immediately told him the news of her possibly being an elf. Rex raised his eyebrows and grinned mischievously. Meenal looked worried. "Rex?"

"Nothing…" he said, the smile still on his lips.

"There is obviously something you know which I do not. Please, I would like to be informed."

He laughed. "Later. Right now, we got a party to attend."

He took her hand, and she frowned as they returned to their bedchambers to dress. Kadmus and Darius watched them go and laughed, Darius saying that it was like a gender-reversed version of Kadmus and Bala. Kadmus, despite himself, nodded and agreed.

Rex and Meenal went their separate ways and prepared for the ball. Rex quietly closed his bedroom door behind him and scratched his head, still wondering what had come over his father during the introduction speech. It was strange. Kadmus had acted nothing like the man Rex knew.

The Registration Act protests were decreasing, possibly adding to his father's hopefulness. Whatever the case, Rex hoped that this change would continue, for he enjoyed this side of his father. The professor and others mentioned that the joyless expression had begun when his mother disappeared.

Pushing those thoughts aside, he readied himself for the ball, slicking back his hair and changing into one of his finest suits: a midnight-blue with a shimmery overtone. He smiled when he recognized that it was similar to Meenal's skin at night, just darker in color.

His mind then swiftly remembered their time at the beach and a chill shot through him, the strange feeling of desperation. Shaking it off, he sighed and finished off his outfit with a pair of shiny dark-blue shoes and a white rose in his pocket. He checked himself out in the mirror and nodded in approval. If he didn't capture the attention of any ladies tonight, he would be a sorry excuse for a Marshall man.

He walked out of his room and turned the corner just in time to see Meenal stepping out of hers. The light from her room poured out into the hallway and spotlighted her exit. A small white slipper holding a blue foot peeked out from the doorway, and slowly she revealed herself.

She was wearing an original design, no doubt about it. Long dark-blue gloves covered her arms up to the elbows, and lace danced around her upper arms, weaving its way into the main part of the dress. The shoulders were elaborate designs of roses, colored white with water-like droplets on them. The bodice was the same blue as the gloves and fitted her body closely. The white skirt flared outward, the cut like a flowing river, and dark blue roses dotted it here and there in no consistent pattern. It ended higher in the front, showing off her shins and ankles, while the back hung low and trailed along the floor.

Once Rex had taken all of that in, he finally noticed her face and hair. The shimmers on her skin seemed to be enhanced, jumping out at him. And her pinned-up hairstyle, encrusted with gems of various whites and blues, finished off her regal appearance. She looked like a princess from a winter wonderland.

Slowly, she turned back to the room and started to rush inside, her train pulling behind her. Leeni was right there, and she pushed Meenal out of the room and slammed the door behind them.

"No!" Leeni shouted, a rare occurrence. "You look beautiful, and I will not allow you to hide all my hard work! Do you realize how long that dress took?! I made it for you and for this night! And your hair, do you know how long it took to hide that purple?! And don't get me started on the glasses! I swear—!"

"Leeni, my friend, please. This is beautiful, and I greatly appreciate your work. I just believe myself not qualified to be presented in such a fashion," Meenal said.

Rex cleared his throat and approached the two, both of them freezing in their tracks. Meenal curtsied gracefully, and Leeni folded her arms with a scowl on her face.

"Excuse me, my lady, I did not know that we were entertaining royalty from Tuyet," Rex said, attempting his best to impress the so-called lady. Meenal's eyes widened as she stared at Rex.

"Please, Rex, it is I, Meenal. I am but a humble sla… translator," she said, curtsying as low as she could.

"Meenal… you look… amazing. Leeni's right too. That dress is too awesome to hide. You make it better! You gotta save the first dance for me."

"First?"

"Yeah… what? You thinking nobody's gonna wanna dance with you? Wearing that, everybody's gonna wanna see who the Snow Queen is."

He winked and extended his elbow. Meenal glanced from him to Leeni, who was still scowling. Meenal sighed and took hold of Rex's elbow with the death-grip. He chuckled and led her to the ball's entrance. One of the guards at the entrance stopped Rex and demanded to know the beautiful woman who was holding so tightly onto his arm. Rex laughed and said, "You'll never guess."

The guard stared at Meenal, and she bashfully slipped down the eye-color-changing glasses to reveal her red eye. His eyes went wide, and he shouted to his companion on the other side, "Dude! This is that translator chick!"

The opposite guard nearly left his post to get a better look at the transformation, but knowing better, he shook his head and watched as they entered. The noise inside the ballroom was loud with bands blaring music and people shouting.

Leenie went off to join Tiffanie as the duo walked through the main portion of the crowds. Meenal noticed that they were creating a path. People stared at her with the same question on their lips, "Who is that?" Never "what" but "who."

She glanced at Rex and saw the confidence that poured out from him. He walked tall and straight. He held the look of money-earned pride. But Meenal could not copy him without feeling as if she were lying to the ones around her. She was no princess, no queen, and no duchess. She was a slave who had been given another chance and that was all.

Yet, they still stared as Meenal walked with fear and doubt, an obvious giveaway that she was not of the royal class. She gripped onto Rex as hard as she could. She was not ready to face the disappointment that would come once the crowd discovered she was a fake. But as Rex led her to the special seat reserved for his one guest, the eyes continued to stare, the jaws continued to drop, and the people continued to whisper.

Meenal decided to turn her attention to the dance floor, searching for familiar faces. She soon found Tiffanie, wearing a common, pretty dress and hovering around her latest boyfriend. She wondered if Tiffanie would have accepted the invitation to be Rex's special guest, had she not betrayed him. Tiffanie appeared happy as she clung to her boyfriend. With her primary element being Air, Tiffanie probably thought little of the hurt she had caused Rex, and this upset Meenal.

Her fists began to clench, and she narrowed her eyes. A gentle touch brushed against her arm, and she jerked her evil stare toward Rex, who looked wide-eyed and disturbed.

"Eh! What the hell I do?" he shouted, his eyes reddening.

"I apologize. I was deep in thought," she said, smiling softly at him.

Titus's booming voice announced that dinner was now served, cutting off Meenal—a perfectly-timed distraction. The crowd cheered, and everyone seemed to be heading toward the buffet lines, causing the loudness of the banquet room to increase. Meenal turned her attention away from Rex and looked at all the different colors of dresses, suits, and skin tones.

She spotted a few of the elves and attempted to compare their appearances with her own. She first noticed their ears and carefully felt hers. Hers were pointy, and she started to feel hopeful, but the more she investigated, the more she saw the differences between theirs and hers. The ears of the elves were long and they elegantly stopped into a single point.

While Meenal's ears were indeed long, they split into three separate points. Her shoulders slumped a bit, and she sighed. Perhaps the professor was wrong; there could be other races with sensitive ears. Once again, Meenal lost her hope.

A plate magically appeared in front of her, and she jumped. She looked up to see a just-as-startled servant. She gave her best closed-mouth smile, and the servant bowed lowly and apologized. Meenal smiled again and dismissed the servant happily.

The food in front of her was possibly the richest and best she had ever seen, and it was fish, her favorite! She looked over at Rex and saw that he had already finished half of the fish. He was currently chatting away with one of the actual royal guests, a duke from Churchland. The duke would occasionally glance in her direction and smile. She always returned the smile, but immediately refocused on her food.

Dinner continued without incident and soon enough, the bands once again blared their music. She waited for Rex and the duke to finish their conversation before stretching out her hand and speaking. "The music has begun, and I do believe that the floors are open for dancing."

Rex grinned and started to take her hand, but the duke cut in front of Rex and took Meenal's hand.

"Yes, they are, my lady. And I would be honored to dance with a woman of your status," the duke said.

Meenal glanced over at Rex, whose eyes quickly flashed red.

She smiled pleasantly at the duke and thought Rex's saying, *Do you... Do you...*

"Your grace, your invitation is most appreciated, and it would be my honor to dance with a man of your status," she said, and they both stood up. She turned to Rex and smiled. "Yet, I would not be an honorable lady if I did not keep my word, for I have already promised my first dance to another."

With that, she removed her hand from the duke's grasp and held it out to Rex. He snatched it up and twirled her once as he stood up. She laughed and steadied herself against his chest.

"You may have the second dance, if you wish," she said with a devious grin. The duke sharply nodded and tried to save face by asking another lady for a dance. The woman seemed to giggle at his previous rejection, but she accepted his invitation and quickly joined him on the dance floor.

Rex and Meenal strolled onto the floor, bumping the duke and knocking him into his new lady friend. Rex grinned and took Meenal to the middle, twirling her as they went. She laughed and fell into the pace of the music, following his lead. She realized that this was the first time they had ever danced together, and while she had no real expectations, she just hoped that this experience would be much better than the one she had had with the Lord Septimus.

Thankfully it was, and Rex was a complete gentleman, staying with the pace of the music and keeping a comfortable distance from her. She had never felt so calm in a man's arms before, and she thrived in the excitement of it all. With the music always varying in pace and tempo, there was always something to keep them on their toes.

The whole crowd cheered as the band exploded into a fantastic ending. The musicians bowed and sent kisses to the crowd. Meenal held the brightest smile on her face, and Rex matched her warm smile with his own. He suggested that they head to the drinks and rest up a bit while the bands changed. She agreed, and they slowly made their way to a table. Rex then gestured to a seat, and with ladylike grace, Meenal plopped down and sighed happily.

"Oh, Rex, this is wonderful. I wish that every day could be this exciting," Meenal said, taking a glass of water from him.

He shrugged and took the seat next to her. "If you wanna get dressed up and deal with snobby rich folk, then all you gotta do is marry a lord or duke or some other royal dude."

"You sound unhappy. I apologize if I upset you."

"It's aiight; I'm just grumpy. I don't like the people stuff like this brings. Speaking of…"

Meenal followed Rex's gaze and noticed that his cousin, Septimus, and their friends were approaching them. Thaddaeus and Jacqueline were among them, and Thaddaeus immediately averted his eyes.

Jacqueline just stuck her head up higher and gave an arrogant smile. The group filled in the rest of the chairs at the table; Septimus sat next to Meenal, and Jacqueline next to Rex, with Thaddaeus taking the seat next to Jacqueline. Septimus grinned at Meenal with that same creepy smile from the night at the club. She tried to resist the urge to scoot away, but she could not prevent her skin from crawling.

"I apologize on my cousin's behalf for not giving me an introduction sooner than now. I am Septimus Maxence, the seventh son of Lord Seneca Maxence of the Emerald Region in Maventa. You are absolutely stunning, if I may be so bold—"

"There is no need for introductions," Meenal cut him off, raising a hand, "for we are friends here. I know each and every one of you, but especially you, Sir Septimus."

Septimus's eyes widened in surprise. He bowed his head and gingerly took her hand and kissed it, just as slobbery as before. She frowned, not hiding at all, and wiped the spittle away on her dress.

"My lady," he said, "I did not know that I was of interest to you."

"I apologize, but you are of no interest to me. We just simply have met before, for you are Septimus Maxence, the seventh son of Lord Seneca Maxence, cousin to Rectavius Marshall and conceited Air elemental."

Eyes shifted back and forth as Meenal spoke, and everyone looked uncomfortable. Rex glanced at Meenal and smirked, nodding once when she glanced in his direction. Thaddaeus looked to Rex and narrowed his eyes, while Jacqueline whispered quietly to Thaddaeus.

"Mis-Miss...?" Septimus stuttered.

"You are a member of Maventa's high society," Meenal continued, "and you believe that those below your superior ranking are worth nothing but to serve and slave for you, especially when that one had been a slave in a previous life. Yet, I will tell you that you are lower than the beggars who hover around the street corners. They have respect for all sorts of persons and treat them as such."

Septimus narrowed his eyes and peered into Meenal's face, recognition slowly beginning to take place.

"You're the mixbreed's slave," he whispered.

"No, I am not a slave. I am Meenal Libéré, official government translator and personal assistant for Councilman Kadmus Marshall. I am a friend of Rectavius Marshall, son of Kadmus and heir to the Marshall inheritance. You, sir, are nothing due to the fact that you are the seventh son and you shall inherit nothing. You have no redeeming qualities, and your friends are only using you for your father's influence in the arts. You yourself are worth nothing."

The table fell silent as Meenal ended her speech and downed the rest of her drink. Rex lost the battle of hiding his chuckle, and even Jacqueline joined in. Soon, nervous chuckling came from everyone except Septimus, who abruptly stood and excused himself.

The music had softly begun to return, and unlike the previous song's fast tempo, this song was slow and perfect for intimate dancing. Thaddaeus and Jacqueline headed off first, and Meenal watched them go, the feistiness immediately gone from her previous encounter with Septimus. The smooth movements between Jacqueline and Thaddaeus were beautiful, and she could have continued to watch them forever.

"Okay, Little Instigator, you ready to dance again?" Rex asked, holding out his hand.

"Instigator?" she started, fear rising inside of her. "Oh, no! Am I going to start a war between you and Septimus? That was not my intention. I just wished—"

"Calm down! Damn, you haven't done nothing worse than I have. 'Sides, he can't really get mad. What you said was true. He's not getting anything as the seventh son. Me, I'm an only child and I'm getting everything. That's one reason he hates me. He also got problems with nonhuman folks, but most upper-class humans do. Come on; I like this song."

She sighed and gave in to him, walking over to the dance floor once more. The song was new, but the slow pace remained, and he carefully gathered her into his arms. She hesitantly placed her hands on his shoulders, but he took one of her hands in his and then placed his other on her waist. He was still keeping a safe distance between them, and their platonic relationship was not questioned by either of them.

Kadmus watched his son, and the slave-turned-duchess interact with each other, Rex having the biggest smile on his face since his mother disappeared. Despite the fact that a slave was brought into his house and he had to clean up the mess that the situation caused, he would definitely do it again, especially if the slave was anything like that magical little girl.

Meenal was kind, sweet, and always thinking of others. She never wanted to cause any unnecessary trouble, like Tiffanie. A hard worker and a wonderful friend, she was exactly what his son needed at this moment in his life. Kadmus was thoroughly grateful for her.

"Beautiful event, Kadmus. You've really outdone yourself," a female voice cooed in his ears. He turned to see his sister, Khthonia. She was the oldest of the three of them, while he was the youngest. However, he was the only male child, and therefore, the heir to the Marshall inheritance.

Khthonia and Karissa were very protective of Kadmus during his youth, raising him from a boy to a man. Their mother, a popular Maventi socialite, was not interested in bringing up yet another child.

When Kadmus became old enough to choose a wife, it was Khthonia who lined up plenty of proper high-society women for him to choose from. He had honestly tried to find any one of them attractive, but they lacked the passion that he had seen in some of the lower-class women.

Eventually, he met Bala, a poor and wandering gypsy who said that she would never stay in the same place for more than one year. Kadmus took that as a challenge and made her stay in Chance by falling in love with him. When he and Bala were engaged, they received backlash from his family, particularly Khthonia. The relationship between Kadmus and Khthonia had not been the same since his wedding day.

"Thank you," he said, staring at his sister. She was pale like him, though she resembled their mother in her own youth almost exactly: pale-blue eyes, long blonde hair, and the perfect hourglass silhouette. She was the girl that all the boys had attempted to woo, but she waited until someone of power arrived onto the scene, and that was Seneca Maxence.

She did not love him on their wedding day and throughout their years of marriage, she had never grown to love him. She loved only her children with Seneca. Yet, she married the man as a business arrangement, knowing that despite her title as oldest child, her gender had cursed her to lose the inheritance. She was determined to make sure that her children would be able to obtain what she had been denied.

"My son tells me that you have a new personal assistant," she said.

"Who are you speaking of?"

"The lovely blue-skinned girl that is currently dancing with your son. Meenal Libéré is her name. She is one of the excellent translators you have assembled for your ridiculous Registration Act. Honestly, there is now an unsightly tattoo on my arm."

"It's an invisible marking on the inside of your wrist."

Khthonia just stared at him with an annoyed look and then sighed. "It is the principle behind the tattoo, not the tattoo itself."

"I really wish not to speak about politics tonight, Khthonia."

"My apologies, for I figured that a councilman lived for politics."

"Khthonia, peace."

She pressed her lips together and shrugged. "I actually wish to speak to you about something of importance. It pertains to Rectavius, a concern really. He is already seventeen years old, yes? A brilliant man with much potential, despite his scandalous reputation as a playboy and now a slave purchaser. However, he is still unoccupied with the world of commerce and becoming increasingly engrossed with the world of pleasure. His cousin, Septimus, who is two years younger than him, is already managing one of the opera houses. It has nearly doubled in profit over the past two months, and it is gaining in popularity. Why has not Rectavius taken to anything political, following in your footsteps? Where is his maturity?"

"Sister, really? I cannot just give Rex a bill and say, 'Here... fight the rest of the council and make this law.' And besides, he is not interested in politics."

"Well, if he is to inherit the Marshall fortune, then you as his father and sole provider must make sure he is responsible enough to manage it. Otherwise, it would be in the best interest of the family to give the inheritance to another Marshall, perhaps Charles, Karissa's second oldest, or even Septimus."

Kadmus glared at his sister, and she blinked innocently, turning to watch Rex and Meenal dance. *The foolish man of the family. Every family has at least one, but of course, it has to be you, younger brother,* Khthonia thought. She sighed and looked back at her brother. "Oh, if only you had remarried when he was young. Though, apparently, you still have charm, for Lady Aellai from the Diamond Region asked of you again."

Kadmus shook his head and walked away, cursing under his breath. Khthonia watched him go with a smile. Her work was done, and it was time to allow Kadmus's overanalyzing mind to finish the job.

CHAPTER 11

THE BALL ENDED WITH A FLOURISH. AS the band struck its last chord, the crowd pleaded for an encore. Four songs later, the band gave its last hoorah, and the members took their bows. Applause rang out in the ballroom as the audience showed their appreciation. Titus once again took the stage and announced the obvious end, with people exchanging contact information and goodbyes. The guests returned to their respective loggings and the night concluded.

The next few days consisted of entertaining the remaining guests and cleaning up the mess of a ballroom. Many of the foreign lords and ladies stayed longer in order to enjoy the company of the Marshalls, as well as the lovely Meenal. Jacqueline and Thaddaeus were among the few who remained, and once they were able to sneak Meenal away from all her adoring fans, they got the gang together and hung out.

Despite having little interaction with the strange-looking girl previously, Jacqueline made sure to commend Meenal on her speech against Septimus.

She never liked the seventh son; he was so prideful and conceited without any worthwhile talents or resources of his own.

She always wanted to say something to the effect of Meenal's words, minus the political correctness, but Thaddaeus always stopped her due to his connection with Seneca Maxence. She could only give respect to the brave girl, and it seemed that the single commendation opened up a bridge to friendship.

Sadly, though, the guests had to return to their duties and families. Life returned to normal at the manor. Rex and Meenal still tutored together with Professor Ostby, Tiffanie got yet another boyfriend, Kadmus continued to put out political fires, and Leeni silently worked on her next masterpiece dress.

Meenal also returned to her studies in elementology with full force. She was confused about her aggressive encounter with Septimus as well as her budding friendship with Jacqueline, who was a Fire elemental through and through.

A pure Water elemental would not openly mock an aggressive person, especially without considering the effects on her relationships. Also, Waters usually did not enjoy time spent around too many Fires, unless the Water possessed a secondary element similar to Fire. Meenal decided that it was time to dive into the latest book she found at the library: *The Facts and Myths of Secondary and Special Elements*.

The first couple of chapters were introductions of the most common and well-known elements: Earth, Fire,

Water, and Air. Despite her expertise in the subject, she learned a number of new traits and powers related to the various elements, for this book was one of the few that listed the strengths and weaknesses. Earth held the strengths of honesty, responsibility, and impartiality, and weaknesses such as indecisiveness, awkwardness, and a strong resistance to change.

Fire was outspoken and passionate, making its elementals fine leaders. Yet, they were competitive, quick-tempered, and too big of risk-takers for most to take them seriously.

Air elementals were outgoing and loved to have fun, being talkative and the life of the party. Their weaknesses were a lack of attention to detail, superficiality, and pride.

Water elementals were still the peacemakers in this book but also artistic and flexible, especially in dealing with big life changes. However, their weaknesses were some of the worst: naïveté, emotional fragility, and cold-heartedness when hurt.

While Meenal did see herself associated with Water, the naïveté bothered her. *I am only naïve because I was not allowed to learn*, she thought. Most Water elementals may have been taught a lesson countless times but would still easily fall prey to the same trick. If that was the case with her, she would have not stood up to Septimus and spoken out against him.

Meenal thought her secondary could be Earth, yet she was not slow in making decisions. And while she was strange looking, she was usually the life of the party, much like an Air elemental. She shook her head and pressed her lips together, frustrated that she could not identify a single secondary element she associated with clearly.

She turned the page and saw the next chapter: "Myth: There are Only Four Elements." Having read the back cover, Meenal realized that the author was obviously referring to Light and Darkness. She continued reading the list of the currently known elements: Air, Earth, Fire, Water, Light, and Darkness.

Meenal started to skim over the rest of the chapter, not wanting any more introductory information. Yet, when she saw the subtitle, "Volcano, the Erupting Elemental," she jumped back to that first sentence. Air, Earth, Fire, Water, Light, Darkness, Volcano, Storm, Mud, and Ice. The last four opened up a world of possibilities for her and her secondary element. Storm and Ice sounded like good possibilities, and she went directly to each of their prospective chapters.

> *Storm, the Emotional Whirlwind elemental, is a rare combination of Air and Water with Air being the primary element. Only ten Storm elementals have ever been found and studied; therefore the information regarding the powerful elemental is limited. Among all the Storms recorded, four personality traits consistently appear. The first of these four is artistic ability, usually a specialization in the performing arts. The second shared personality trait is being judgmental, which*

comes from the Air half of Storm. The third shared personality trait is loquacity, or talkativeness. Storms can easily be mistaken for Air elementals by this trait. From time to time, however, there is the "calm before the storm," in which Storms act more like their Water half. If a Storm is quiet, one should beware. The quiet actually leads to the final quality: sensitivity and emotional fragility, a trait shared with Water elementals. Yet, unlike Waters, Storms are not silent about their pain and usually become violent, attacking the person who harmed them with their power of weather manipulation, particularly lightning.

Meenal flipped through the pages of Storm's chapter and sighed. She sounded nothing like a Storm, which appeared to be little more than a bipolar and trigger-happy Water elemental. She turned to Ice, hoping for information that better suited her.

According to the book, Ice was another rare combination, this one being Water as primary and Air as secondary. Ice elementals typically inhabited colder and snowy regions, though they could be found in other water-dominated regions.

Ices were often confused for Waters because some Waters were able to manipulate water in all states. However, that was where the similarities between the two types ended. Ices were cold and calculating, taking life seriously, especially in business matters.

They could be cutthroat if it benefited them in their endeavors. While Waters were emotionally invested in their relationships, Ices were detached from others, often appearing robotic in their movements and voices. They hated mundane conversations and thrived for serious topics such as business, politics, scientific news, or their favorite topic: themselves.

Yet, the most distinctive trait of Ices was their perfectionistic outlook on life. They were usually diagnosed with obsessive–compulsive personality disorder, in which the person attempted to be perfect, and could become violent when perfection was not met.

Ice was more of a disappointment than Storm for Meenal. She sighed and shoved the book away. The other special combinations, Volcano and Mud, held less of a chance to be her element.

Volcanoes, a combination of Earth and Fire, appeared be an elemental with a case of multiple personality disorder, switching back and forth between an Earth-dominated side and a Fire-dominated side and having no memory of the switch.

Muds, a combination of Earth and Water, were calm, friendly, and lazy followers, rarely doing much of anything out of their own incentive, including aiding others. Upon further reading, she discovered that the combinations could only be sole elements, not allowing the possibility of any of them to be her secondary.

Meenal had thought she was a Water elemental, but the fact that she was not a spineless doormat and not overly expressive led her to believe that she was something else. She turned to the next chapter on Light and continued to read.

> *Light appears to be one of the rarest elements to have, no matter if it is the primary or secondary element. There have only been thirty cases of Light elementals, usually possessing Light as a secondary element. Current researchers are unsure if Light is rare itself or if Light elementals have been confused for other types of elementals. Lights can easily pass for several different elements: Water because of their helpfulness, Air due to their outgoing nature, Fire for their righteous passion, and Earth considering their honesty. White is the total absorption of all colors, and therefore, one could look at Light elementals in the same fashion in regard to their strengths.*

> *One myth about Light elementals is that they have no weaknesses. While they are some of the kindest and most helpful people, they are not without their weaknesses. One such weakness is the plague of self-righteousness. They believe themselves to be the personification of goodness, so they tend to have very big egos, which also leads them to judge others harshly. Two common traits among Light elementals seem to contradict*

their haughtiness and judgmental attitude: being naïve and too trusting. A constant struggle of trusting and distrusting people usually make Light elementals paranoid and jumpy, adding to their awkwardness and high standards.

The next chapter was about Darkness, and Meenal hesitated. This was the last chapter and her last chance. If she was not a secondary Dark elemental, then she was something completely different. That would require more research and discovery, speaking with other elementologists, and pouring over more writings and books. Taking in a deep breath, she began reading the final chapter.

Darkness is the opposite of Light, not the opposite of goodness, which is a misconception people have had from the beginning of time. Each element has an opposite: Earth and Air, Fire and Water, Volcano and Ice, and Storm and Mud. Therefore, it is only natural for Light to have an opposite.

Darkness, like Light, is rare to have as one's element. Yet, depending on the location, that may not be the case. This is particularly true in the Drow Lands, where most inhabitants usually possess Darkness as their primary element. In the Elfin Lands, on the other hand, having Darkness even as a secondary element is rare and considered a curse. In the more liberal and diverse lands, a person having Light or Darkness as an element matters not. It all depends on location.

Another similarity between Light and Darkness is the ability to pass for other elements. By their fun-first attitude, Dark elementals can easily be confused for Airs. Their impartiality and spontaneity allow them to blend in with Earths and Fires respectively. And depending on the individual, they can be considered Waters by their calm and quiet nature. Similarly to how black is the absence of color, the element of Darkness is always lacking at least one key trait of the main four elements in order to avoid it being classified as such. For example, a Dark could be rational, impartial, and quiet, making him appear to be an Earth elemental, but lack a resistance to change and instead be comfortable with or even welcoming changes.

One trait that is unique to Darks is being expressionless. While it is true that most Darks experience feelings of happiness, sadness, and anger, they are not as expressive as some of the other elementals. Often one cannot tell if a Dark is joyful or depressed. The elemental wears a blank face. Darks have been used for spy and similar missions due to this ability, along with their ability to blend into any environment, assuming that their looks allow them to do so. While this is viewed as beneficial to governments and other similar operations, Darks themselves often consider it a hindrance, especially when attempting to build meaningful relationships. Friends and family judge them as emotionless, and therefore the Dark elementals are constantly misunderstood.

Darkness… Am I a Water-Dark elemental? Meenal thought, pressing her lips together. It was a strong possibility; she did exhibit traits of all four main elements and she was not expressive at all. Yet, she was emotional and searched out opportunities to promote peace and aid her friends.

True Dark elementals acted for the benefit of themselves, using whatever charms and tricks they could. The rare few even loved chaos and cruelty, two things that Meenal had seen more than enough of and desired never to see again. She looked down at her hands, seeing them shake. She tried to settle her breath. Suddenly, a hand rested on her shoulder and she jumped.

"Sorry, didn't mean to scare you," Rex said, looking down at her, concerned.

"It is no bother. I am in need of leaving my quarters," she said, standing shakily. Rex noticed and took her arm, helping her up and leading her out of her room. She did not know if she could trust her own feet. The discovery of her secondary element shook her to the core.

Eventually they left the manor and entered one of the three gardens that surrounded it. This one in particular contained mostly flowers and healing herbs, giving the place a calming effect on even the most furious. The sounds of hummingbird wings and the trickling of the small fountain toward the center added to the serenity.

They sat on a bench near the fountain, and after dismissing a couple of gossiping servants, Rex held Meenal's hands.

"I know what I am…" she whispered and closed her eyes.

"What?" Rex drew in closer to hear her better.

"Water-Darkness, that is what I am. That is my element."

"Well, hot damn, you did it! Congratulations!"

"Congratulations? My friend, how can you congratulate me on such an occasion? I am Darkness, the element shared by some of the most infamous murderers in all of history."

He sighed and rolled his eyes, squeezing her hands. "One, you're only at most half dark, but honestly, you're probably more dominated by Water. And two, are *you* one the most infamous murderers in all of history?"

"No… but I am not ignorant of what I am capable of if pushed."

Rex gave her a puzzled look, and she stood up from the bench, walking closer to the fountain. She stared at the water and tried to listen to the calming song. She wrapped her arms around herself, but her body would not be still. Rex followed her and watched the water with her. They remained silent for minutes until he asked, "What?"

"Certain Dark elementals have the ability to know the fears of a person. The stronger elementals can know a person's deepest fear, and the strongest of the Dark elementals…" She heard someone approaching and turned around. Rex, not hearing anything, followed her gaze and saw Leeni, bowing low.

"What is it?" he commanded, sounding more like the son of a lord than the friendly companion they knew.

Leeni's frown deepened as she barked back. "Your father wants you."

With that, she turned and retreated back into the manor. Rex groaned and pulled away from Meenal as she watched him go, easily reading the frustration in his walk.

As his angry footsteps marched down the empty hallway, Rex reflected on Meenal and her cryptic message. Dark elementals did not openly identify themselves, almost always picking a basic element similar to their current mood or actions. He was greatly intrigued by them, especially if Meenal considered herself one.

Their powers of shadow manipulation and the manifestation of dark emotions were fascinating. If fear knowledge was another, a powerful Dark could be nearly unstoppable. Still, Meenal spoke of those who could do more than simply know others' fears. Could they control it? Increase it? It did not seem logical to Rex, for that would require them to control another's mind and no elementals held that ability.

He pressed his lips together and soon enough found himself standing in front of his father's study. The imposing door mellowed out his rage, turning it into a mild irritation. The large knockers of lion's heads stared back at him with shame and disgust as they proudly held the family's coat of arms inside their mouths.

Two griffins battled, one red and the other white, as a single sword separated the two beasts. His family's coat of arms symbolized the power and strength of warriors and peacekeepers coming together to form a strong, single unit. He glanced away, silently cursing his last name, and knocked.

Rex heard a muffled reply and opened the door, figuring he had been invited inside. Immediately, he was greeted by bookshelves upon bookshelves of books with all sorts of different covers. Reaching high up to the ceilings, the books almost seemed to stretch forever, and he felt insignificant in their presence. He perused some of the titles, most of which were about war strategies and business practices.

He glanced over at his father and tried to imagine him as an army general or some other war leader. He kept drawing a blank. His father was an Earth elemental, according to Meenal the guru, and therefore was not ashamed of fighting. Yet, it had to make logical sense and not conflict too much with his secondary of Water, the complete non-combatant. If his father had his way, he would discuss, argue, and debate any issue before ever picking up any of these war books.

Moving away from the books, Rex dragged one of the many guest chairs closer to the desk, plopped down, and kicked up his feet onto a table.

"Sup, Pops," he said and smirked.

Kadmus looked up and sighed, shaking his head.

"Afternoon, Rectavius. Thank you for coming quickly," he started and stood up from behind his desk, joining Rex in one of the guest chairs. "This meeting is of the utmost importance."

"Everything's always of the utmost importance," Rex muttered and crossed his arms.

Kadmus ignored the comment and continued, "Your Aunt Khthonia has alerted me of news regarding your cousin, Septimus. She claims that he is running one of his father's opera houses and generating a profit."

"Aunt Toni is a habitual liar, you know."

Kadmus cut his eyes at Rex, and Rex mimicked his glare.

"I know this, and that is why I checked, spoke with Seneca, and attended the opera house myself. It's—"

"Who'd you go with?"

"Well, I invited Professor Ostby of course and a few other associates within the council. The professor decided to invite Meenal as well, and she attended, enjoying herself grandly."

"Meenal went—?"

Kadmus chuckled. "Yes—by force of hand, but yes. Concerning the opera house, Septimus renamed it from the Bronze Street Opera Hall to the Teatro Lirico—or the Lirico, for short. Most of the operas showing are classics. The inside was done with the Maxence flashiness, but it works for the neighborhood. I can see why his parents are proud of him."

"Yay for Sept. Don't tell me you brought me here to brag about your nephew?"

Kadmus sighed. "No. It is just that Khthonia has a point—"

"And what's that? *Your point*... don't go throwing Aunt Toni under the bus."

"Your cousin Septimus is busying himself in the world of commerce; your cousin Charles has written two books, both receiving high marks among the critics, and your cousin Barak is sponsoring quite the successful cattle ranch. All of them are younger than you and have already created names for themselves and given honor to their families. They are proving themselves ready for adult life and responsibilities. What have you done to prove your readiness to enter into official adulthood?"

"I've done lots of stuff!"

"Name them, please, for I am growing old, and my memory fails me."

Rex fell silent as he thought about it. He nearly mentioned his freeing Meenal, but he remembered all the difficulties he had gone through in order to obtain legal-resident papers for her. Once his father discovered her, the situation was out of Rex's hands, and his father had to hasten the process in order to maintain his good standing among all the abolitionists. Nothing else came to mind, and Rex silently admitted defeat.

"Don't be sarcastic. It's not a good look for you."

"My point exactly. Like you, I cannot name any proof of your maturity. You have partied, toyed with hearts, and created one of the worst reputations within Chance, most recently as a slave purchaser. You have proven your immaturity, if nothing else. I believe that my sister has reason to give the inheritance to another Marshall."

"What?!" Rex jumped out of his seat, his voice echoing off the books.

Kadmus studied his son and waited for his eyes to settle back into their original brown color. Rex glared at his father and fought the urge to slit his throat for even contemplating taking away his inheritance. His breathing labored to steady itself, and his thoughts ricocheted between logic and violence. Forcefully, he sat down with a growl.

"Allow me to explain, please," Kadmus said quietly. "This is not an easy situation for you or for me. What disgrace could be bestowed on our family if I gave the inheritance to anyone other than my *son*? I would face ridicule for being an irresponsible father, for misusing the Marshall inheritance, for not marrying another woman to provide you with a mother—"

"I don't want no mom," Rex growled.

Kadmus nodded. "I know. I do not want another wife, but people will accuse me of not providing for you."

"I'm gonna find her."

"Who?"

"Ma… I'm gonna find her."

"Rectavius, we have not seen her in years. She is most likely—"

"No! She *is* alive! I'm never gonna give up hope, like you!"

Kadmus sighed and closed his eyes, cursing under his breath.

"Rectavius, you must accept the truth that your mother is gone. Give up the childish dream of finding her and begin to concentrate on your future. These admirable yet unrealistic goals are holding you back from your full potential. Finding your mother is similar to freeing Meenal. You—"

"How the hell's that similar?!"

"You believed that a single righteous action would spur an entire nation to abolish slavery."

"Course not! But it helped! Lots of slaves have been freed since I saved Meenal."

Kadmus started to speak and stopped himself. Rex's red eyes begged him to continue.

"Most are not generous like you and I. They have tricked their slaves into endless indentured servitude. They are still slaves, unable to live how they wish. Other masters have indeed released their slaves but only into the wilds of the streets, allowing them to become slaves once again, to be deported, or even to be killed. Your revolution was unsuccessful."

"This isn't a revolution! I'm fighting slavery! I'm doing what folks who have balls would do!"

"No, Rex! It is a revolution, and a revolutionary is the last thing this family needs! We need an upright citizen, not some reckless playboy rebel!"

Rex stood and rushed toward the door, not daring to stop, despite his father calling his name. He slammed open the heavy doors, cracking one off its hinges. The shouting faded as he continued into a run. He ran out of the empty hallway, through the gardens, across the manor, and finally up countless flights of stairs. He shoved open a door at the top of the stairs and stepped out into the breeze. He leaned against the door and ran his fingers through his hair. He stared at the sunset, his mind drifting back to his childhood.

Five-year-old Rex was leaning against that same door, only it was a lot heavier and bigger to him back then. He was crying after enduring another hard piano lesson with his father. His small hands and tiny fingers did not allow him to reach all the keys, and

Kadmus expected perfection from his son. Yet with each lesson, he only received disappointment.

He remembered hearing soft footsteps and a knock on the door. Despite his protests, the person begged and pleaded until Rex finally gave in. It was his mother.

Time could do nothing to distort the face of that special woman: soft brown eyes, long and dark eyelashes, a flat pudgy nose, and the warmest smile. Her skin was a flawless cinnamon brown, and her thick dark brown hair added to her beauty. He was looking up at her, and she smiled back at him. He sniffed away a tear, and she easily lifted him into her arms, snuggling him.

"Aww, what's the matter, little man?" She kissed him on the cheek. Rex remembered mumbling something about his father being mean and how he hated him. But Bala quickly corrected him.

"Now, don't be like your nasty Aunt Toni. Your father loves you, and he just wants you to be the best you can be. You and me, we're all he got."

Rex blinked and looked to his left, expecting to see his mother. But no one was there.

"Ma… he only got me now. I don't hate him anymore; I think he hates me."

Depressed, he left the old watchtower and trudged back to his room. Meenal noticed him and started to follow, but he slammed the door in her face. She stumbled and started to knock on the door but refrained and returned to her own room.

Rex collapsed onto his bed and heard a crinkling sound underneath him. He rolled over and noticed a crumpled note in his father's handwriting. He narrowed his eyes at the note and finally decided to open it.

Rex,

I want to apologize for my rash accusations and I want to reassure you of my love. I am just concerned that someone else in the family will force my hand in regards to the inheritance, claiming your unsuitability. Despite my sisters' innocently sweet appearances, they are cutthroat.

I realize that you are not interested in the traditional sense of politics, but I do see that you have a love for people and are an excellent and motivating speaker, able to convince even the most stubborn of listeners. Therefore, I have a proposition for you. This will show your maturity to the family and show that you are more than what your reputation declares. The Saldur Empire has requested that an ambassador be sent to their capital, Rajsatish, in order to establish an alliance and trading relationship. As I am sure you know from your history lessons with the professor, the Saldur Empire was once the biggest and the most powerful nation; however, much of that changed with several of their states fighting for and winning independence. The empire has now become a nation of landlocked desert states and is in desperate need of an alliance to a wealthy country with seaside access. This is where Maventa comes in. We are small but wealthy, and having a militaristically strong alliance would aid us greatly in these trying times against the Jaaks.

I have been assigned to be the ambassador to the Saldurs. Yet, with the riots and disturbances in the streets regarding the new Registration Act, I feel that I am needed more here instead of chasing after some whimsical call of the former powerhouse nation. I will alert the council of your abilities immediately, and I am confident that they will agree that you would be the best man to send in my place. It is up to you to accept or deny the opportunity. I strongly urge you to think this over, consult your comrades, and decide.

If you accept, you will be traveling with an interpreter since many of the Saldurs, especially the royal family, do not speak Jeletho, being that it is a human language. I have an interpreter already in mind, and I believe that he and you will get along swimmingly.

My son, I again wholeheartedly apologize. I wish not to fight. I only want the absolute best for you and this is the only way I know how to give it.

Sincerely,

~~Your Father~~
Pops

CHAPTER 12

REX TWIRLED THE NOTE FROM HIS father in between his fingers, rolling it from his pinky to his pointer. He thought about the decision he had made to be the ambassador to the Saldurs, wondering if it was the right one or the wrong one, and wondering what he would be doing instead if he rejected the offer.

Whatever the case, it was all a game of what-if, and he lacked creativity to imagine anything different. Therefore, he concentrated on the task at hand, opened the note, and reread his father's words concerning the empire.

Rex's interpreter stirred across from him in the carriage, and he cracked a smile. Her lips were slightly parted, and her hair was falling out of her perfectly formed bun. Her skin still glittered in the moonlight, and her light eyelashes mimicked her skin.

He leaned a little closer to her and saw that she was sound asleep, comforted by the small rocking of the carriage. This would be her first trip out of the country as a free person. It had taken some fancy talking on Rex's part to convince Meenal to come along. It took even fancier talk to convince his father to allow her to go.

Kadmus had brought several logically sound arguments against Meenal being the interpreter: the reception of her strange looks, her lack of skill in translating the language, and her inexperience in traveling as a free person.

The original interpreter—an old fart, even compared to the professor—had been raised in the empire and knew the language and cultural nuisances like the back of his hand.

Yet, Rex convinced Kadmus that Meenal would be a better choice than some random guy with a ton of knowledge. Knowledge could be transferred, but the ability to calm Rex down in seconds could not. Finally, Kadmus agreed and allowed Meenal to go.

However, Rex was not completely free from his father's watch. Simon, a burly half-dwarf, half-ogre family friend, was part of the accompanying party. Rex also managed to convince Jacqueline, an expert in fire creation and manipulation, to join at Meenal's request. Jacqueline's request was to bring Thaddaeus. The last to join were Alcon, to care for the horses pulling the carriage, and Lucas, a strong healer.

They would arrive in Rajsatish in the morning and thankfully, they would make their official introductions after they had time to bathe and energize themselves from the three-month-long journey. He could tell that the trip had worn out Jacqueline and Thaddaeus, seeing how they were slobbering in their sleep.

Lucas sat next to him with his head on Rex's shoulder, despite Rex's efforts to make sure the fairy leaned his head and obnoxious silver wings in the opposite direction. Yet, any movement made by the carriage pushed his head back onto Rex's shoulder and eventually, Rex just learned to deal with it.

Sometime later, the sun shined brightly on Rex's face, and he heard talking around him. He sat up and saw that the others in the group were awake, and excitement buzzed throughout the carriage. Jacqueline and Lucas were looking out one set of windows; Thaddaeus and Meenal were looking out the other. Rex pulled Thaddaeus back and lightly pushed him toward Jacqueline, taking his spot. Meenal smiled at him and then quickly returned to looking at all the different kinds of people in the town's center.

Skin tones ranged from pale to black. Eye colors varied: the deepest blues, the brightest greens, the warmest reds. The dominant species was elf, their pointed ears giving them away. However, none of them had the same three-pointed split ears as Meenal, and watching her eyes dart from person to person, Rex knew that she was searching for someone like her. He placed a hand on her shoulder, and she turned away from the window, smiling at him. Her smile did not fool him, though. It did not reach her eyes.

Soon they passed the town's center, drawing closer to the palace's entrance. The buildings turned into trees, and eventually, there was nothing but sand. The scenery once again became boring, and all the tourists sat back inside. The carriage stopped moments later, and Rex stuck his head out to see the front entrance to the palace: a large golden gate heavily protected by guards. Simon's booming voice announced their desire to enter, and after a second of confirmation, the gates creaked open and the guards allowed the carriage to pass through.

Silence fell over the carriage as they traveled through the courtyard of the palace. The guards, with their black skin, red eyes, and fierce expressions, separated into two lines and surrounded the visitors. Meenal grabbed Rex's hand and scooted closer to him. He wrapped a protective arm around her, fighting down his nerves. While his father, the professor, and culture experts had given them a complete rundown on the Saldurs, nothing could have prepared them for the actual face-to-face meeting.

The carriage halted, and Simon barked for everyone to exit. Rex was the first, followed by Meenal, Jacqueline, and the rest. Rex straightened his posture and bowed lowly to the black-skinned men in front of him. The rest awkwardly followed suit.

One man bowed lowly, his hand swiping across the sand, and he started speaking in a rough voice. Simon narrowed his eyes, obviously feeling insulted, while Rex looked dumbfounded, glancing toward Meenal for help. She stepped forward very slightly and bowed once again and began to speak with the same harshness as the man. The man's red eyes lit up in surprise and quickly started directing the guards in various ways.

"What's happening?" Rex whispered to Meenal. She shushed him harshly. Rejected, he frowned and moved back into his place in line. Minutes passed, and soon only the man who had first spoken remained. He barked something again, and suddenly, beautiful Elfin women appeared from the sides.

Each stood in front of a visitor and curtsied, though the one in front of Simon nearly stumbled at the sheer size of him. He rolled his eyes and looked toward Meenal, who was speaking again. The man nodded, and then she turned to face them.

"I apologize for the confusion. We have arrived a day earlier than they anticipated. These women will show you each to your room. If you want to share a room, alert me now, and we can get that settled straight away," she said in a loud and clear voice, sounding much unlike herself.

The rest of the Maventi all looked at each other, and Jacqueline was the first to raise her hand, wanting to share a room with Thaddaeus. Simon asked if there was a room big enough for him and as Meenal asked, the main man in charge looked Simon up and down, nodding enthusiastically. That was a first, and even grumpy Simon had to smile.

With the rooming situations settled, the visitors left with their companions, and despite not knowing the language, Rex attempted to flirt with his. He figured out her name, Náriel, and that was all he could understand of her weird words. At least she giggled a lot when he tried to imitate her. She dropped him off at his room and curtsied before leaving.

He stepped inside and whistled low. The room was gorgeous! It had a complete living room set of precious stone, namely emeralds and diamonds. His bed was in the corner and had velvet green blankets and fluffy pillows. The sole window in the room was more like a door, allowing him easily to step in and out to view the beautiful gardens surrounding him. Despite being a desert, Rajsatish was lovely. He would have explored more, but the bed was calling to him and within seconds, he crashed into dreamland.

Hours later, he felt someone poking him in the head and whispering. He groaned and opened his eyes to see Thaddaeus, Lucas, and Alcon looking down at him. Simon was outside, his back turned to the three younger men. Slowly Rex sat up and pushed the boys away. He rubbed his head and asked, "What time's it?"

"Time for you to get up, sleepyhead!" Thaddaeus sung. Rex growled, whacking his friend with one of the pillows.

"Seriously speaking, though, dinner is going to be served in maybe a half-hour. You should probably look presentable," Alcon said.

"Right, yeah… ugh, where's my clothes?" Rex stood and stumbled around the room. Thaddaeus laughed, and even Simon and Alcon joined in. Lucas looked worried and frowned.

"We probably should have taken that extra day to rest," Lucas said, his quiet voice barely heard above the laughing. Rex shrugged and then nodded, trudging off into the bathroom. After cleaning up and shaving off the small beard that he had grown during the journey, he emerged from the room and found an outfit picked out for him, laying on the bed.

His friends were outside on the porch, laughing their heads off about something, so Rex quickly dressed and combed down his hair. He joined his friends and showed off his new digs. They approved, though Thaddaeus made some stylish changes, which received great mockery from the rest of the boys.

A gong sounded outside the bedroom door, and the boys rushed toward it. Rex shooed away the others and opened it, revealing his companion from before, Náriel. Her long blonde hair was down, and her green eyes fluttered as she presented a note on a golden plate. She gurgled something and nodded toward the note.

Rex blinked and slowly took the note, hoping that it would not be in whatever language she spoke. Thankfully, it was in Jeletho and it was his invitation to dinner. He gathered the rest of the men, and they followed Náriel, heading toward a gazebo-like dining area. She gestured toward the chairs, and they all took seats, discussing the differences between their female guides.

The conversation died down as others were spotted in the distance, four of them. The men watched to see who was approaching, but it was not until they came into the light that they saw Jacqueline, Meenal, and their Elfin companions.

Jacqueline wore a red regal dress with a tiny waist and a large skirt, and Meenal had on a simple lavender halter dress and long white gloves. They walked slowly, seemingly in deep conversation.

As they approached, one of the servants was speaking Jeletho and entertaining Jacqueline with a story about one of the princesses, Omvati. She was something called a chaotic Drow, but the servant knew nothing of what that could mean. Meenal and the other servant were conversing in the strange, gurgling language from before. Rex tried to catch her eye, but she seemed to be thoroughly enjoying whatever topic they were discussing.

Suddenly, trumpets blared, and everyone turned toward the noise. The boys stood and saw lights coming from the same direction the girls had come from. It was the royal family, fashionably late like most royalty.

Yet, this was no party; it was a meeting between nations, and the realization of what was about to occur slapped Rex into full alert. He swallowed hard and calmed himself. His father had told him to just be himself and to speak the truth. That was easy for a confident Earth elemental to say. Rex hoped he would be able to fake at least half of his father's confidence.

The first to appear from the shadows was the emperor of the Saldur Empire, Raaghib Kumur of the Saddijaeo tribe. The history of the Drows was shadowed by various lies and deceptions, in order to keep the truth out of the hands of non-Drows. However, for the past five thousand years, the abridged history of the Saddijaeo tribe had been known due to the Kumur family.

The Kumurs were known to be ruthless at times and were more prone to invade than to debate. Murders, assassinations, bribes, and kidnappings were commonplace in the family. Yet, looking at the patriarch of the current Kumurs, one could not imagine the famous murderous tendencies of the Saddijaeons.

He held the traditional appearance of a Drow: black skin, red eyes, and white hair, though his eyes did not have the harshness common to most. More than anything else, they looked tired and ready for the endless sleep of death.

The next to appear was the crown prince and heir to the throne, Rissien Kumur. His eyes were the complete opposite of his father's. They looked full of life, determination, and rage. Rex noticed that they were not the classic blood red; they were an orange-red.

The next three to appear were women, all having the same black skin, red eyes, and white hair, though one of them was obviously older. She was the empress, and the other women were princesses.

The royal family was presented, and all the guests bowed. The emperor gestured for everyone to take a seat, and after they complied, he gave a tiny smile and addressed Rex in the harsh language.

"He wants to thank you for traveling to visit his country and hopes that the lodgings are up to your standards," Meenal whispered.

"Oh, yeah! Tell him we like it a lot," Rex said. Meenal repeated, her face void of much expression. The emperor nodded and then clapped his hands, signaling the servants to disappear; they reappeared with gold wash bowls, even bringing a large one for Simon. The big man laughed softly and nodded thanks to the servant.

Meenal shifted her eyes toward the emperor, but he seemed not to notice the lack of respect. The emperor, instead, seemed to be studying her more so than anyone else. She quickly avoided eye contact with him and carefully cleansed her hands.

The emperor then clapped again, and the bowls were replaced with salads. All waited for the emperor to take his first bite, and he glanced around, narrowing his eyes and then barking something. The royal family began eating, and Meenal quickly translated, "He does not want anyone to wait for him. He finds it irritating."

With that, all the guests greedily ate the food in front of them, sighing happily to finally have a decent meal. The salads were replaced with large platters, and one by one, a servant brought out the dishes. There were pounds of strange meats and soups and sauces, but after the servants described each dish, the guests felt reassured.

During the main course, Prince Rissien paused in his eating and clapped his hands, calling for attention. Everyone put their utensils and food down, except for Simon, who still chewed the leg of a desert bird. The prince frowned and rolled his eyes. Simon, finally getting the hint, put down the leg and looked at the prince.

"Your language hard," the prince started, his voice deep and his accent thick. "But I try. I no want woman speak for me."

Meenal lowered her eyes, and Rex narrowed his. He had been told that Drows, at least those in the upper class, did not respect women and considered them to be treacherous creatures that could never be trusted.

"Fine," he grumbled through clinched teeth, and Meenal jabbed her fingers in his thigh. *Right... the respect thing.*

"Your Jeletho is very good," he said, hoping to recover from his mishap. The prince gave a smug smile and crossed his arms.

"Your slave speak good Majah." The prince nodded toward Meenal, who sunk lower into her seat.

"She is not a slave. She is my friend. These are all my friends," Rex said, gesturing to his party. It had grown silent during the prince and Rex's conversation.

The emperor looked back and forth between his son and Rex. The empress and one of the princesses continued to pick at their food, but the other princess, perhaps the younger of the two, watched with understanding and intrigue.

She briefly made eye contact with Rex and smirked, showing a pointed tooth. He gave a tiny smile back and returned his focus to the prince, who had been watching the interaction between them. He narrowed his eyes and barked something in Majah.

The younger princess looked at her brother and stuck out her tongue, an obvious sign of disrespect. The emperor glanced at the prince, waiting for something. The prince spoke more Majah, and the princess responded back, a rebellious tone in her airy voice.

Suddenly, a smack came across her face from the empress. The sound echoed into the darkness, yet nothing followed it. Not a sniffle or cry or shout. The princess looked as stoic as her family around her.

Rex did not understand what had been said to warrant a slap and humiliation. He clenched his fists repeatedly, hoping to abate his rage. Coolness touched one of his hands, and he glanced over at Meenal. She was not looking at him, but she squeezed his hand so tightly it probably would have hurt anyone else. To Rex, however, it was a blessing, bringing him back to the delicate situation before him.

"I apologize for my rudeness," the younger princess said with the same airy voice and little accent. Rex was surprised by her fluency with the human language, but the prince took over the conversation before he was able to ask.

"Women no respect, ja?" he said, and reluctantly, Rex nodded. "Mah fahja say to you come and you come. Many thanks chou. We want sea. What you want?"

"We want military aid."

The prince scrunched his eyebrows in confusion and turned to Meenal, commanding something in Majah. She replied back, gesturing to Rex. The prince nodded and leaned over to his father and whispered something in his ears. With a solemn nod, the two leaders parted.

"You want help fight, ja?" the prince asked. "We help. We friends now."

The prince clapped, and the servants returned, clearing away empty plates. A second round of food appeared, and the intensity of the previous scene was gone.

The emperor and prince talked enthusiastically with Rex, asking him about life in Maventa, the trading climate, and the health of the economy overall. Rex asked the same questions of the two men, though their answers were much vaguer than he was hoping for. However, it was more than what most received or even expected.

Finally, the dessert course was ending, and Rex was emotionally drained. There had been too many ups and downs throughout the conversations, especially when dealing with the cultural variances. Yet, the prince was not done. He spoke to his sisters, a first since the slap, and they nodded. The empress nodded proudly and said something in Majah. The emperor bellowed something, and the princesses stood up.

Some of the servants also left their posts and joined the princesses at the front of the table.

"They dance for you. Watch and be 'appy," the prince commanded. Rex nodded, turning his full attention to the rebellious princess. She caught him staring and playfully winked at him. *That's new.* Rex had never heard of a Drow showing any other emotions besides anger and boredom.

He stared at her, mesmerized. Music suddenly surrounded them, and the stoic maidens came to life, swaying their arms and hips to the rhythm of the drums. Their feet crushed the sand underneath, and their flowing dresses twirled in the wind.

Soon, the servants backed into the shadows, and the princesses took center stage. Wearing similar styles of dresses and hairstyles, they could easily have passed for twins, but their personalities vibrantly shown through their dancing. The older sister moved with precision, her eyes closed and her hands gliding across the music. She had clean movements without any unique styling of her own.

Her sister, on the other hand, added a little shake here and wiggle there, even moving closer to Rex and wrapping her scarf around his neck. She gave all sorts of hints, welcoming his wandering eyes. At the end of the dance, the princesses and the other servants bowed. Everyone applauded loudly, and the rebellious princess twirled once before returning to her seat.

The emperor said something in Majah, and all the Majah speakers chuckled, even Meenal. She looked toward the emperor, and he nodded, allowing her to translate.

"He said that the princess has found another toad, which is not an insult. She likes you," Meenal whispered, smiling through her words. Rex's eyes widened, and he glanced at the princess again, catching yet another wink. Seeing her spunk, he had to like her too.

The emperor spoke again, and the prince translated, "Many thanks for journey. Rest now. Big days a'ead."

With that, they were dismissed and guided to their rooms, all with ideas as to what the "big days ahead" could entail. Meenal constantly reassured Rex that he had done a splendid job of handling the situation. Both Simon and Alcon gave their reassurance as well. Rex doubted the legitimacy of their words but appreciated them all the same. He hoped that he had not completely screwed up this mission and by extension, the entire country of Maventa, by insulting a militaristic powerhouse.

$$\Delta$$

During their first few weeks in the empire's capital city, the Maventi got the red-carpet treatment: autograph and interview sessions from the major reporters, write-ups about each one of them in the newspapers, and gossip circles about who might be dating whom. Both Alcon and Thaddaeus had cult followings and were crushes among the Elfin population, which did not work out so well between Jacqueline and Thaddaeus.

Eventually, though, Jacqueline started to gain her own fans, who loved her fiery disposition and beautifully rare red hair. The citizens of the Empire found Lucas adorable, Simon fear-inspiring, and Meenal abnormal in all contexts. Rex was the obvious Drow crowd favorite, mostly due to his unique eye-color change, which had only happened twice during the trip thus far. His straightforwardness was a different trait that both the Elfin and Drow populations appreciated, and he was well-respected, from the poorest to the richest. When his father received news of his son's growing popularity, he smiled and bragged to everyone, but especially to his sisters.

CHAPTER 13

EVERY CELEBRITY NEEDED A NUMBER-one fan, and that person for young Ambassador Marshall was Princess Omvati. Their first meeting had left an impression in her mind, and she could not concentrate on much else.

According to the papers and the reports she had received prior to his visit, he was the local flirt with a fiery temper and love of people. While his father was a serious councilman fighting for the freedom of all, Rectavius rarely had dabbled into the world of politics until recently, when he bought the freedom of his interpreter, an ugly and strange-looking girl named Meenal.

Someone with a sick sense of humor had to have given her the Majah name meaning "gem." Omvati laughed to herself. Yet, she gave credit where it was due, for the little weirdo was intelligent and talented at learning languages.

Toying with her braid, Omvati glanced out the window, watching the ambassador and his strangely assembled party lounging in the gardens. Even if Rectavius was not in a position of power, she probably would still have been interested in him, but power was much more attractive and useful than good looks, which faded with age—for lesser beings, anyway. She smirked as she turned from the window and called a slave.

"Tell Ambassador Marshall that his presence is needed in the East Gem Garden at once," she commanded. The slave started away, but not before the princess quickly added, "And tell him that his interpreter is not required."

Δ

My friend Alcon,

I just wanted to say that you are very brave for accompanying Ambassador Rectavius on the first visit by an outsider to the empire in over one thousand years. We love outsiders; outsiders don't love us so much.

I heard about the betrayal of your former woman. That was cruel of her. Believe me when I say I have many daughters who would never abandon you. Please visit us and see. One makes a delicious dragon eye soup! Another has an excellent singing voice. My second oldest has the most beautiful eyes anyone...

"...has ever seen! Directions to my residence are as foll—"

"Cut it out!" Alcon shouted, and a burst of laughter erupted among the group. Alcon snatched the letter away and folded it carefully, placing it with the rest of his fan mail. Jacqueline teased him, saying that he was keeping it for later, and the laughter erupted once more as Alcon glared at everyone in disgust.

Jacqueline started to read one of hers, deepening her voice to sound masculine. "I am much more of a man than your current boyfriend. You should leave Thaddaeus to ride off into the Red Sun with me."

"I am no wimp!" Thaddaeus declared, pouting like a baby. Teasing and laughter echoed through the garden as the Maventi—or "outsiders," as they were known throughout the city—celebrated their fame.

Meenal tapped Rex on the shoulder as she noticed a servant approaching. He turned and stood, helping Meenal up in the process. They straightened their clothes, attempting to look more like country representatives than the teenagers they actually were. After exchanging bows, the servant began explaining her request, and Meenal's face darkened. Rex looked from the servant to Meenal and frowned.

"What's up?" he asked.

"Your presence has been requested immediately in the East Gem Garden and an interpreter is not required," she said and stepped back, but Rex held her arm.

"I'm not going anywhere without you. They might be treating us like we're famous or something, but we're still outsiders. I don't trust nobody but my crew."

"Rex, you cannot deny a request like this. It is obviously very important."

"Tell her I'm not leaving without you."

Meenal sighed and translated, noticing the changes in the servant's demeanor. The servant pleaded and dropped low to the ground in front of Rex and Meenal.

The others looked on to see what was happening. Rex rolled his eyes and picked up the servant. She looked dazed and frightened, but he smiled and gestured her to lead. She pointed at Meenal and shook her head. Rex smiled and gestured again. The servant slowly pulled herself out of his grasp and started to walk away. Rex glared at Meenal. But from her time with the Marshalls, Meenal realized what that meant: *I hate this, not you.*

Rex turned away from his friends and continued after the servant, having no idea where the East Gem Garden was located. He tried to converse with the servant, but she looked more confused than before. He sighed and allowed her to continue in silence as she directed him to the garden.

Upon entering the mysterious place, he saw the bright colors of the flowers, each resembling a precious stone. They shimmered like diamonds and glittered like rubies, but they were genuine flowers. Astonished, he continued to investigate the garden, seeing each flower and matching it to its gem counterpart. The Drows were not the most creative race, judging by the name of the garden, but they were certainly brilliant for engineering these flowers.

Looking up from a tiger's eye flower, he noticed a person sitting on a bench in the middle of the garden. He cleared his throat, hoping to catch the person's attention.

"Ambassador Rectavius, I appreciate you accepting my invitation," Princess Omvati said in Jeletho, standing slowly. She wore a long braid, her white hair reaching down to her hips. Her red eyes held a flirtatious glint, and her black skin was perfect. She wore a purple and gold sari, her midriff exposed. She waltzed over to him and gently touched his shoulder. "I had begun to believe you would deny my request."

"I apologize for the delay," he said, putting his speech lessons to good use.

She shrugged, moving away. He followed her.

"I assumed that you would be hesitant about leaving your interpreter," she said.

"I trust Meenal, and she is a talented translator."

"Indeed. But I do believe you can admit that she is not needed when we are together."

Rex said nothing, and the princess turned toward him with a sly smile. She continued to stroll around the garden as she spoke, "I wish to better know the first ambassador to my country in over one thousand years. But I want to know *you*, the man behind the title. So, who is Rectavius Marshall?"

"Prefers the name Rex to Rectavius. Son of Councilman Kadmus Marshall and Bala the Gypsy. Appointed ambassador to the Saldur Empire as a replacement for my father," Rex said, crossing his arms.

Omvati rolled her eyes. "Oh, I know all that. That's the same as you knowing I'm Princess Omvati, youngest child of Raaghib Kumur and Susheela Bishshari, Emperor and Empress of the Saldur Empire. As I said, I want to know *you*. What is fun for you?"

"Uh… I like exploring the market and walking on the beach. People watching is always fun."

"Beach, as in the ocean? From what I know of it, it sounds lovely, though Drows don't particularly care for water. But I'm a little different from other Drows."

"You've never seen the ocean?"

Omvati gave a deep sigh and walked away from Rex, heading towards a blue flower resembling the shade of a sapphire. She cupped the flower in her hand and tilted her head. Rex looked at the crisp blue against the blackness of her skin, never seeing such a combination of colors before. It was beautiful to him.

"Unfortunately, no. I have never seen the ocean, though this here is my ocean."

"While the flower's pretty, there's no comparison to the actual ocean. You should come visit. My backyard is the ocean."

She faced him, grinning a bright white smile. Then suddenly, her red eyes flickered once and the smile disappeared.

"Thank you for the invitation. I doubt that will happen, though. Soon, I am to be engaged—how wonderful. And you know who my husband will be? A spineless, dimwitted *kalkallayi!*"

Rex chuckled, "I think you just swore."

Omvati huffed and placed her hands on her hips. "What? Did you expect a sweet and calm princess? Think again."

"I never said that. But why are you marrying someone you don't love?"

Omvati laughed, a good hearty one. "Politics, never love. It's the only part I can play in my family since I never get anything right and I don't fit in anywhere else. It's the best I can do."

She plopped down onto one of the stone benches within the garden. Rex joined her with a sigh.

"You sound like me," he said. "I'm the odd man out in my family. They're rich, snotty humans and I... I don't really know what I am. I don't fit in, never have."

"Really?"

"Yeah."

"Tell me more."

Δ

As Rex continued to meet with Meenal, Emperor Raaghib, and Prince Rissien to construct the alliance between the Saldur Empire and Maventa, he also continued to meet with Princess Omvati. He spent less time with his comrades, using every excuse to spend more time with Omvati.

She taught him about her culture and her life in the empire. She spoke of the history of her oldest sister, Princess Jumanah, who was banished from the country for treason, but not before her tongue was cut out to prevent her from speaking any more governmental secrets.

Omvati spoke of her tribe, the Saddijaeo, and how they were the descendants of Saddi and Jaeo, the oldest son and daughter of the first dark elves. She spoke of her hatred toward her parents for using her as a bargaining chip in another possible alliance. She would curse and swear, speaking more like a sailor than a princess. Yet, she presented herself as a person rather than a figurine, and Rex became romantically attracted to her.

Dinner had just finished, and Omvati requested his presence in her private chambers within the next twenty minutes. He readily agreed and started to head to his room to change into some relaxed clothing. He felt a tap on his shoulder and saw Meenal. He looked at her, wondering what she could possibly want.

"I wish to speak with you, Rex," she said and bowed. He saw her worried eyes and sighed, gesturing for her to follow him into his room. She bowed again and ducked under his arm. He closed the door behind him, and she turned to him with a deep frown on her face. He touched her shoulders, staring directly into her eyes. He saw that she looked more than worried. She looked scared. If her skin tone would allow it, she would have been pale.

"Sharky, what's up? You not looking good," he said and gestured for her to sit down. She shook her head and stood her ground, wiping off the worried look and replacing it with determination.

"Rex, our friends have noticed a change in you since your encounter with Princess Omvati. You have been avoiding us and preferring to spend your time with the princess," she said.

"Having friends of a different nation's suddenly a crime now?"

"Rex, we are glad that you have established a relationship with the princess, for she and her brother are quite close, and he values her opinion. But a line has been crossed. You wish not to explore the town with Thaddaeus, your best friend. Alcon and you have not had a sparring match in three weeks. And Jacqueline and I are ignored directly when we address you. We are worried that you are becoming too close to her, wrapping your entire life around her as you did with Tiffanie."

"What you getting at, Meenal?" His eyes hardened, fading to red.

"Are you falling in love with her?"

"What?"

"This situation is very delicate. You must remember that she is already promised to another."

"No, she isn't. It's not finalized."

"You must realize that it will be soon. Would you jeopardize this mission for temporary bliss?"

"You sound like my dad—only caring about this bloody mission! Screw this mission!"

"I care about *you*. You are my friend. I do not wish to see you hurt. I myself believe that this relationship with the princess is not healthy for you. She is changing you."

"No, she's making me know who I actually am. The black sheep of the family, just like her. Different, just like her! She's the only one who really gets me!"

"Rex, please, listen to reason—"

"No!"

He pushed past her, knocking her over. Meenal yelped softly in pain as some of the gem furniture cut her upper arm. She looked to him and tried to call after him, but he was gone, rushing toward the woman who was more similar to him. He zoomed through the hallways, knowing the direction by heart.

Reaching Omvati's door, he started to raise his fist to pound on the door, but then froze, remembering where he was. This was not his home; despite his closeness to the princess, he was an outsider, so he stepped back and took deep breaths to calm himself. Slowly, his eyes reverted back to their brown color, and his breathing returned to normal.

He knocked, and Omvati immediately opened the door, looking lovely as ever. She smiled, a pointed tooth showing through her lips. She curled a finger at him, inviting him inside. He followed and finally noticed that she was wearing a very see-through black robe. He was unsure if there was anything under the robe and he swallowed hard.

"I apologize for the delay, Omvati. I got... caught up," he said and glared at the door.

"No worries. Wine to calm your nerves?" she asked, holding up a gold cup. He shook his head and took a seat on one of the living room chairs. Omvati frowned and sighed softly, setting down the cup and taking a seat on his lap. He blinked at the sudden contact and saw that she wore solely her underwear beneath the robe. He looked away, and she wrapped her arms around his neck.

"Do you wish to speak of your problems?" she cooed, running a finger across his cheek.

"No, I mean... It's just that—" he sighed, frustrated. "Meenal came into my room and said that us together isn't healthy for me. She says I'm changing."

"Changing into what? You are becoming who you should be... Strong... Powerful. What does that weak, ugly mixed-breed know?"

"What you call her?" Rex's eyes turned red, and the princess blinked. She touched the corners of his eyes, the red already fading.

"Beautiful..." she whispered, and this caught Rex off guard.

"What?"

"Your eyes... they were so red, so beautiful. Make them red again."

"No. They only turn red when I'm angry, and I don't wanna be mad at you."

"You do not have to be mad at me. The mixed-breed said we are dangerous together. Whoever her father is should be ashamed for bringing such an abomination into the world. She should have been killed in order to end the disgrace brought to his family."

Heat radiated from Rex's body, so much so that the princess jumped from his lap, her legs scorched. Rex chased after her, taking hold of her neck in two strides. His eyes were fully red and locked onto hers. She tried to speak, but he squeezed harder, allowing no sound to escape. Her eyes glanced frantically around for help. Her neck sizzled. She punched against his arm and chest, but they had become rock solid. She clawed at her neck, hoping for release, but she received a tiny chuckle for her efforts.

"You shouldn't be so quick to assign death. You might be facing it yourself, huh, princess?" he hissed, squeezing harder. Her eyes started to flutter, her strength weakened, and eventually, her body went limp in his grasp.

Rex dropped her, satisfied, and breathed until he returned to his normal self. He blinked and flexed his hand, feeling it was stiff. He finally looked down and saw the body of Princess Omvati with a pinkish white scar on her neck. Her eyes were open, and her throat collapsed on itself. Panic set in, and Rex stared at his shaking hands.

I have to leave.

I have to hide.

He looked around and saw that the door was the only exit. Holding his breath, he opened it, and after checking the hallways, he dashed out of her room and away from the haunting body.

I killed her... I killed her... Murderer... Killer...

The thoughts raced through Rex's head as he hurried toward... toward... He was unsure where. He kept envisioning the princess's burned neck and the indentation on her throat. She was dead, murdered by his hands, over a stupid insult and a mock threat of Meenal's death.

Was it a mock threat, or had the unfortunate princess been speaking the truth? There had been no playful glint in her eyes. Her eyes... they stared back at him, lifeless. Rex pushed faster, dodging this group of people and that bunch of slaves. He stopped in front of a door—Meenal's door. He pounded on the door and within seconds, it flew open, and he collapsed into her arms, whispering, "I killed her..."

CHAPTER 14

A DAUGHTER'S LOVE IS LIKE A DIAMOND, *the strongest precious stone of all. Unbreakable, a daughter's love is able to withstand all trials from the turbulent world she lives in. My love has been put to the test, and I have failed, where in other situations, more extreme, more trying than this, I have soared. For the sake of love, I have lied, stolen, and cheated. For the sake of love, I have lost my true love. For love, I have betrayed my eldest sister. For the love of my father, I have committed great evils, only causing my love for him to grow as I received praise and glory from him.* As Omvati stared at the ceiling, her thoughts tormented her for failing her father. *For while a daughter's love is like a diamond—unbreakable, it can be scratched by another, stronger, love; it appears as if I have finally encountered that type of love on this forsaken day.*

Women in white gowns circled around her, their light faces strange to her eyes. She searched for another black face, a familiar face, and soon enough she spotted Rissien. He stood in the corner, his arms folded and his orange-red eyes fierce with rage. Their eyes locked, and she stared at him, searching his face and attempting to decipher its meaning. His eyes hardened, and he looked away. She stared at him longer, wanting him to return her gaze, but he kept his eyes toward the entrance. Eventually, she drifted back to sleep.

Hours later, the sun was just hitting the horizon, and Omvati welcomed the morning, signaling the start of a new day with new opportunities. She slowly rose to a sitting position and stretched. She turned toward the shadows, rolling her eyes.

"I can feel you, come out," she commanded in Majah. Three figures emerged: Rissien, her sister, Fadilah, and her good friend, Nishith, Rissien's highest-ranking general. The three of them all held the same solemn expression on their faces, and Omvati sighed dramatically.

"I'm all right. It was just a shadow clone. There was absolutely no physical harm done to me," she reassured them, but Fadilah cut her off.

"It was still very foolish of you to meet with him alone, shadow clone or not. After your fainting, you were vulnerable and at anyone's disposal. He could have stayed behind instead of running away, and you would be dead," she said, her words cutting deep wounds into Omvati's heart. Omvati frowned and hugged herself, shuddering.

"Don't remind me. But I got what Father wanted, yes?"

Rissien nodded. "Yes, though we have no idea how to harness that power to our benefit. It appears that he is a true Maventi, hating racial injustice and the like."

"What if it is more than that?" Nishith said, and all eyes turned to him.

He cleared his throat and continued, "What if he himself is biracial? Perhaps being part human and part... something else?"

"A mixed-breed?" Omvati shouted, disgusted.

"Can you think of another reason for his strange red-eye color change?"

"Yes, he may be Sonnareian. He does look like those beasts."

"Perhaps, but Sonnareians tend to stay in their own country. Also, that trait is only passed from father to son, not mother to son. His resemblance is strongly linked to his mother's appearance, at least at the time of her vanishing."

"Someone did their homework," Omvati snapped and crossed her arms.

"We do appreciate your work, my friend," Rissien said, and Nishith nodded.

"Tell us more about his mother," Fadilah said.

"His mother, named Bala, was a gypsy. She traveled with a group of gypsies for a couple years around here, having a home base inside the Trees of Som. Her gypsy band left the empire and traveled, eventually arriving in Chance, Maventa. There, she met Kadmus Marshall, and he wooed her and went against his family's wishes by marrying her. Their marriage, despite the lack of familial support, was happy, and the birth of Rectavius brought much joy. However, five years after their child's birth, Bala mysteriously vanished from the city. She has not been found alive or dead.

"Her personality was very similar to Rex's. She was loveable, flirtatious, and passionate about equal rights, which are the traits that attracted Kadmus to her in the first place. She shared the same eye color change as her son when angered, but she usually forced her rage down and never lashed out with physical violence. She was known to be unusually strong for a woman of her small size and quite sarcastic. Her disappearance crushed Kadmus and enraged Rectavius."

"So, that is where the strength for throwing a man twice his size comes from," Falida said with a smirk.

"Indeed. Nishith, how should we proceed? According to reports, the ambassador believes that he has murdered the princess in his rage," Rissien asked.

"Apparently, after leaving the princess's room, he raced to his interpreter's room and collapsed, where he remains now. Make it seem as if he dreamt the entire event. Princess Omvati, you should be the one to visit him. Shock him and make him believe that he dreamt it. It could push him to want to know more about his mother, which is what we need."

Omvati nodded with a sigh. *This is all for Father.*

Δ

"Rex, what happened to you? I do not understand… Killed who?" Meenal whispered to a sleeping Rex. He looked in pain and exhausted, covered in sweat and mumbling endlessly. She wondered if this mission had been too much for him. Councilman Marshall had put great faith in his son and believed that he would be able to complete it without much difficulty, especially with Meenal by his side to keep him calm. Yet, the proof against Kadmus's claim was right in front of her.

Rex seemed mad, fidgeting and fighting against a horrible dream or a horrible reality. She could not tell which, and it frightened her. She checked his pulse and felt the rapid beat, a frown deepening on her face. She sighed and took his hand. She brushed back some of his hair, and his grip on her hand tightened as he muttered, "Ma. Momma."

Suddenly, there was a knock at the door, and a nurse answered it, declaring that it was Princess Omvati, and she wished to see Rex. Meenal narrowed her eyes briefly, but quickly reset her face to its normal expressionless state to welcome the princess inside.

The princess looked well-rested and regal as usual, wearing another colorful sari, this time an orange and yellow one. Her hair was down for a change, but this only added to her already immense beauty.

She gazed around the room as the servant allowed her entrance. For a moment or two, she seemed to avoid Rex's sleeping body, before finally walking over to the other side of the room, opposite of Meenal.

She took a seat and stared down at him with more emotion in her eyes than what Meenal had seen from other Drows. She remembered Rex's words from the night before, declaring that he and Omvati were the same: different from the rest of their kind. Omvati appeared to be like any other Drow from her appearance. Perhaps her difference was somewhere else.

"How is he doing?" the princess asked in Majah.

"The healers have said that nothing is physically wrong with him. He is just having an emotional struggle within himself. He has not awakened since his collapse yesterday," Meenal answered back, looking down at him and brushing away the sweat from his brow. "What occurred between the ambassador and you, princess?"

"Nothing occurred between us besides a brief conversation. My brother called him away, and they discussed something, which exhausted Rectavius. He fell asleep in my chambers directly afterwards. He woke up screaming and raced out of my room. I do not understand what happened. He seemed to be peacefully at rest before… nothing like this."

Omvati glanced down at the fidgeting Rex and sighed. "I do hope he comes out of this."

"He will," Meenal said with a sharp tone.

Omvati widened her eyes. "Do you love him?"

Meenal said nothing as Rex began to stir, his eyes fluttering open. He groaned, and Meenal quickly reached behind herself and took a glass of water. Slowly, Rex sat up and regained his balance as she handed him the water. He grimaced at it and shook his head.

"Please, Rex, you must drink. We are unsure of your condition," Meenal said, switching back to Jeletho. She forced the glass closer to his face. Reluctantly, he took it and drank a little before pushing it away from him. Meenal frowned and placed the water back on the side table.

"Morning, sleepyhead," Omvati smiled.

Rex jumped at hearing her voice, scrambling off the bed. His eyes went wide, and he panicked as he pointed to Omvati, stammering something about death. Meenal followed him and tried to hold him and calm him down, but he fought her.

"Who the hell are you?!" he roared, his eyes changing from brown to red in rapid succession. Mesmerized by the change, Omvati did not answer immediately, and Rex yelled again, growing more hysterical. She attempted to reassure him that she was the real princess, and Meenal did the same, but he seemed not to believe either of them. He paced, screaming and clawing at his head.

"Rex!" Meenal shouted and cautiously approached him. He jerked, but she managed to get ahold of him. She kept her arms wrapped around him and stayed on him, despite his sharp movements and yanks. She gritted her teeth as she held on with a death-grip, and gradually, the jerking stopped.

She looked up. "You have killed no one. The princess is safe. You have not shed innocent blood," she whispered. His eyes finally settled into their brown color.

"Rectavius, I am fine. It is all a dream. No harm has been done to me," Omvati said quietly. She gently touched his shoulder, lingering longer than Meenal preferred. But Meenal did not flinch, focusing instead on keeping Rex calm.

"I think I need some food or something," Rex mumbled. Meenal nodded and started to turn, but Omvati had already barked an order to the servant watching the scene. Meenal thanked her and slowly returned Rex to the bed. Soon enough he was asleep once more, much more soundly this time.

Meenal and Omvati watched Rex for about fifteen minutes before Omvati spoke.

"How did you know the source of his pain?" she asked, brushing some of his hair out of his eyes. He smiled in his sleep and mumbled an incomprehensible name.

"He had been talking in his sleep before your arrival; he screamed about a connection between death and you. Listening is a useful tool for solving problems," she said matter-of-factly. Omvati glared at her. Eventually, she took her leave with a promise to visit later. Meenal nodded with many thanks.

Omvati kept her promise and periodically visited throughout the day, seeing the ambassador eat and return to his normal state of health. By the night, he was fully recovered but he still lingered in Meenal's room, and she watched Omvati like a hawk. She did not care for the princess and cared even less if she knew it. Soon, the princess deemed it late enough, and she bided them goodnight, wishing for more pleasant dreams for the ambassador.

Rex had remained at the window since recovering the strength to stand. His friends visited after hearing what had happened, and they continued to reassure him that he had done nothing—the princess was in perfect health. Yet, despite having seen the princess himself, he did not believe any of them. It felt too real to be merely a dream. Rex had felt the heat and her skin melting off. He shook his head and felt a hand on his shoulder. He jerked his shoulder away and heard a quiet voice.

"Shut up," he said.

"Rex, please listen to me." Meenal touched him again and again, but he jerked away.

"I don't need you telling me, 'I told you so.' Not now, aiight?"

"I was not going to, for that is counterproductive to my objective. I simply wish for you to abandon your mission."

Rex turned to face her. He was shocked; that was the last thing he thought would ever come out of Meenal's mouth. He studied her face and saw that her two-toned eyes were stern. Her arms were crossed, and she held a deep frown on her lips. She meant business.

"You're joking, right?"

"This is no joking matter. At the start of the mission, you handled your annoyance of cultural variations well. Yet now you are easily agitated around the emperor and prince. Previously, your eyes were always brown, but lately they have been red for longer and longer periods. The Maventi have been inseparable, but now you abandon us to enjoy the company of a near stranger in Princess Omvati. We must not forget your latest misadventure: dreaming of murdering the princess, whom you claim as your new best friend. The evidence is clear: the longer this mission continues, the less stable you become. It is growing more difficult for me to calm you. We have already established enough of a relationship with the Saldur Empire. I believe it is time to return to Chance."

"No."

He turned his back on her and stared off into the distance. Meenal shook her head and stood directly in front of him, blocking his view. His eyes faded to red, and she narrowed hers, daring him to put her to the test.

"Do not dismiss me as some *slave*," she hissed. "I am your equal and your friend, and I deserve more of an answer. I am looking out for your best interest."

"Leave me alone, Meenal," he growled. She raised her head higher in protest. Irritated, he pushed her out of the way and walked further into the room.

"What draws you to this place? Is it the fame, the fact that you are a celebrity here while you are nothing more than a councilman's rebellious son back in Maventa? Is it the power that you have, holding a fragile relationship between two countries in your hands? Is it the infatuation you have with one of the most influential women in the land?"

"Shut up!"

"I will not, for I am seeking truth. What keeps you here? There is no use for your presence any longer."

Rex gave off a low growl, sounding more like a dog than a human. Yet she continued, walking after him, citing plenty of situations wherein he differed from his usual course of action. He yelled and cursed at her, his voice growing increasingly distorted.

"Rex, please, you are putting everyone at risk by remaining here. One day, you actually might kill—"

Her words stopped short as Rex slammed her against the wall. She could not breathe from the impact. Pain rushed from her head down her spine. Her arms dropped limp at her sides. The pressure on her neck tightened with each breath. Sharp pricks dug into her waist, and she felt blood beginning to flow.

She looked at Rex and saw the villainous glint in his red eyes and the cruel grin on his lips. The grin broadened with each wince she made. She tried to talk, but his grasp tightened and a haunting laugh followed soon after.

"Might kill someone?" he said.

Meenal tried to speak but only a whimper came out. Rex laughed, gripping tighter on her neck and waist.

"Oh, I'm sorry. You trying to speak? It's better if you don't. You're annoying the hell out of me. This is better—much better." He grinned as he watched her fight for air. With each of her movements, he tightened his grip.

"Rex! What are you doing?!" a voice shouted. He looked to see his mother, not having aged a day. She rushed over to him and shoved him away. Meenal's lifeless body slumped to the ground. His mother backed away from him, shaking her head.

"You are not my son," she whispered.

"Ma, I didn't mean to! Momma—" Rex cringed at the change in his voice.

"You are not my son! You are not my son! You are not *my son!*"

"Ma, please!"

She continued to shout, cursing Rex and disowning him. He reached out for her, but she shrunk away until she faded and completely disappeared. He stood there, searching the air for his mother—or rather, the apparition of her youthful self.

A soft call of his name brought him back to the present, and he turned to see Meenal, bleeding from her stomach. Rex glanced down at his hands and saw that his nails had transformed into blood-covered claws.

He looked toward Meenal again and saw her still breathing. He stumbled away and ran out of the room, going two rooms over. He pounded on the door and an eternity passed before it opened, revealing a smiling Thaddaeus, who immediately glanced down at Rex's hands.

"The hell...?" he stuttered. Rex pushed past him and yanked Lucas up, half carrying, half dragging him into Meenal's room with Thaddaeus following. There, he dumped Lucas in front of Meenal, and silently Lucas emitted a cool blue light around her wounds. Thaddaeus looked at Rex's hands and the wounds in Meenal's side and shook his head.

The silence continued throughout the healing process, and slowly, the bleeding stopped, and the puncture holes closed. Meenal's breathing became less labored, and carefully, Lucas looked her over.

"Physically, she is fine," Lucas said quietly. Rex glared at him and then stared back at his hands, the claws still there. Rex flexed them and sighed, trudging off to the washroom. Thaddaeus watched him go, but looked back at Meenal as Lucas helped her up.

"What the hell happened? Rex looks like a freakin' sabertooth!" Thaddaeus said.

"I attempted…" Meenal winced slightly. "I attempted to tell Rex that we should leave and return to Chance due to his instability. But he disagreed and upon my harassment, he lost control."

"He could have killed you," Lucas said.

"I know, but perhaps that would have made him actually want to leave. Being here is not good for him, especially being around Princess Omvati. I believe she has done something to make him more aggressive."

"Self-sacrifice, I guess, Meenal. I'm just glad ya safe," Thaddaeus said, shrugging.

Rex reemerged and could not make eye contact with Meenal. She was breathing fine, sitting up, and still alive. Yet, the image of her lifeless body still plagued him, and he could not get it out of his mind. He sighed and started toward the door, but Meenal stood up and stopped him. He turned and waited for her to berate him, to curse him, to scream at him for harming her. Yet she said, "I apologize for my action. I did not know that it would involve your mother."

"What are you talking about?" he said, his voice weak.

"I am a secondary dark elemental and I have the ability to know others' fears and to bring them to life."

"So, you… you did that?"

"Yes… I am sorry."

He glanced away, raising his clawed hand. "Did you do this?"

She looked away, shaking her head.

He stared at his hand again and then sighed. "It's nothing to do with the fame, power, or Omvati. I wanna stay here because I feel my ma. I can feel her blood, the blood of her kind—our kind—in this land more so than at home. That probably doesn't make sense, but I feel connected with her here and I know just as soon as I leave, it'll be gone, and she'll be gone too."

"I understand, but it appears as if it is more of a curse than a blessing. You have already attacked two people."

"Two?" Thaddaeus asked. "The princess is fine. He didn't do anything."

"It matters not whether it was reality or fantasy. He still attacked a person."

"So, what are you gonna do? 'Cause I'm with Meenal; we gotta get the hell outta here before something real goes down."

Rex clenched his fist, the claws cutting into his flesh. "I'm gonna find my ma."

CHAPTER 15

REX EXPLAINED HIS PLAN, OR RATHER his skeleton of a plan. He would ask the prince for a tour of the empire while he searched for information about his mother. Using the information found as well as his strange connection to his mother, he would finally find her.

After discovering that Rex would have to cover the treacherous Saldur Desert in order to reach the rest of the Empire, Thaddaeus furiously shook his head in disagreement.

"The hell you are!" Thaddaeus screamed. "You got any idea what sort of nasties are out there in the wild?! Even the Drows don't go out in the desert 'less they wanna die!"

"There also is not much time to prepare." Lucas said.

"Yeah! And another thing. Your ma's been missing for over ten years. What makes you think you gonna find something now?"

Meenal squeezed her brow in frustration. The only logical solution was to leave the empire, but he wanted to venture out into the unknown.

"Please reconsider," Meenal pleaded. The stubborn frown and the determination in his eyes caused Rex's ears to stop working. She groaned and tried repeatedly, to which she received the same response, as did Thaddaeus and Lucas. Rex was not to be swayed.

"Maventi men, we will leave within the day, possibly tomorrow. The women will stay and keep an eye on the royals."

Eventually, Meenal, Thaddaeus, and Lucas reluctantly agreed.

Early the next morning, Rex set up a meeting with the emperor and prince to alert them of his wanting to leave the capital city. He was prepared for their refusal with a list of why his departure was not a threat but a requirement for his mission.

When he told them about his desire to see more of the empire, the prince gave a small but warm smile and granted his request, even asking if a guide would be necessary. The prince explained that a tour of the less glamorous parts of the empire would prove their honesty in needing a wealthy ally. Rex nodded and mentally celebrated.

The emperor, after Prince Rissien translated, told Rex to enjoy his time out in the desert and to be safe. Rex bowed lowly and then allowed the emperor to leave as the two younger men went out to meet the guide for the trip.

They left the main section of the palace and walked quite a distance to reach another building of a similar sandy color but less grand in size. The prince and Rex walked in and saw bunches of black-skinned and white-haired Drows and a few earth-toned elves, making their beds, laughing, and playing cards, each wearing a sand-colored militaristic outfit.

As one man by the door noticed who had appeared, he shouted, "Dohmiro Rissien!" and stood at sharp attention with a straight back, feet together, and left fist on his breast. The men immediately stopped whatever they were doing and stood at attention.

Rissien nodded, and Rex followed him throughout the barracks as he inspected the soldiers with a keen eye. Once the prince deemed everything to his liking, he barked something in Majah, and the men went back to their previous activities. Rex thought about the military in Maventa and frowned, knowing that its soldiers were not as disciplined or respectful to higher-ranking officers. *These soldiers would eat ours alive*, Rex thought. *Gotta applaud Rissien and his country for their efforts.*

They eventually approached a door at the back of the room and without knocking or announcing himself, the prince opened it and invited Rex inside. Upon entering, he saw a Drow soldier at a desk, writing something. The man stood and gave the same salute as the other soldiers, but Rissien quietly said something, and he immediately relaxed.

As Rex looked at the soldier, he saw that he had the same black-as-night skin and white-as-snow hair as all the other Drows, but the one distinctive characteristic that he lacked was the red eyes. His eyes, instead, were a dark color, possibly black or brown. He wondered if he was different—like Omvati claimed that she was, though she looked no different. Rex pressed his lips together and dismissed his thoughts of the princess, knowing that it was foolish to be thinking about her. He had to concentrate on the meeting at hand.

"Friend, friend," Rissien said, pointing to Rex and to the Drow soldier who bowed. Rex mimicked him, unsure of what else to do.

"Nishith Aiimyath. Rex-tah-is Mar-zall," the prince again spoke, pointing to each of his friends and completely butchering Rex's name. Rex fought back a laugh and extended his hand to the soldier.

"Rectavius Marshall, Ambassador of Maventa, but Rex is best," he said, and the soldier, Nishith, shook his hand firmly.

"Nishith—or Nish, if you prefer. I can answer to both," he said in strongly-accented Jeletho, but Rex could understand him, and that was the main issue. While Rex liked the prince well enough, his accent and lack of knowledge of the language got in the way of communication.

Rissien spoke something to Nishith and then saluted him. Nishith saluted back and then gestured for them to exit. Nishith followed them out, and the soldiers once again saluted upon exiting. On the way back to collect the men and prepare for the journey, Nishith and Rex spoke of the goal for the trip.

Rex thought about lying but decided against it. The lie would get too complicated as the quest went on. Instead, he said that his mother was a longtime resident in one of the towns near the Trees of Som, and he wanted to find out more about her and her disappearance. Nishith nodded in understanding and said that he would give his all. He sounded sincere and this reassured Rex.

Nishith met with the Maventi men and gave them a crash course on the wilderness in between Saldur towns.

"From bandits to giant sandworms, any and everything hostile lives in the wilderness, and only skilled adventurers or soldiers cross it alone or in small groups," Nishith said.

Rex was fired up for the journey and attempted to stir up excitement in his men. Yet, it seemed he had done more harm than good with only Simon displaying any excitement. Alcon was only going to repay the debt he owed Rex for telling him the truth about Tiffanie. Lucas was concerned about his skills in such a hostile environment, and Thaddaeus whined like a baby about wanting to stay and protect Jacqueline and Meenal.

"Alcon, I can't blame you for your unenthusiastic attitude, and Lucas for your worry, but come on, Thaddaeus. You're a yellow-bellied wannabe aristocrat who's as worthless as a dried-up, old goat."

"Screw you! At least I still got my wits about me, not killing imaginary princesses and chasing after ghosts," Thaddaeus shot back.

"You know nothing!"

"I know when give up something lost."

"What about Jackie, huh?"

Thaddaeus rushed and pushed his face into Rex's face, pointing him hard in the chest.

"Lay off Jackie! Could say same with you and Tiffanie. She never loved you and you know!"

Rex lunged at Thaddaeus, but Simon caught him and led him out of the room. Thaddaeus spat on the ground as Nishith held him back.

Alcon and Lucas glanced at each other, "Do you think we'll even get out of the city limits alive?"

"I'd bet against it." Lucas said.

Things calmed down, and after both men apologized, the trip was back on schedule. They planned to leave the following morning. The Emperor held a grand feast in honor of the men, and it consisted of some of the richest food any of the Maventi had ever tasted. They feasted like the mighty men they were not and regretted it. Holding their stomachs, they all retired to their rooms early.

As Rex groggily prepared for bed, he heard a knock and shouted for the person to enter, hoping that they actually spoke his language. Meenal tucked her head in and stepped fully inside, bowing.

Rex smiled widely. "Hey, Sharky."

"I want to wish you luck and prosperity in your travels," she said, bowing again and then turning to leave. Rex quickly walked over to her and took her hand. She froze. Seeing this, he let her go.

"Meenal, what's—"

"It is late," she cut him off, "and I do not want to deny your sleep any longer. I have overstayed my welcome."

She turned to leave again, but he stopped her, refusing to let her go.

"Why are you running from me? Are you... Are you scared of me?" Rex asked.

Meenal stood silently and lowered her head. Rex let her arm go, and she walked toward the door.

"I am not afraid of you, for you are my friend," she said and opened the door. "I am afraid of the monster you have become."

As she walked out, her words echoed in Rex's mind and tormented his sleep.

CHAPTER 16

THE RED SUN COOKED THE MEN AS THEY traveled across the desert. Their camels dragged their feet along the sand and carried the unconditioned travelers. Water was rationed, food was scarce, and only ten days had passed since their departure from the capital city.

Tensions were running high, and patience was low. Sweat beaded down their faces, their expressions ranging from exhaustion to agony to rage. Even Nishith was not accustomed to such brutality. He looked up toward the sky and whispered a prayer, asking the Sun Goddess why she detested him and these foreigners so. He received no response, and the sun continued its unbearable punishment.

Silence dominated the majority of the trip once they entered the desert. They barely had any energy for walking, so walking and talking at the same time was completely out of the question. Grunts and groans were the only sounds they heard for miles as they went.

After two weeks of traveling, they had not yet arrived at a town, and the Trees of Som were still in the distance. Everyone was growing anxious.

On the sixteenth day of travel, Thaddaeus hysterically exclaimed, "I left my girlfriend for this! This mess is ridiculous! I'm out! Y'all losers can go on and search for someone that's good and dead. I'm headin' back to the capital!"

He turned his camel roughly around and started in the opposite direction. The others glanced at one another and watched as their comrade left. Nishith called after him, but with a feminine wave of his hand, Thaddaeus dismissed him and continued on, his camel happily returning home.

"Your friend is deserting us," Nishith said to Rex. "What shall we do?"

"Leave him; he stupid enough to go traveling by himself, so let him," Rex snapped and continued on.

"I'll get him," Simon sighed, ignoring Rex's order and marching after Thaddaeus, who continued on his way back to the city, tuning out the discussion he heard behind him. "I'm the only one smart enough to turn around before we're all eaten alive by some crazed troll or betrayed by the Drow general," he muttered. "I want a classier death if I am to die at all. I refuse to become anyone's meal or target practice."

"Boy, get back here!" Simon yelled. Thaddaeus gave the same feminine wave and continued on.

Simon trudged after him but slowed when he felt the ground shifting beneath his feet. A low rumble followed and grew louder as the ground shifted more. Simon looked down and cautiously moved back toward the group, continuing to yell at the stubborn pretty boy.

Nishith watched the strange movements of the big man, and his eyes widened. He demanded silence from the rest of the group and listened, shaking his head. The rumble sounded again, but more distant. Small and worried chatter started, and Nishith again demanded silence. Rex tried to catch his eyes. Whatever that rumbling was, it certainly had Nishith concerned.

"Nish, what's—" Rex started, but frantic screams captured their attention. Thaddaeus's camel was gliding across the sands, zigzagging in a random pattern. Thaddaeus had been thrown and was on the ground, his right leg obviously broken. The rumbles faded to silence as the camel sank deeper into the sand, its cries vanishing with it. Suddenly, it was eerily still.

Simon and Alcon jumped off their camels and raced to reach Thaddaeus. The rumbling grew louder once again as they approached, and spikes emerged from the sand. Thaddaeus screamed and reached out for the men, who quickened their pace. He called to Simon and Alcon just as the spikes disappeared again. Only a few more steps until they reached him.

Sand exploded around Thaddaeus and obscured his vision. Growls encircled him; he could not see how to escape. Pain registered in his mind as his bloodcurdling scream filled the air. The creature dragged him across the sand in the same fatal pattern as the camel.

"Thaddaeus!" Simon screamed. He received no response from the unconscious boy. The creature dragged Thaddaeus down to its home below.

"Dammit! He's gone…" Alcon said.

Unsure of what to do, they stopped their pursuit and turned toward the group, instantly noticing that Rex was missing. Lucas looked frightened enough to soil his trousers, and Nishith actually paled.

"Where is Rex?" Simon shouted.

Lucas pointed at the ground with a shaky hand. They looked in the direction he pointed but did not see anything. They rejoined the other two men, and Alcon immediately shoved Nishith.

"Where is Rex?!" he snarled, gripping Nishith by the collar and bringing him lower to face him eye to eye. Nishith tried to speak, but fear had a tight hold on him. Alcon shook him, demanding an answer.

Lucas tried to calm Alcon, but the return of the rumbling stopped all the noise. No one breathed. Alcon released Nishith and readied his bow. Simon and Nishith unsheathed their swords. They surrounded Lucas as he tried his best to remain calm.

"Get ready…" Simon whispered.

Heat burst from the ground. Ashes covered the sky so thick that they could barely see their weapons. There was no sound, no growling, no gnawing of teeth. Complete silence. As the ashes cleared, they spotted a column of fire. It took the form of a man and it carried something—someone—in its arms. As the column approached, the men saw that it was Thaddaeus being carried. They glanced at each other, whispering questions as to what the column could be.

The column seemed to slow down as it came closer. Lucas's eyes widened in recognition.

"It's Rex," he whispered, placing his hands on Simon's sword. "Put the weapons away. Something is happening to him."

"Forget that! I'm not puttin' anything away," Alcon spat. Nishith agreed with a silent nod.

Lucas snuck out from under the men's protection and ran over toward the column of fire. Simon yelled after him and tried to snatch one of his wings, but Lucas was too quick.

The three fighters stood their ground, but Simon grew increasingly anxious as Lucas approached the fire. Lucas gazed in awe at the man of fire and held up his hands to show that he was unarmed. The man tilted his head to the side and placed Thaddaeus on the ground.

Lucas knelt down and looked at Thaddaeus. His tanned face was scarred badly with a deep cut near his left eye. His shirt was ripped and falling off, showing his bruised chest. Wounds decorated his one good arm, while the other was a stubby knob. His right leg was grotesquely twisted with a bone sticking out of the skin. Lucas opened one of Thaddaeus's eyes, and they stared blankly ahead. He frowned and started the healing process.

Rex glanced down at his friend, then turned away as Lucas worked. "Dammit. Why did I even let this stupid idiot get as far as he did?"

According to the crash course on the Saldur Desert they'd received before the journey, there was strength in numbers, especially when dealing with the sandworms. They were similar to the African lions of old who attacked the young, sick, or alone. He glanced down at his hands, still engulfed in flames but not burning. His nails had turned into claws once more.

Lucas stood and gestured to his best friend. "He'll live."

Rex nodded and stared at his hands again, the fire still going strong. He reached out toward Lucas and croaked, "Now help me."

His feet wobbled, and he collapsed. The fire around him started to dwindle, and he became cool to the touch. The three other men rushed over, finally seeing that it was indeed Rex. Simon lifted Rex onto his back, and Alcon took Thaddaeus. Lucas walked in the middle, and Nishith brought up the rear, always checking behind him.

"The oasis is not far. Let us hurry, for the blood will attract more creatures," Nishith said.

"About damn time," Alcon said.

The worms did not make a reappearance throughout their seven-minute journey to the oasis, and Thaddaeus seemed to be recovering well enough; Rex not so much.

Each of the men settled into precautionary positions around Thaddaeus and Rex, who were sprawled out in the middle. Simon stayed near Lucas, with Alcon toward the edge, sharpening a knife, and Nishith keeping watch of anything off in the distance.

Periodically, Alcon and Nishith would come and stare at the two injured ones. Thaddaeus, while still slightly bruised and missing most of one arm, slept soundly. Lucas finished his healing session with him and turned his attention to Rex, frowning.

Rex fought in his sleep, his claws scratching his chest and the ground around him. More than once, Lucas had to duck in order to avoid getting cut. Rex growled, mumbled, and yelled, making the healing process harder than it should have been. Eventually, Lucas abandoned trying to heal Rex and simply kept his temperature regulated. "This is the most I can do," he sighed.

"Don't get down on yourself," Alcon said. "Why don't you get some rest?"

"Good idea. We should all get some rest." Simon said.

"Somebody must keep watch," Nishith cautioned, volunteering to take the first shift. There was no dispute from the Maventi. It appeared that the distrust of him was gone. Despite the injuries, the worm attack held some benefit.

Nishith watched them all lie down on their sleeping mats and quickly drift off, Simon the giant being the last. He relaxed and stared at the night sky, the stars and moon lighting up the surroundings and making the fire almost unnecessary. He sighed and looked at his strange companions, wondering what his mother would think of his company.

She would probably ridicule me for even volunteering for such a stupid mission, risking my life for a mixed-breed, the highest all of abominations. Nishith knew of the far-reaching good this mission would do for the empire, yet he almost regretted the plan that the prince and princesses were putting into play. Maventa would fall, and he would bear much of the blame.

Rex jerked roughly in his sleep and awoke. His eyes searched around and settled on Nishith. Seeing the wild glint in Rex's eyes, Nishith gripped hold of the hilt of his sword, waiting for the attack. He remembered the details Omvati had provided regarding the different rates of eye color change and how they corresponded to the ambassador's level of control. Rex's eyes were completely red and remained so, which signaled trouble. Nishith truly did not wish to harm him but would do so out of self-defense or to protect the others.

"Nish..." Rex groaned, the color in his eyes flickering to brown before returning to their fiery color.

"Yes, Ambassador, it is I," Nishith said. "What troubles you?"

"Pain—everywhere. I want it to stop... but Luke can't—"

"Please, calm yourself and rest."

Nishith neared Rex and placed the back of his hand against his forehead. He quickly drew it away, nearly burning himself. Taking off his coat, Nishith wrapped it around his hands and took hold of Rex's hands. Rex gave him a questioning look as Nishith dragged him off his sleeping mat and toward the water.

Stripping Rex down to his undergarments, Nishith pushed him into the shallow part of the lake. The water steamed as soon as it came into contact with Rex's skin, but it comforted him.

Minutes passed, and Rex returned to his usual state, red eyes gone. He nodded toward Nishith and said, "Thanks. I probably would've passed out or something."

Nishith shrugged. "I do not care to see comrades in pain."

"We comrades now? Well, yeah, you kinda did save me." Rex raised his hand out of the water and offered it to Nishith.

Nishith glanced down and raised his white eyebrows, but decided that Rex's hand would be cool enough by now; he took it and shook it warmly.

"Since we friends now, I'm gonna ask you some very personal questions. Don't gotta answer them if you don't want, but it makes for good conversation. And since sleeping tonight is completely shot for me, and you on watch, we can be company."

Nishith blinked and waited for the first question expectantly, while Rex waited for a response. After an awkwardly silent minute, Rex decided to just go on with the questions.

"So… what was it like growing up here?"

"One could ask that question to over one thousand people and each answer would be different. It depends on the person."

"Aiight, smart aleck, what was it like growing up here *for you*?"

"I was born near the western edge of the empire but grew up inside the capital. My father was a general in the army, and my mother taught dark arts at the university. I suppose that my childhood was similar to that of any other Drow child. Upon reaching young adulthood, I entered into the military and eventually received enough praise to become a general."

"Wow, y'all got boredom down to an art."

"I apologize. Do you wish for more detail?"

"Nah, but why'd you move to the capital?"

"More opportunities for my family."

"So, you got brothers and sisters?"

"I have a younger brother and sister, who should be reaching adulthood soon, within the next twenty years."

"Twenty years! Oh yeah, I forgot, y'all pretty much immortal."

Nishith shrugged and stared at the sky. "What is your family like? How is it different from my own?"

"Well, for starters, I'm an only child. I live with my dad now, since my ma disappeared when I was five. Got friends, ladies, and money. Though with the anger-management issues and all, folks be scared."

"You are not fully human, as most clearly must know. Do *you* at least know what you are?"

Rex laughed. "Nope! I kinda always hoped I was something awesome like a werewolf. But that's the real reason why I'm out here. All this craziness been happening now. My ma came from here before coming to Maventa and meeting my dad. I can almost feel her, like she's right here with me. It probably don't make no sense, but I wanna visit the towns around the Trees of Som and see if anybody remembers her."

Silence settled between them, and soon enough, Rex jumped out of the water and stretched. Nishith looked up and saw that Rex was still going to join him on his watch.

"What is the name of your interpreter?" Nishith asked.

"Random, but okay. Meenal," Rex said.

"I have heard that she was a slave before her work as a government translator. Is Meenal her given name?"

"Uh… I dunno. I think so. She called herself that when I first met her."

"It is just a strange name for a non-Drow to have."

"Why?"

"The name Meenal means gem in a tribal language of the Drows. I have only seen Drows with that name. I find it odd that a non-Drow would possess it."

"That's cool. She's on this kick about finding who she is and stuff. She found out she's probably Elfin since she got kinda pointy ears and they're pretty sensitive. She also knows that she's a Water-Dark elemental."

"A Dark-Water elemental?"

"Nah, Water-Dark. Water first, then Darkness. She's *really* into elementology."

"Perhaps she is Drow, for an elf would never mate with another who possessed the Darkness element.

Elves believe that being a Dark elemental is a curse, and while most Drows are not liberal, many are willing to mate outside of their race. Another, more likely possibility is that she is the result of a rape, the mother being some sort of elf. The mother would be shunned if she raised the child herself, and therefore, she sold it."

Rex pondered this and then asked, "What about her skin tone then? She's blue, remember?"

Nishith smiled. "Yes, she is quite blue. Her mother may have been a snow elf. There are accounts of elves with blue-tinted skin. It may be more pronounced in Meenal due to her father's blood, which could be a number of different types, for Darkness is common among certain races."

Silence returned again, and they watched the rising of the sun together. Nishith felt reassured that the interpreter was not an Earth elemental. He could redeem himself in front of the prince and princesses.

Princess Omvati had blamed Nishith for not finding the truth of Meenal's element. Secrecy was essential for the mission to overtake Maventa, and having an Earth elemental so close to someone in power was not good. Yet, the explanation that Meenal gave for knowing the source of Rex's fear did not convince Omvati.

With Nishith knowing Meenal was a secondary Dark elemental, he could put the puzzle together. Meenal was one of the rare Darks who could read emotions, translating them into thoughts either by assuming or knowing their subject well enough. It was easy to confuse them for Earth elementals, but the major difference was that for Dark elementals the emotion connected with the memory had to be negative; otherwise, it would be lost to them. Earth elementals could read all memories.

Around midmorning, Nishith and Rex woke the rest of the group. Alcon and Simon were hesitant about Rex, watching him with hawk eyes, but he had returned to his normal self, minus the claws.

Lucas woke in good spirits. "I'm happy to see that you and Thaddaeus are recovering well. I think it would be best that we continue toward the nearest town to look for an Earth elemental who could replace Thaddaeus's arm."

Rex disagreed. "I would probably be a threat to the town. I really think we should continue toward the trees; we're so close."

No one else was quite sure what they were close to.

"I promise there is an inn inside the forest with comfortable beds and warm food and refreshing baths." Nishith said.

This easily rejuvenated the group to good spirits, and they agreed to continue on.

Δ

After two more days of traveling, they finally reached the Trees of Som. Towering over the men, the trees' burnt-orange wood appeared like hardening lava rock. Their roots cut the ground, making it difficult to maneuver the camels. The sun disappeared behind the thick, black-colored leaves, adding to the difficulty. Night fell too quickly, and due to the Maventi's inexperience in dealing with rough terrain, they had not reached the inn, and visibility for everyone except Nishth was zero.

"Dammit, I wanted a bed tonight," Thaddaeus whined.

Simon's stomach grumbled loudly. "At least you aren't starving."

"If you ate like a normal person, you wouldn't be hungry, Fatty."

Alcon rolled his eyes. "Why don't you try to run off toward the capital again? You still got one arm left."

"At least I know a whore when I see one," Thaddaeus spat back.

"Really now? There was a pretty little redhead in my bed before we left, and I gave her a night she'll never forget."

Thaddaeus lunged at Alcon and attempted to punch him in the jaw, but Alcon spun out of the way, grabbed his arm, and swung him toward a tree. Losing his balance, Thaddaeus tripped over a tree root and landed in some mud.

Alcon and Simon laughed at him, but unwilling to be defeated, Thaddaeus threw a good chunk of it at both Alcon and Simon. The mud hit Simon on the cheek and Alcon right in the mouth. Bows and swords came out. Lucas stepped in, speaking of peace and friendship, but he was ignored. Nishith and Rex turned around to see what was happening.

A fireball appeared between the three of them, and they instantly stopped. They turned to see Rex's eyes red and his fist smoking.

"I'm tired and I wanna make camp. Get your bickering selves in gear before I aim a little higher," Rex said in a strangely calm and quiet tone. The rest of them looked at each other and decided to call a truce. Alcon helped Thaddaeus up, and Simon allowed Lucas to go ahead of him in order for him to bring up the rear. Rex's eyes remained red despite the calm, and he glanced down at his hand, the smoke finally disappearing.

They eventually found a clearing and made camp, building a generous fire. There was no talking as they ate and settled in. Simon took the first watch, and once Alcon strengthened the fire, they all slept—or at least tried to. Alcon, Thaddaeus, and Lucas quickly drifted while Nishith remained awake for some time before finally falling asleep.

Rex tossed and turned for the majority of the night, his dreams plagued with murder and dead princesses and friends. Each time he awoke, he was drenched in sweat and covered in claw marks.

Eventually, Rex grew tired of constantly waking up and stood from his sleeping mat. He stretched and looked at those around him, his men: Simon, his father's friend and the older brother he always wanted; Thaddaeus, his cowardly best friend with a sense of style; Lucas, the healer with too soft of a heart to be a healer; Alcon, a rival turned comrade; and Nishith, the Drow, whom Rex was still unsure about but liked better than Prince Rissien. It was a strange group if one actually looked at them, for nearly all the major races were represented.

Rex smirked and then decided that it would be good to check the perimeter just to make sure everything was okay. He tried to make another fireball to build up the fire, but nothing happened; he gave up after a couple tries. Disappointed, Rex got some of the wood that Simon had chopped and added it to the dying fire. He glared at the fire and tried once more, receiving nothing for his efforts.

Rex walked around the campsite and saw nothing out of the ordinary, but something that sounded like a scream perked his ears. He ignored it and continued on, returning to the campsite.

The scream came again, and it bothered Rex enough to wake up Alcon. "Hey, I think I heard a scream. Come with me to check it out."

"Ugh… If you hear it again, I'll go with you."

After a minute of silence, Alcon told Rex to go back to sleep.

Simon was snoring too hard to be woken up, and Rex didn't want to take Thaddaeus or Lucas since they would do more harm than good. He at last tried Nishith.

"Wake up, dude!" Rex said, shaking Nishith's shoulder.

Nishith's eyes snapped open and in a split-second, he had a knife against Rex's throat. Rex's eyes widened. Upon seeing who had disturbed him, Nishith put the knife away.

"What is it?" he asked.

"Just listen. There's somebody out there, and they need help."

They listened for the scream, and seconds later, Rex heard it. Nishith shook his head and said, "I heard nothing. The forest tends to play tricks on the ears. Please ignore the sounds and return to sleep." Nishith said, rolling over.

Rex narrowed his eyes and left the campsite, following the noise and calling out to the voice. The closer he got, it became noticeably female, and there was no way that he was not going to investigate, forest playing tricks or no. He was deep in the forest when he heard someone calling, "Please! Help!"

"Hello?"

The voice called out again, inching Rex further away from the campsite. He entered into a clearing and saw a woman with raven hair and a hole in her stomach. She was bleeding and with a bloody hand, she reached out to him.

"Help me, please," she said, her dark eyes pleading with him. Without thinking, Rex rushed over to her, scooping her up into his arms.

"I got you," he said. She winced as he lifted her up.

"There… is a lake… healing properties. Please…"

The woman pointed her hand straight ahead, and Rex broke off into a run, holding the woman tightly to minimize the bumping around. She held onto his neck, and he felt the blood against his skin.

Rex tried to keep calm, knowing that becoming enraged at her assailant would only bring her harm. He focused on the direction ahead and slowly heard the trickling of water. Moments later, they arrived at the lake, and he laid her down in the shallow parts of it.

As the water touched her skin, it began to glow, lighting up the entire clearing. The cricket noises dwindled and peace came over the entire area. Rex watched in wonder as the blood slowly transformed into water, and the hole in her flesh shrunk. Her skin soon had a healthy glow, and her eyes fluttered open as she gasped for air. She reached for him, and he helped her up out of the water. She rested her head against his chest, catching her breath.

"Thank you. I owe you my life, young man," she said in a sultry and confident voice.

Rex blushed and shrugged. "I couldn't just leave you there."

"Nevertheless, I greatly appreciate it. Please tell me my savior's name."

"Rex. Yours?"

"I go by many names, but my favorite is Aurelia."

Slowly, she removed herself from his arms and returned to the water, hiking up her dress to reveal her thighs. Rex watched her sashay, her wide hips taunting him. Her hair was long, reaching slightly above her backside, which was just lovely. She moved with grace and beckoned him to the water.

Rex followed and stood looking down at her. She was short compared to him, maybe coming up to his chest; he usually found that unattractive. Short women were usually pushy and domineering, but she was soft and kind. She smiled at him and took his hands.

"I wish to express my gratitude toward my savior," Aurelia said, her voice husky. Rex's eyes widened. He glanced around for any of his comrades. With the coast clear, he returned his eyes toward Aurelia, and she pulled him toward her.

"Rex..." she whispered, softly brushing her lips against his. But instead of flesh, she felt fire. She cried out in pain and stumbled away, holding her mouth. Rex was jarred back as he looked at her, her skin black and pink—like Omvati.

"What did you do to me?" she cried, tears in her eyes, and started to run away.

He chased after her. "Please, I'm sorry! Wait... Aurelia!"

Rex managed to take hold of her hand, and she screamed in pain and jerked her hand away, revealing the same severe burn. He cursed and continued to follow her, but she raced away, and his surroundings started to fade. Slowly, everything went black.

CHAPTER 17

"MISTRESS? MISTRESS AURELIA?! YOU all right?"

Whimpering and groaning echoed in the trees as hurried feet rushed through them. The groans grew fainter the closer the young man got. "This is not a good sign," he muttered.

He had been off collecting wood for the night when he heard the scream of his mistress. *Why did I leave her in such a vulnerable state?* he berated himself.

She had insisted—strongly—that he go away and leave her to her work. While he did not fully understand the effort needed for her to earn the trust of her future meal, she was always close to the prey. With closed eyes, she had leaned in and touched her forehead to his, her hands cupping his face.

Sweat had decorated her brow, and her face wore a series of concentrated looks, ranging from anger to hunger. She had assured him afterwards that the time alone was needed, but he always worried. He loved her and wished for no ill to come to her.

Hearing her distress, his blood was pumping and his adrenaline was rushing, forcing him to run faster toward his love. *I will not lose her!*

Upon reaching their little clearing, he first spotted his mistress on the ground, gasping for air. Her lips were burned badly, and there was a deep black and pink burn on the ivory skin of her left wrist. She shook violently and slowly turned her head to face him.

"Ru-Rudo…" she wheezed.

"I'll-I'll get Grandmother!" Rudo said, nearly tripping over himself to reach Grandmother Zipporah. While she was no one's biological grandmother, she was the personification of the word: long white hair, dark wrinkled skin, a joyful and crooked smile, and a healing hand.

Rudo found Zipporah, and with a single glance at his panic-stricken face, she ordered him to lead and she would follow. They raced back to Aurelia's den.

Zipporah immediately spotted her friend's latest prey hanging unconscious in her spiderweb, a young dark-haired and dark-skinned lad. She looked down at the ground and saw Aurelia, who was lying completely still. Zipporah went to work, her hands glowing and sending energy to the burns. Slowly the damaged flesh disappeared and new, baby-soft skin formed. Aurelia returned to her natural beauty, but still she lay, unmoving.

"Can't you do anything else?!" Rudo snapped, but Zipporah ignored him.

Minutes passed, and Aurelia still did not respond. Rudo began to sob, and Zipporah stepped away. Just as they were leaving, a giant gasp escaped from

Aurelia. Gaining recognition of her surroundings, she began to struggle to stand. Rudo quickly rushed to her side, but she brushed him away.

"I do believe I can manage. I have eight legs and two arms after all," she said and chuckled. Zipporah looked on with concern, but Aurelia shrugged a shoulder. "The boy was more than what I could handle. Apparently, he's not as human as he looks."

"Indeed," Rudo mumbled. Aurelia shot some webbing that sealed his mouth closed. Ashamed of his backtalk, Rudo lowered his eyes and retreated into the trees. Satisfied, Aurelia moved back toward her captured prey, and Zipporah followed cautiously.

Despite having been friends with the woman for years, Zipporah still got chills whenever she saw a person caught inside Aurelia's web. This time was no different. Zipporah sighed, knowing that he was another one of those young and dumb knights, believing in the screams of a maiden in distress.

"How did you catch this one, Madame Arachnid?" Zipporah asked.

"He was actually easy to catch, already in a fit of confusion. I used my usual lure, and he ran to my aid. Though it was hard to keep him focused. His mind was everywhere, and I was getting impatiently hungry. I wanted to sink my teeth into him," Aurelia said, crossing her arms and tapping her front two legs.

"Must you be so graphic?"

"Must you be so squeamish? You're a healer, of all things! You've *seen* worse."

"Irrelevant. How did you get burned?"

"Well, I'm assuming that he burned me. I dove into his subconscious and created a lovely little forest area with a lake. He seems to have a great interest in water areas, especially in connection with something called a mee-nuh. After he healed my wound, I said that I wished to show my appreciation. We started to kiss and after barely touching, I felt a pain I had only felt once before. He tried to apologize, reaching out to me again, and proceeded to burn my wrist. I had to get away. I dissolved the fantasy and returned him to unconsciousness."

Zipporah nodded as Aurelia stepped closer to the young man, running her fingers through his hair.

"He is almost too beautiful to eat," she sighed, dragging her hand against his chest. "Just like Rudo. Their names even start with the same letter, R."

"What's the boy's name?" Zipporah asked.

"Rex, just as strong and handsome as the owner. I mean, just look at him, Zippy!"

Aurelia lifted the boy's head and revealed his face. Zipporah shouted and stumbled away. His head instantly fell as Aurelia jerked back.

"What?!" she demanded. "You act like you just saw a ghost!"

"I just did. Look at him, Aurelia. Can't you see her?"

"See who?"

"Bala."

Irritated, Aurelia roughly lifted the boy's head again and stared, trying to find the lost woman in his face.

She saw the same untamable hair and lovely skin. His facial features were harder, most likely resembling his father, but those eyes—the shape and color—were all his mother, Bala.

"Zipporah…"

"Wake him and get him something to eat. There is much we must discuss." She said, beginning to walk away. "I'm going to find Lloyd. He will be interested in this."

Δ

"He looks just like her!"

"Their eyes are definitely the same."

"They could be twins!"

"I doubt twins…"

"What? Have ye no faith? Look and see, for the eyes tell all."

"Please, for Joseph's sake, just talk normal."

"Pardon, but I know not of any Joseph. Would you be willing to offer me an introduction?"

"'Ey! Shut up. I think he's starting to wake up."

"Probably from all the noise."

"Oh, isn't he just lovely?"

"Don't eat him, Arachnid—Oh wait, you tried that already."

"You will not insult my mistress!"

"Shh! He stirs—"

Rex heard voices all around him. There was a high and squeaky one and a low, manly one. Another with an accent, but he couldn't place the region. Still another held a soft and kind tone, sounding much like his grandmother, Prissy. He couldn't tell exactly how many there were, but he knew that the Aurelia woman was among them. She was the one who called him lovely. He found it creepy that she was watching over him as he slept.

His eyes slowly opened, and he saw Aurelia looking down at him with a pleasant smile on her face. The burn on her lip was gone. *Is this all a weird dream, like Omvati's murder? But why would I dream about someone I've never met?*

Rex sat up, and she backed away. Holding his head, Rex groaned and finally noticed the others. It was quite the group. There was Aurelia, completely beautiful with her flawless skin and long hair. It seemed shorter than he remembered, only coming to her shoulder blades. That was odd.

There was a young man standing next to her. He was about the same size as Rex, towering over Aurelia. His arms were crossed, and his purple eyes glared at Rex. His skin was pale, and his hair was a soft blond. He looked to be only about fourteen or so, but that hardness in his eyes made Rex question whether this was correct.

Next to the boy stood a tall man with broad shoulders—the classic soldier's build. He carried a large bow and there was a nice stack of arrows strapped to his back. His eyes were small, slanted, and dark brown. His skin color was one that Rex did not see very often. It was a strange yellowish-brown color. He assumed that this man had the deep voice he had heard.

He scanned over the rest of the crew: a fairy with light blue hair and eyes, a very plain human girl with dark hair and pale skin, and a short dwarf-looking man with a long brown beard and bald head. *Interesting bunch indeed.*

An old elf walked toward Rex, which was something he had never seen before. The old elf—a woman with gray hair, soft green eyes, and skin like bark—tilted her head at him and grinned, showing a crooked smile. He smiled back, utterly lost in this situation. She pinched his cheek and grinned harder. *That hasn't been done to me… ever. Weird. This whole thing is weird. Who are these people anyway?*

"See, he looks like her, just like her," the fairy with the squeaky voice exclaimed, clapping her hands together.

"All he did was frown. How can you tell?" the short man said.

"It's the same scowl!"

The fairy rolled her eyes and fluttered over to Rex, who was slowly beginning to stand up. She helped him the rest of the way up and beamed a bright white smile at him.

"Hi! I'm Nidawi!" she squeaked. Aurelia looked at her with annoyance while the old elf shook her head.

The fairy, oblivious to it all, took Rex by the hand and dragged him over to the other members of their group.

"We're gypsies! We make ends meet by traveling from town to town and doing random things, but usually we just perform."

They stopped in the center of the misshapen circle, and Nidawi twirled once in the air. She certainly was excited to see him. He watched her with curious eyes, never seeing someone so bubbly before.

"Let's introduce everyone else! You've already met Aurelia. She was trying to eat you, if you were wondering."

"Wha—?"

"Over there's Zipporah, but everybody calls her Grandma. She's like the leader of all of us, taking us in when others won't. We all love her. Oh yeah, next to Aurelia is Rudo. He doesn't like you since he thinks that you're gonna replace him as Aurelia's servant."

"I don't—"

"Over there, that tall guy, that's Kang-Dae, but I like to call him KD. It's more cooler, hipper, whatever-er. Then that's Lloyd, or Mr. Grumpy Pants."

"I am not Mr. Grumpy Pants!" Lloyd yelled, but Nidawi, true to her nature, continued.

"Finally, that's Cedron…"

Nidawi stopped her rambling and grew extremely quiet. She shook her head and started again.

"Just don't mess with her and things will be good, okay? Okay."

Rex stared at Nidawi and decided to trust her. Cedron did give off that creepy vibe, but part of him was drawn to her; he wished to learn more about her. However, the bubbly fairy had other plans for him, which included a tour of their current campsite and potential travel movements.

According to Nidawi, they rarely stayed in the same place for too long since they had to go into various towns for supplies. "There is only so much makeup you can make from berries, you know."

Despite her giddiness, Rex enjoyed his time with Nidawi as well as with the others. Cedron was actually quite nice, though still a little creepy. At times, she would become extremely quiet and disappear—literally, slithering into the shadows or a ray of light. Seconds or hours later, she would return, more talkative though still creepy.

KD, who allowed Rex to use his nickname, was calm, logical, and not really patient with Nidawi's flightiness and short attention span. But they were at least friends.

After their initial greeting, Aurelia and Rudo isolated themselves from the rest of the group, only returning at dinner. Aurelia never ate, which led Rex to conclude that she ate people, but never the boy, Rudo.

Rudo received his meals at dinner, and after he finished, they would take their leave, though not before Aurelia could flirt with Rex.

Lloyd and Zipporah seemed to be the leaders of the group, being the oldest. Despite their headship positions, they always asked for the others' input about their travels and other gypsy business.

During his first couple of days, Rex enjoyed the company of the misfits. He listened to their tales of their various travels and adventures. They also spoke of times when they were in Maventa, knowing all about the Mystic Quartz neighborhood, the debate on slavery, and the various clubs and opera houses.

Yet, Rex's mind nudged him about his comrades. They were probably searching for him, and he was safe, comfortable, and satisfied. Before his disappearance, they had been running low on food and other supplies. Thaddaeus was still missing his arm and they needed an Earth elemental powerful enough to completely heal it.

On his third day with the gypsies, Rex spoke to Zipporah about his troubles. She nodded wordlessly and then told Nidawi to fetch KD and Lloyd. She explained the situation, and with no words of complaint, they left. Rex was awed.

He had only known these people for a couple days, and they were willing to risk their lives to find his friends, who might attack them, feeling threatened. Repeatedly, Rex expressed his gratefulness to the men before they left, but he still felt it was not enough.

The following evening at dinner, the women and Rudo seemed not to notice the absence of their comrades. Rex was particularly bothered by this.

"Y'all aren't worried about KD and Lloyd?" he asked, annoyed.

"Kang-Dae is a strong and capable warrior and prospers with a mission. Lloyd has lived in this forest since his youth. There is no reason to fear, newcomer," Cedron said.

"Cece's right, Rexxy-boo," Nidawi chimed in. "They are big, strong men. They can handle themselves. This is our territory."

"KD, yeah sure, I'll give you that one, but Lloyd? Dude, he's a midget!"

"Those quick to judge are easily fooled," Cedron quietly whispered and suddenly disappeared.

Rex shivered and sighed. "Yeah, okay. Whatever."

Silence lingered as they roasted pieces of bird. Minutes later, Cedron reappeared, and Rex glanced at her, giving her a nod. She stared at him for much longer than what was necessary. Eventually, he turned away and decided to directly address the thought that was troubling him.

"Why y'all helping me?" he asked, not looking up from his roasted bird.

"Why would we not help you?" Zipporah asked soothingly.

"You barely know me, only for two days, and you're willing to leave yourselves vulnerable by sending out your two best fighters on a wild goose chase. You don't even know where to start looking for my men! It don't make sense!"

Nidawi and Cedron glanced over at Zipporah, who sighed and gave her crooked smile.

"You're right. We don't know you very well. But we know where you come from."

"Maventa! Really? You're helping me because I'm from Maventa? We some of the most crooked, greedy, cheating dirtbags who ever walked this planet! If you're doing this because I'm Maventi, y'all got—"

"We know your parents!" Nidawi said, exasperated.

Cedron stood and announced her leave. Nidawi caught sight of her and followed without a word. There only sat Rex and Zipporah.

"Right… Of course you know my parents. You must mean the councilman…" he started, but Zipporah lifted a single hand.

"I was friends with your mother, Bala, even before you were born. She was part of our strange little family. She stayed with us until she met your father and then she became a non-traveling gypsy. We stayed in Maventa until a month before her disappearance. When we received the news of her being missing, we searched everywhere, but we could not find her. I'm sorry."

Rex blinked. These were the gypsies that he had heard so many stories about, the family of his mother. He realized that he should be happy, jumping for joy at this discovery. He should be loading Zipporah and the others with questions on top of questions about his mother, but there was only one question he truly wished to have answered.

"What was my mother?" he asked, finally looking up into the soft eyes of this grandmotherly woman.

"I do not know and I did not, and still do not, wish to know," she began, as Rex looked away. "There are secrets among this family, and we respect them. I do not know from where Kang-Dae comes. I do not know what happened to Nidawi's tribe or Lloyd's clan. I do not know why Aurelia keeps Rudo around, even when he has offered himself to her in times of distress. I do not know Cedron's father and I barely knew her mother. And of course, there are stories of mine I do not wish for the others to hear."

Zipporah stood and slowly walked over to Rex. Perhaps it was his destiny never to know and to deal with this curse that had been placed upon him. He sighed and ran his fingers through his hair, fed up. A hand touched his shoulder and as he looked up, he saw Zipporah's classic, crooked smile. She removed her hand and fished inside her jacket, pulling out a yellowed paper. Rex narrowed his eyes and watched as she held it out to him.

"What's this?" he asked.

"It's a letter from your mother," she said, her smile broadening.

Rex, with hesitant hands, took the letter and slowly opened it. He had never seen her handwriting before, but he immediately recognized the nickname she used to call him. He felt tears beginning to fall, but he fought them back. He did not wish to ruin these last words from her.

> *My little man, my Rex,*
>
> *I know that I have been away, probably for a long time, but do not, not for a second, think that my absence means I don't love you. I love you with all one-half of my heart. The other half belongs to your father. You'll have to fight him for that.*

The story behind my leaving cannot be explained in a letter. It is too long and complicated. Even if I did attempt it, you would be left with more questions than answers and you deserve more than that. Also, I do not wish to expose you and your father to dangers unnecessarily, for I am a hunted woman.

All who have been associated with me have been tortured and/or killed in order to locate me. They do not take pity on the young or the inexperienced, for I am accused of taking one of their young and inexperienced. I have lost so many friends thus far and I will be damned before I lose my family. Therefore, I beg, I plea, that you do not look for me. Stay away and live your life. I do not wish to lose you any more than I already have.

Please, my little man, live for yourself, for your father, and for me.

Love,

Your mom

Rex stared at the letter, stunned at the words of his mother. He had assumed, childishly, that she would welcome him back into her life with open arms. She was supposed to embrace him with kisses and unbreakable love. At the very least, he expected an explanation from her.

The child in him felt utterly abandoned. He understood the reasons for her choice. She would rather leave than lose what was precious to her. Still, pain caused his heart to ache. Why had his mother left? What danger could she be in? Why had she not asked his father for help? How could she leave him at such a young age with an emotionally fragile father?

The letter shook in Rex's hands as tears of rage streamed down his face. He crumbled the paper in his hands and dashed it to the ground, never wanting to read those words again.

Zipporah bent down and placed her hands on his shoulders, but he shook her off, standing up. He had to get away. Fury was boiling inside him.

"I placed my friends in danger. I allowed my best friend to lose his arm—all for nothing. I have no answers, no hints, absolutely nothing for my efforts. Ma gave me nothing, thinking it would be better that way. But she don't know me." Rex roared in pain.

Zipporah shivered as she watched Rex walk out of the clearing. It was so inhuman, so animalistic. The fear he struck would not leave her. She needed to know what upset the boy so much. She picked up the crumbled words and shook her head. "Bala left that poor child with little more than a warning." She pressed the paper to her chest and sighed. "Bala... you're torturing your baby."

"Zipporah!" KD shouted. She quickly turned, spotting him and Lloyd with a group of five men, one of them a Drow. *Rex is more like his mother than he probably realizes, spending time with such strangely diverse groups of people*, she thought.

Zipporah folded the paper neatly and returned it to Rex's original spot. The men looked at her, some with worry and others with caution. She scanned over them and instantly spotted Thaddaeus and his missing arm. She pressed her lips together and demanded, "Young man, your name and what happened to you."

Thaddaeus stammered, "Th-Th-Th-Thaddaeus, ma'am. And a sandworm got to it, though thanks to Rex I managed to escape alive."

"How did he save you from a sandworm? Those are very vicious creatures."

"I don't remember. I got knocked out pretty early, losing blood and all that." He laughed, shrugging. Zipporah cracked a small smile, liking his easygoing attitude.

The Drow stepped forward, and she noticed that his eyes were black, not the classic red. *Halfbreed, interesting*, she thought, nodding toward him to speak.

"Upon seeing Thaddaeus being dragged underground by the sandworm, Ambassador Rectavius transformed into a column of fire and went after the worm. Moments later, he reappeared with Thaddaeus in his arms, still on fire, but not burning himself or anyone else," the Drow said, bowing.

"Your name?" Zipporah asked, smiling at the formalness of the recount.

"Nishith Aiimyath, m' lady."

"Please, all of you, call me Zipporah—or Zippy or Zip, if you wish. We are family here. No need for formalities. Thaddaeus, right? Come here and let me fix that arm. Whoever did the initial healing did a nice job for a quick fix."

Thaddaeus turned toward Lucas, who was hiding behind Simon, and pulled the boy by the arm. Lucas squeaked and followed Thaddaeus toward Zipporah. The old woman had a warm smile on her face, and slowly Lucas relaxed.

The two healers worked together on fixing Thaddaeus's missing arm. Lucas managed to handle keeping the talkative man asleep as Zipporah gave him a brand-new arm. Once finished, Lucas returned his friend to consciousness and Thaddaeus, thoroughly surprised, hugged and kissed Zipporah on the cheek. They laughed, and he ran off to show Rex his new arm.

Talking was heard in the distance as Nidawi and Cedron returned. Nidawi squealed upon seeing KD and Lloyd. She flew up to them and gathered them into a group hug. She twirled around KD and tried to dance with him. He sighed and allowed her to swing his arms back and forth. Lloyd and Cedron glanced at each other, and she gave a tiny smile. He nodded back and turned to Zipporah, a look of concern on his face.

"What was that roar?" he barked, and Zipporah blinked.

"Oh, that? Just Rex... He's embracing his nonhuman side, I think," she said with a shrug. "I finally gave him the note from his mother. Though it was a little earlier than I had wished."

She gave a sharp glare at Nidawi, who stopped her dancing. She looked down at the ground and retreated behind KD.

"You're some of the people he was looking for," Alcon said, and Zipporah nodded.

"Yes, we were friends of his mother's, even before he was born. The note his mother left him was not the most encouraging. She wants him to stay away from her, saying that she is a hunted woman."

"Hunted as in how?" Simon asked.

"The note does not say, and I do not know. She never spoke of her past before meeting us and while we were curious, she was a stone wall, not letting any of us truly in."

Thaddaeus and Rex came back, Thaddaeus looking less joyful than when he left. Rex was covering his eyes and breathing heavily. Cedron copied his movements, covering her eyes. Her lips trembled.

"Unspeakable evil approaches…" she whispered.

"Cedron? What's the matter?" Nidawi asked, peeking over KD's head. He narrowed his eyes as he glanced at the copied stances of Rex and Cedron.

"Unspeakable… unspeakable…" she said, growing louder and raising her hand to point at Rex.

Thaddaeus followed her finger and cautiously backed away from Rex. A deep growl came from his throat, and Thaddaeus quickly moved to the side, standing next to Zipporah. Simon and Nishith drew their swords as Cedron continued to chant, "Unspeakable, unspeakable."

KD and Lloyd mimicked their fellow soldiers, and the four slowly neared Rex. Cedron's chant continued as she slowly removed her hand from her eyes. Rex mimicked her. His eyes were red, while hers were black. Rex gave off another menacing growl, hunching forward.

Cedron swayed back and forth, unsteady on her feet. Rex stepped forward once, the ground cracking underneath his weight. Simon glanced over at Nishith, who kept silent and gripped tighter on his sword. Simon nodded and followed suit. The growling grew louder as Cedron's voice rose. The four finally encircled Rex as he crouched onto the ground, his fists digging into the dirt.

"Unspeakable evil… unspeakable," Cedron chanted. Rex's back suddenly arched dramatically.

"What is she doing to him?!" Simon hissed. Zipporah shook her head.

"I-I dunno. Cedron, honey…" she called, but the chanting continued.

Rex's fists dug harder into the dirt, twisting and turning as he growled and snarled at the four around him. His back flexed, and his head shook back and forth as tears streamed down his face.

"She left me nothing," he said, his voice distorted by the beast's takeover. "She left me *nothing, nothing*!"

He hugged himself as he fought the wide range of emotions flooding his mind: the abandonment of his mother, the weakness of his father, the isolation of his childhood, the loneliness of being unwanted, the fear of being different, the anguish of wanting to kill. He gnashed his teeth together, wanting to fight off the change that was overcoming him. He did not want to turn into the beast, not again.

A giant whoosh nearly knocked them all off their feet as Rex suddenly jumped and launched himself high into the air. Their eyes followed him as large, black wings ripped from his back and fire exploded from his mouth. In an instant, he was gone.

All stood staring at the night sky, wondering if Rex would return. Cedron's black eyes began to fade as her skin paled. She kissed her hand and lifted it to the sky, saying, "Unspeakable evil and beauty has awakened. Embrace this new side of yourself, Rectavius." With that single wish for luck, she closed her eyes and collapsed.

Hearing the thud, Zipporah and Nidawi turned in the direction of the noise. Nidawi was the first to reach Cedron, flying past everyone. She crashed right next to her friend and scurried on her hands and knees, reaching for her and cradling Cedron in her arms.

The person she held in her arms, however, looked nothing like her friend. Ashen skin had replaced the healthy pink it had been before. Her hair, once a luxurious black, was now dull and brittle. Her body was like a paper origami, weightless and fragile. Despite her appearance, Nidawi tried to wake Cedron by calling her name, poking her, and even shaking her. She received no response.

Once Zipporah and the others reached the two girls, they instantly knew that she had died. Zipporah, unable to stand the sight, turned away and buried her face in KD's chest. He held her tight as he stared at Cedron. She had died the same way as her mother, as a shell of herself.

"What happened to her?" Lucas asked.

"Dragon…" Zipporah mumbled into KD's chest.

"Dragon?" Nishith said, staring at the ashen girl.

"What does a dragon have to do with Cedron's death?!" Nidawi cried, clutching her harder to her chest.

"Everything…"

Zipporah's word hung as a single roar echoed in the distance.

CHAPTER 18

A GIANT SHADOW RACED ACROSS THE sky. The mighty wings of an eagle shaded the creatures below. Boyish giggles chased after it; little brown hands reached up to join the eagle in its flight.

A woman watched her son with loving and protective eyes. A warm smile brushed her lips as she listened to the beautiful noise her child made. He shouted and laughed, dancing around the open fields as the eagle swirled and swooshed about him. Finally, it continued on its journey, leaving the boy and his mother.

The boy looked to his mother and pointed at the sky eagerly.

"Momma, I wanna fly!" he said, jumping high, flapping his arms and tucking his legs. He tried and tried again, but gravity continued to bring him back down to the ground. His mother, joining him, giggled and opened her arms to him. He raced over to her and squeezed her tight.

"Rex, humans can't fly, silly," his mother said and kissed him on the cheek.

274 | ELEMENT UNKNOWN

"I know, but I wanna fly! I'm gonna fly someday! You just watch!"

Rex raced away from his mother and ran toward a high rock. He got to the top and looked down, seeing his mother's worried expression. He grinned and jumped, flapping his arms. He hovered for a split second before falling once again to the dirt.

He grimaced and looked at his elbow, seeing a scrape. He stood, pouting, and trudged back to his mother. She opened her arms up to him, and slowly he nuzzled into her chest. She scooped him up and carried him away from the rock.

"Maybe one day you'll fly, my little man," she whispered in his ear. "I flew once."

Rex peaked up from his mother's chest, and his eyes widened in awe.

"You flew once?" he gasped.

"Yes, long before I was your mom."

"But you just said humans can't fly!"

Bala smiled and nuzzled her son. "I know."

Δ

Trees collapsed all around Rex as he tumbled onto the ground, rolling incessantly and running from himself. Big black wings followed him wherever he went, despite his countless attempts to rip them off. He dashed his nails against trees, rocks, anything that would break them. He roared, searching for a way to remove the beast that had finally been unleashed.

This was not who Rex was. He was Rectavius Vitus Marshall, son of Councilman Kadmus Xavier Marshall, son of Vitus Anacletus Marshall. He was heir to his family's inheritance and ambassador to the Saldur Empire for Maventa. This monster that was rumbling through the forest and destroying everything in its path was not him. This was not him.

"Embrace this new side of yourself, Rectavius." Cedron's last words to him. Rex swayed and shook his head. *I cannot embrace this. I cannot even accept this! This is not me!*

Whispers circled around him.

"H-Hello..." he called into the darkness. The whispers grew louder. He called again, and still louder they grew. He squeezed his eyes shut and hunched into a ball, banishing the voices out of his head. He gritted his teeth and clawed at the ground.

"Leave me alone!" he hollered and slammed his fist against a tree, breaking the tree in half.

"Don't fight it," a distinctive voice shined through the noise of the whispers. "Please, embrace the change, my love."

"Stop it!"

"Embrace this, for it is who you are. You are my son."

"Ma?"

"Embrace this. Embrace you."

"But..."

"Fly!"

He shot up into the air, stretched his wings, and flew.

Dawn had broken by the time the search party located Rex. He lay in the middle of destruction: trees broken into pieces, animals torn in half, claw marks drilled into rocks, and plants burned to a crisp.

Lloyd held Zipporah back to prevent her from rushing to Rex. KD drew his sword and approached him first. His back was bruised, and covered with two long and spidery markings going from his shoulder blades to his waist. Claw markings decorated his arms and puncture wounds were everywhere on his legs. KD lifted Rex's face and saw the dirt, dried tears, and blood. He was barely recognizable as Bala's son, but this was him.

KD nodded, and Zipporah pushed Lloyd out of the way, running toward Rex. She wished to heal him as quickly as possible. The window was small already and closing by the second. She knelt next to him and turned him over onto his back and gasped, seeing the damage done to his face. She closed her eyes and calmed herself. She would not break the promise to her old friend.

"Dammit, Rex, don't you die on me," she hissed, and her hands began to glow. KD and Lloyd watched as Nidawi fluttered over to his other side, staring at him with terror, hatred, and grief. While he had killed her best friend, he had found his other half, which Cedron willingly helped him do. Rex had blood from the strongest of all elemental creatures: dragon's blood. Cedron was merely a rare mixed-breed, a Dark-Light elemental. She had to have known the possibility of death. And yet, she had blessed him with her last words.

Nidawi shook her head and stood, moving away. She raced over to KD and hugged him. She cried into his chest and he, unsure of what else to do, patted her back in the hope of giving her some relief.

Nishith and the Maventi emerged and stared at the damage Rex had caused to the forest and to his own body. Lucas immediately went to Zipporah, who instructed him on what sections to work on.

Anxiously, everyone watched the two healers work to save their friend. Hours passed with still no response from Rex. Lucas started to sit back, but Zipporah demanded that he continue. He shook his head and stood, looking toward the group.

"We need to get back to the palace and send someone to alert the councilman," he said softly.

"No! He's not dead. There's still a heartbeat!" Zipporah yelled.

Lloyd approached her and lifted her up from Rex's body; she fought him, kicking and biting him. KD aided Lloyd and held Zipporah as she sobbed uncontrollably. Nishith and Alcon quickly made a makeshift mat and laid Rex upon it. They hoisted him into their shoulders, and the group mourned with each step they took toward the palace.

The gypsies, despite repeated pleas against it, decided to accompany the men back to Rajsatish, the capital. They all made the fortnight-long journey, and upon entering a neighboring city's outskirts, rumors had already spread of the ambassador's return to the capital city.

The word went from the streets to the palace slaves, and eventually to the ears of Meenal and Jacqueline. Princess Fadilah was entertaining them over a cup of coffee when one of the slaves came and whispered something in her ear. Meenal and Jacqueline looked expectantly as the slave retreated and Fadilah smiled, speaking something in Majah. Meenal brightly smiled.

"What?" Jacqueline said, annoyed that she could not keep up with the conversation.

"Thaddaeus and the others have returned!" she squealed, and Jacqueline frowned.

"Already? I had expected them to be gone at least two months. Knowing Rex, he would want to visit multiple cities for at least a week and a ha—" Jacqueline's eyes grew wide. "Ask her what's wrong."

Meenal frowned and asked the princess about the state of the men. The princess held a stone expression, but her eyes quivered for a split second, and Jacqueline instantly recognized it. Jacqueline stood and swore at the princess, demanding to know what their backstabbing guide had done.

Meenal quickly stood and pulled Jacqueline away from the stoic princess. Obscenities flew out of Jacqueline's mouth during their entire exit. Princess Fadilah sat in silence, watching them leave. Once they were out of earshot, she sighed, "Why is the human upset? It is not her love that is dead."

Days passed, and there was still no news in regards to the men. The rumors continued, declaring that they had been in the capital city for weeks; that they were attacked just before arriving at the city's gates; that an unexplainable disease struck them all in the desert.

Jacqueline worried excessively about Thaddaeus, screaming at all the false comfort the Saldur slaves attempted to give her. She banished them from her room and refused to come to any meals most days, demanding that Meenal bring her food.

One night, as Meenal brought yet another dinner to Jacqueline, the fiery redhead glared at the food and then her friend, her green eyes calling for blood. Meenal frowned.

"Jacqueline, you must eat," she said and pushed the food tray toward her.

"I will not eat until I receive news," she said and crossed her arms.

"You are being unreasonable."

"*I'm* being unreasonable?! *I'm* being unreasonable?! Those Drows are being unreasonable by not giving us any information in regards to our people! They probably did the dirty deed themselves!"

"You do not have any proof of their hands shedding blood."

"I don't? Then why all the secrecy? Why haven't we been alerted about anything? Why hasn't a search party been sent out to collect them? That's proof right there!"

"Jacqueline…"

"Don't *Jacqueline* me! I know what I'm talking about. It's those nasty pieces of filth!"

She pushed herself out of her seat and marched away from Meenal, cursing all the Drows and calling for their deaths. Meenal sighed and looked away from Jacqueline. She was unable to comprehend the great fear and worry that her friend felt.

It made logical sense to be concerned about their health, but the curses of death were unnecessarily evil to Meenal. She thought of Rex, Thaddaeus, and the others, knowing that they were a strong group of men who could withstand just about anything. She thought there was nothing that Jacqueline should be concerned about.

A knock on the door pushed Jacqueline out of her rage. She raced to the door, pulled it open, and spotted Thaddaeus. She squealed and launched herself at him, giving him the tightest hug Meenal had ever seen.

Thaddaeus's eyes seemed to bug out and he coughed a bit. Finally, Jacqueline released him, kissing him repeatedly and berating him for being late. He apologized again and again, holding her in his arms and never wishing to let her go. Meenal watched the strange greeting with curiosity and unease. She was unsure if she would enjoy being grappled and tugged as Thaddaeus was.

"Oh my, oh my, oh my, I missed you soooo much! What happened? What took so long?" Jacqueline said, kissing him quickly before he could answer.

"It's a long story, but Meenal might wanna check out Rex," he said and looked in her direction. Meenal tilted her head to the side and blinked, confused as to why she should check on Rex. Unless it was some political dispute that required a translator, she was not needed. She wished to hear the long story of their journey.

"Meenal... Rex is in a coma, and it don't look good."

Jacqueline stepped away from Thaddaeus and gasped, covering her mouth. She turned to look at Meenal, who stood like a statue with wide, frightened eyes. Meenal had never imagined a life without Rex. He was her benefactor, her rock, her friend. He was a constant force behind her, telling her what was okay for freed people and what was not. She jumped as Thaddaeus took her hand.

"Come on, I'll take ya to him."

Thaddaeus led Meenal and Jacqueline down to Rex's room, where it was silent. He stopped at the door when he saw someone else sitting at the bed. Meenal looked around the corner, seeing a dark-skinned older woman with long, beautiful white hair and wrinkled hands. Her clothes were tattered and covered in sand and dirt. Pieces of sticks and a few leaves decorated her mane of hair, and she resembled a nature goddess of old.

The woman was looking down at Rex, and while Meenal could not see her face, there was a connection between Rex and her. She lovingly caressed his cheek and squeezed his hand.

Meenal stepped into the room and left Thaddaeus and Jacqueline, mesmerized by the scene in front of them. She walked behind the woman and stared at the cuts and bruises on Rex's face and body. It was strange seeing him so still, for he was always pulling her to go somewhere, tapping his foot in church, or talking about nonsense. To see him actually at rest was unreal. Meenal stepped forward and accidentally touched the older woman. She sighed and slowly started to stand.

"It's time to go, huh?" she said softly, "All right, we can go."

Meenal said nothing as the woman bent down and gently kissed Rex on the forehead, lingering for a bit. Meenal stepped back as the woman straightened and faced her. She held a look of surprise and recognition instantly. Meenal bowed deeply and said, "I apologize for my rudeness. I did not wish to disturb you."

"No need to apologize, Meenal. I've been hogging him up for too long in the first place," the woman said, her voice warm and loving. "My, look how much you have grown... and your eyes! You've finally grown into your beautiful eyes."

"Ma-Madame? I am sorry, but I do not believe that you and I have been introduced..." Meenal said.

"But we have been, even if briefly."

"I have never seen you in my life."

"You probably don't remember. You were just a baby."

"Ba-by? I don't... Who are you?"

The woman laughed and gave a very crooked grin. "I birthed you. You were my third."

Meenal's world, everything that she had taken for truth, came to a screeching halt as this woman proclaimed that she was her mother. Her very first owners, the ones that she had adopted as her parents, had told her that she was orphaned.

They said they found her near their home, covered in dirt and dried blood. They hurriedly gave her goat's milk, a warm bath, and decent clothes. Weeks went by, during which time the child grew like a weed, and despite the hardship of raising her, they continued.

Within months, the childless couple was blessed for their kindness by becoming pregnant. They kept Meenal, at first like a good luck charm, but then they grew to treating her as their first child. They nicknamed her Asha, meaning hope, for she had given them the hope to continue.

While Meenal had given them hope, they had given her lies. Everything they'd said about her family was a lie. They never had any last words with her father. Her mother never squeezed the lying woman's hand. A rage Meenal had never felt before flooded her body and she glanced away from the older woman, an elf, her birth mother.

"Meenal? Are you all right?" her mother asked.

Meenal flexed her hands and slowly raised her head, staring her mother in the face. She looked for any similarities in their appearances but found few. They both possessed pointed ears, confirming that she was indeed Elfin. They both had green eyes, but Meenal found her mother's to be lighter than her own. She glanced at the hair and wondered if it was white naturally or due to age.

So many questions flooded her mind; she could not keep them straight. Meenal started to speak but stuttered and then shook her head, disappointed in herself for showing so much emotion.

"I have just met my mother after having been lied to about her death. Judge for yourself if I am all right," Meenal snapped and then glanced away, cursing herself for reprimanding her mother for something that she could not control.

The woman looked at her with sad eyes and slowly shook her head. "Oh, you poor thing. You must pardon my Jeletho. I am not your mother, but her midwife. And your mother lives but I have not seen her since your birth."

"What?"

"Yes, your mother was a human woman named Isolda, with some of the most beautiful eyes I have ever seen. They are like yours in that they are different colors, yet while your two colors each own a separate eye, her two shared: green on the outer rim and a light brown on the inner. Otherwise, she was a very plain-looking woman. Your mother and Rex's mother were very close, sisters, actually. Bala brought Isolda to me one night. Isolda had been attacked and both your life and hers were in danger. We managed to save you both, but your mother and

Bala left immediately after your birth, telling me that they would return soon. But they never did. I don't know what happened to them."

The rage fled from Meenal, and she swayed from the sudden release of energy. The woman, quick for her age, caught Meenal and guided her to a seat. After resting for a few seconds, Meenal asked, "What is your name?"

"My name is Zipporah, but many call me Zippy or Grandma. It's because I'm all old and such," she said and gave a little laugh. "But on a serious note, you probably have many questions about when you were little. I'll tell you, but you must promise me that you will not tell Rex. It was my last promise to my friend, and she was like the daughter I never had."

"You are an Earth, deeply connecting with your friends and feeling obligated to care for them as mother and grandmother."

"You're good."

Meenal gave an awkward shrug and then said with a stern voice, "I only have one question. My mother, Isolda, as you call her, left me in your care. Why, then, did I not stay in your care? Why was I brought up by an Elfin couple?"

Zipporah closed her eyes in pain, shaking her head. She sighed and nodded. "Apparently, your mother was a wanted woman. The very next day after your birth, me and my fellow gypsies were attacked and you were kidnapped. We searched for weeks, believing that your mother would be back. However, we did not find you and we all thought that you were dead. It was soldiers who attacked us, masters of the dark arts. I have no idea as to what those people would have done if they found Isolda as well."

Meenal stood abruptly and gave a sharp nod, thanking Zipporah for her answer. The elf attempted to stop Meenal in order to learn more about the woman she had become, but Meenal wished to be anywhere but in that room with the woman who robbed her of a normal childhood.

CHAPTER 19

REX THOUGHT THAT HE KNEW HIS identity. He was confident and outspoken. He knew eventually he would inherit his family's fortune and awesome house. He would get a job doing something, get married to a sweet girl from a good family, and have bunches of kids.

As he sat in his subconscious, Rex second-guessed everything. He wondered if he was truly Kadmus's son. Was he the legitimate heir to the Marshall's family inheritance? Had his mother actually committed adultery, proving unfaithful to her still-devoted husband? Was he even human or some other kind of beast, the product of lust?

The rational side of Rex's mind repeatedly told him that his mother had the same traits: brown skin, dark brown hair, eyes that changed color in rage. He was his mother's son—her clone, according to many, including his father. Yet the doubt constantly weighed on his mind, never giving him peace.

He groaned, cursing himself for all the confusion in his mind. He wished that he could just sleep peacefully like he had in the past. Eventually, he grew tired of the fight and opened his eyes, seeing Meenal and his father hovering over him. They were in deep conversation. He closed his eyes again and listened.

"She did not say when Bala brought my mother to her, but I would assume that it was after her disappearance. She claimed that Bala wished for secrecy, but that seems illogical to me," Meenal said, her tone darker than usual. To hear such feeling in her voice was a nice change, despite the fact she sounded as if she were about to kill someone.

"The note that the Drow general gave me, from Bala herself, claimed that she was a 'hunted woman.' She wished for us not to follow her, saving us from harm," Kadmus said.

He sighed deeply. "She was always very independent, hating to ask for help, especially at the expense of her friends."

"Still, even if that was the case, she left no trail, and therefore it would have been futile to keep this secret from Rex. I do not understand their logic, and it is frustrating."

"You wish to know more about your mother."

"Yes… I had always thought that my parents were dead. To discover I have a living mother… I cannot—"

Rex started to cough and cursed. *So much for being sneaky.* He opened his eyes and saw Meenal. Her eyes were intense, and she held a frown on her face. He narrowed his eyes and slowly sat up.

"Thank you for finally rejoining the land of the living. A late arrival is better than none at all," Meenal said and crossed her arms.

"Shut up. Don't need you telling me something I already know. You think I did it on purpose?" he snapped.

"Yes, for at least the last few minutes. It matters not. It is in the past. Now, we must concentrate on returning to Chance and preparing for the Saldur Empire's ambassador."

"I'm not going back."

Both Kadmus and Meenal looked at Rex in disbelief. Kadmus narrowed his eyes and stood up from the bed.

"What do you mean you're not going back? You must go back! There is nothing else for you to accomplish. Your mission is complete. For heaven's sake, Rex, you almost died! I need you back in Maventa where I can keep you safe."

Rex glared at Kadmus. "No! You need me back in Maventa to keep an eye on me to make sure I don't screw up anything else! You wanna make sure that this boy you've claimed don't mess up your family's name!"

"Boy I have claimed? What are you talking about? You are my son, the son of Bala and me."

"You sure? Why don't I look like you then? There's nothing, absolutely nothing, on me that's yours! The rest of your family believes my mother to be a whore, so perhaps it's true."

Rex stood and faced his father. Kadmus held his ground despite the reddish tint growing in his son's eyes.

"If I am your son, how the hell can I do this," Rex yelled and raised his hand, showing claws. He stepped back and hunched forward, dropping to his knees. His screams echoed throughout the room as his back cracked and his skin split. One large black wing tore its way out of his back as the other followed its lead. His cries grew louder still as they transformed into roars.

Footsteps rushed down the hallways, and a group of men barged into the room. Nishith, leading the men, froze in fear. His eyes widened at the scene unfolding, and his ears pounded from the loudness of the roars. His men blocked the doorway as Jacqueline and Thaddaeus came running.

Jacqueline pushed her way in and pulled Thaddaeus through. As her eyes stared at the transformation, she protectively hugged him and steadied a fireball in her hands, waiting for any hint of attack. One of the soldiers saw the flame and grabbed hold of her wrist, extinguishing the fire. She glared at him and released Thaddaeus to fight when a loud roar stopped everyone.

The large black wings stretched and Rex directed his attention to Jacqueline and the soldier. Nishith quickly stepped in front of them and bowed, asking for peace. The other soldiers followed his lead, and Thaddaeus hid behind Jacqueline, who held her head high and once again readied her weapon of fire.

Rex turned toward Kadmus and spoke, his voice dark and deep, "Still wanna claim me?"

Kadmus stared in fright at his son. "What are you?"

"Dragon," Nishith said and looked back at Jacqueline. "Your fire tactics will have little to no effect on him. It will only enrage him. Please, extinguish the fire."

Jacqueline glared at Rex, sighed, and finally waved the fire away.

"Beautiful…" Meenal whispered and immediately Rex went to her.

"What you say?" he growled, and she dropped her head. He neared her and lifted her head to stare into her eyes. "What did you say?" he repeated.

"Beautiful. I apologize. I meant—"

"Shut up. She said that same thing. What happened to her?"

"Of whom do you speak?"

"Cedron…"

"She died, sir…" Nishith said quietly as he prepared an attack, waiting for the rage to begin. Rex's eyes darkened into a blood red, and his breathing was labored. But seeing this, Meenal touched his claw, and the subtle changes vanished. The red from his eyes withdrew, and his wings collapsed into his back. He swayed and then fell into her arms.

Nishith and another soldier took him and returned him to the bed. Meenal rejoined his side with Thaddaeus and Jacqueline.

Kadmus stared at his son resting, unable to believe the transformation he had witnessed. His hands shook. He glanced down at them, willing them to stop, but the fear returned and shamefully, he backed out of the room. His feet dragged against the stone as he returned to his bedchamber. Closing the door behind him, he pressed his back against it and stared at his shaking hands. Mortified at his fear of his own son, he bowed his head and cried.

The sun was still beneath the horizon when Rex woke again. His body was sore, and it protested violently as he moved. He accidentally kicked something at the edge of his bed and cursed at the hardness of it. Then he saw a streak of whitish hair. He narrowed his eyes and nudged the thing with his foot. It moved, and he saw Meenal, rubbing her shoulder.

"I apologize for not—"

"Shut up with all the damn apologizing!" Rex said and sighed. Meenal bowed her head and fully sat up, sitting straight as usual.

"How was your rest?" she asked.

"I didn't get any really. I got knocked out. The hell you do to me?"

"I cannot tell you."

"What you *mean* you can't tell me? Oh, it's some super-secret Darkness thing that only Dark elementals know about. Otherwise, they'll experience a horrible and painful death?"

"No, I legitimately cannot tell you, for I do not know myself. However, if I learn more, you shall be the first to know."

Rex frowned and took Meenal's hand. She looked down at their hands and then tilted her head.

"What are you doing?" she asked, looking up and seeing him look away.

"I'm leaving. I'm not gonna go back to that city, that old life I had, especially not with becoming a monster every freaking time I get angry. I'll end up killing somebody."

"You already have. Why are you so frightened by that?"

"Hers… was different. She sacrificed herself."

Meenal stared at him, confusion evident on her face.

He sighed. "It don't matter why, just know that I'm leaving and probably not coming back for a bit. I'm saying goodbye."

"Goodbye?"

"Yeah, I gotta go and find my ma. I know it's weird, but I can feel her and I know exactly where she is. I'm gonna meet her and demand to know what happened back then."

"I wish to accompany you."

Rex smiled and pulled her into a hug. She froze like a piece of ice, and he quickly released her.

"Sorry, but I don't want you coming with me. It'll be dangerous and stuff. You're fragile."

"Says the man questioning his identity."

Rex narrowed his eyes, and they began to glow red in the dim light. Ignoring it, Meenal continued, "You will need an interpreter, and I am volunteering. Allow me to travel with you."

"You don't need his permission to go. We're going no matter what he says," another voice said and Jacqueline jumped down from the windowsill. She had a bag over her shoulder and she was dressed in her traveling clothes. Her long red hair was in a single braid, and it draped over one shoulder. She flicked it off and glanced over at the window, seeing Thaddaeus struggling to get inside.

She sighed and pulled him through, causing him to crash onto the hard stone floors. Rex stared at his friends and shook his head, starting to speak, but Thaddaeus gave a thumbs-up and a big grin. Jacqueline mimicked the thumbs-up, and Meenal, after looking at the first two, copied the gesture as well, though her smile was forced and small.

"Look, this something I gotta do alone," Rex said.

"Dude, this ain't no epic adventure. We're going. Just say when," Thaddaeus said.

He gave another thumbs-up and grinned. Jacqueline lifted up one of the bags they had brought, throwing it across her shoulders. She returned to the window and faced Rex and Meenal.

"We'll be waiting outside. Nishith is coming too. He wants to help, strangely enough, and he knows his way around this side of the continent. We're not waiting for your decision because we already know what it is; we're leaving in five minutes," she said and jumped out the window. Thaddaeus, struggling with his own bags, followed after her.

The room was silent once again as Rex and Meenal sat on the bed. Noticing that they were still holding hands, Meenal squeezed his and stood, pulling him with her. She gave a tiny smile and then let his hand go, walking over to the desk in the room. She looked around briefly and found what she was looking for: a piece of paper and a pencil. She returned to Rex and handed them to him.

"You should write your father before our departure," she said.

Rex sighed and wrote.

> *Dad,*
>
> *I'm just as freaked out as you. That's why I've left. I'm gonna find my mother. I know it sounds weird, but I know where she is because now I know what I am. I won't be alone. Meenal, Jacqueline, and Nishith, the Drow general, are coming too. Oh, and Thad too, but you know how he is.*
>
> *I'm gonna bring her back to us. She belongs with us, being the bridge between us two stubborn mules. Don't miss me too much.*
>
> *Rex*

He finished the letter and reread it countless times. He went away and got dressed, coming back to reread the note a few more times. Then he checked on Meenal, helped her pack, and once again returned to the note.

He tried to find better words to describe his relationship with his father, putting his tutoring sessions in vocabulary to work. Yet nothing came. While they did have a strained relationship, he loved his father and would miss him more than he would like to admit. This would be their last communication for a while, possibly forever. He briefly bowed his head and accidentally crushed the letter in his hands. Meenal came up behind him and patted his shoulder.

He turned to her and asked, "You think it's enough?"

Meenal glanced at the letter and nodded. "What more is there to say?"

"That I'll be back; that I'm not abandoning him too; that I'm doing this for the right reasons…"

"That is unnecessary. Your father will infer those thoughts. If you have doubts, please act on them now. Jacqueline and the others are waiting."

Nodding, Rex sighed and stared at the note. Meenal placed her bag over her shoulder and climbed onto the windowsill. Rex looked up and watched her long ponytail fly as she jumped down, leaving him alone.

He uncrumpled his note and glanced at it once again, feeling no doubts concerning his choice. He was determined to go, but he just wanted to add one more thing. He quickly grabbed the pencil and scribbled down a couple of words. Satisfied, he placed the note on the desk and lifted his own pack. With a single look back, he jumped out the window and disappeared into the night.

P.S. I love you

ACKNOWLEDGMENTS

FIRST AND FOREMOST, I WANT TO THANK Jehovah God for giving me the gift of creativity, the guidance in life, and the strength to continue. Without him, none of this would be possible.

I also thank my friends and family for encouraging and supporting me through this long process, especially my siblings for their expressive thoughts on my writing.

Many, many thanks to those who have read the book in any and all of its various forms, starting from the first draft (the ugly mess that it was) to the final production. Particularly, my good friend, Adriene, and my aunt, Auntie Ann, deserve my gratitude. Adriene, you are my first and favorite fan! Thank you so much for your enthusiastic thoughts during the early drafting phase. Auntie Ann, I deeply appreciate the suggestions and commendation you gave me. They definitely motivated me to keep going.

I really want to thank Scott Alexander Jones, my editor. You seriously made my book better and gave me suggestions that made me think about it in different ways.

Lastly, I wish to thank Mrs. Lisa Pelto and her team at Concierge Marketing. The frank feedback and instruction I received greatly prepared me for entering the literary world as an author.

ABOUT THE AUTHOR

BRITTANI S. AVERY IS A COMPUTER programmer with an artsy side as a creative writer, novelist, and poet. Brittani is also a gamer, a reader, an avid NBA follower, and a graphic artist. Her other interests include psychology and personality types, especially the Myers-Briggs Type Indicator (MBTI).

Brittani lives in Omaha, Nebraska, and values spending time with her friends, family, and her Olde English Bulldog, Meshach.